THE
HIGHLANDER'S
BRIDE
TROUBLE

MARY WINE

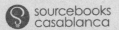

sourcebooks
casablanca

Published by Sourcebooks Casablanca, an imprint of Sourcebooks, Inc.
P.O. Box 4410, Naperville, Illinois 60567-4410
(630) 961-3900
Fax: (630) 961-2168
www.sourcebooks.com

Printed and bound in Canada.
WC 10 9 8 7 6 5 4 3 2 1

This one is for Deb Werksman, for believing in me and having the patience to guide me. You're a truly gifted editor with a vision that inspires me and motivates me to reach higher. Thank you for everything.

One

"YE MAY BE DISMISSED FOR THE NIGHT."

Abigail Ross, the Earl of Ross's daughter, didn't really look at her maid, Nareen Grant. She was too busy breaking the wax seal on the letter she'd just received. Her cheeks flushed and her eyes sparkled as she unfolded the parchment. Its crinkling echoed loudly in the quiet chamber. She was well past the blush of youth, but it was clear affection had no time limit. Even in her late twenties, Abigail was excited by her love letter.

Although, perhaps "liaison letter" might be a more appropriate description. Abigail enjoyed her lovers, and she enjoyed knowing she didn't owe them the obedience a wife would.

"Go on, Nareen. I know ye like yer sleep."

Abigail drew out the word *sleep*. She looked up for a brief moment, making it clear she knew what Nareen would be doing under the veil of night.

Abigail knew Nareen's weaknesses too. It was the

only reason Nareen served her, so she might enjoy freedom as well.

"The moon is full," Abigail muttered before looking back at the letter. There was a subtle warning in her tone, indicating she would turn a blind eye only if Nareen returned the favor.

Nareen inclined her head before leaving the bedchamber. Once she passed through the arched doorway that separated the bedchamber from the receiving chamber, she allowed her pace to increase.

She wasn't interested in sleeping, and luckily, her mistress didn't have any issues with her nighttime rides. Of course, in return, Nareen was expected to ignore the unmarried lady's lovers. So it wasn't luck, it was an agreement. One Nareen enjoyed benefits from as well.

She shuddered, a tingle of fear rising from the dark abyss where Nareen had banished several memories she never wanted to think about again. Sometimes it was very hard to forget her cousin Ruth and the horrors Nareen had suffered while with her kinswoman.

Yes, the arrangement made it possible for Nareen to escape being under the care of her kin, and the unsavory plans Ruth had been making for her.

Nareen turned her attention to the moon. She could see it glowing through the seam in the window shutters. Just a faint sliver of yellow light, it was like a beacon, drawing her toward joyful abandon. The whisper of chilly night air coming through didn't bother her a bit. In fact, it was invigorating.

Outside, she didn't have to worry about being trapped within stone walls.

Nareen steeled her expression as she went through the doors that led to the stairs. Two Ross retainers stood there, making sure the earl's daughter was well guarded throughout the night. They each held a five-foot-tall wooden staff topped with a wicked and deadly looking spear top. The metal gleamed in the moist Highland air. Their gazes followed Nareen as she left, and they stiffly pulled on the corners of their knitted caps.

No one really spared her much attention as she made her way through the partially lit passageways. Several of the torches had been blown out by the vigorous wind.

Nareen skipped down the stone steps, making the three stories to the ground floor in a flash. Abigail would be traveling again soon, if the letter held an invitation. That meant Nareen would be on a tighter leash once the highborn lady found a way to wheedle her father into granting her permission to return to court. The earl had sworn he wouldn't allow it, but Nareen knew he'd soften. Once the wine began to flow, the Earl of Ross lost his will. Abigail always exploited her father's weakness to suit her whims.

So tonight, Nareen would ride.

Many would tell her it was the demons causing the gusts of wind. Nareen scoffed at them. There were legends that went back farther than the Church. Tales of Celtic lore that were still told around the winter fires. She preferred the stories that told of strength and daring, to the Church's teachings that tried to convince her to fear the witching hours.

Nareen pulled her arisaid up from where the length

of Grant tartan draped down her back, and laid it
over her head. During the day, the piece of wool was
secured at her waist, and of little use except to make
it clear she was proud to be a Grant. But at night,
it would shield her from rain and keep her warm.
She pulled it around to cover her shoulders before
venturing into the yard. Most of the Ross retainers
taking their ease in the yard looked her way, but
they returned to whatever they were doing once they
recognized the Grant colors.

She was just the mistress's attendant.

That position suited Nareen well. She didn't regret
leaving her cousin's keeping, not even when it reduced
her to being a personal servant. At least she need not
worry about Ruth selling Nareen's maidenhead.

Nareen shuddered. The woman held no power
over her now. Nareen had seen to that.

The horses greeted her when she entered the stable.
Her mood improved as she reminded herself that she
was free of Ruth and her unsavory plans.

Her mare tossed its mane in greeting. Nareen
murmured softly to it in Gaelic as she eased the bridle
on. Her mare pawed at the ground, eager to stretch
her legs.

"Me thoughts exactly," Nareen said as she slid onto
the back of the animal. The gate watch raised the gate
for her, but not without a stern look of disapproval.

Nareen didn't bother to look back. She leaned low
over the neck of her mare and let the animal have its
freedom. The horse picked up speed, chilling Nareen's
cheeks as they raced across the open land that surrounded the Ross castle.

❧

Saer MacLeod turned his head, listening to the night. He kicked dirt over the small fire he'd built to cook his dinner, and it died, leaving him in darkness.

It wasn't that dark. He'd endured nights that were as black as a demon's eyes, and this one wasn't anywhere near that deep.

But there was something—someone—riding toward him. There was no way he was going to greet that stranger anywhere but on the back of his horse.

There was a whistle from his man. Baruch held up one finger.

Saer didn't reach for the pommel of the sword strapped to his back. A lone rider wasn't that much of a threat.

"I thinks it's her…" Baruch rode up close to his laird's side. "Just like the Ross lad told me, she's riding by moonlight…"

"Good," Saer muttered. He felt a surge of impending victory and savored it.

Nareen Grant had turned him down and dismissed him the last time he'd seen her.

He intended to make sure she knew he was not so easily brushed aside.

❧

Nareen was sure her heart was beating as fast as her mare's. The animal slowed, having spent its first burst of speed. Her arisaid had fallen back, baring her head, but she enjoyed the bite of the night air. She laughed, at ease for the first time all day. But her elation evaporated when her mare's ears lifted. Nareen tightened her grip on the reins as she searched the shadows. "Who is there?" she demanded.

"Ye take a risk by riding out at night, lass."

Her company emerged from the shadows cast by the edge of a woodland patch, where the forest trees thinned and gave way to the slope.

"But yer command of the mare is impressive, Nareen Grant."

He was a large man. She could describe him as huge, but resisted the urge because there was already a chill tingling on her nape. If he knew her name, it was possible he was an enemy of the Grants. She tightened her knees, making ready to flee.

"Ye have naught to fear from me." He nudged his horse farther away from the shadows. Her heart froze as the moonlight illuminated his hard body. There was no mistaking his prime condition, and his voice was deep and young enough to confirm she might be in true peril if he turned hostile.

"Name yer clan," she stated boldly. She lifted her chin and stared straight at him. A weak plea would never do.

There was a husky chuckle from the stranger. "Are ye sure ye are in a position to demand things of me, lass? Most Highlanders do nae care for a lass who spits fire."

"I do nae care for anyone who will nae speak the name of their clan without hesitation. Such actions mean ye have no honor."

He rode a full stallion, the horse just as impressive as its master. The animal was prime quality, telling her he had coin in his purse, but that fact didn't reassure her. Many times, noble lords were far more unscrupulous than a common villain. The law favored them in every way, and they took advantage of it.

He nudged the beast with his knees until it turned and the moonlight washed over his face. She gasped, recognizing him instantly. And a little too well for her liking. A rush of heat flooded her cheeks, for she had just accused a laird of having no honor.

"What are ye doing riding on Ross land in the dark of night, Saer MacLeod?"

He moved his horse closer to her mare and leaned down to pat the neck of the sturdy beast he rode. Her attention was drawn to his hand, fixating on the way he stroked the animal. There was a confidence in his motions that sent a tingle across her skin. He was more than bold, he was supremely at ease in the night—so much so, she envied him.

More heat teased her face, this time flowing down her body.

"This is hardly dark," he said at last.

She jerked her gaze up to his face to find him grinning at her. She tossed her long braid over her shoulder, detesting the way he made her feel vulnerable. "Ye're right, it is hardly dark, which is why I am enjoying it. Good-bye, Laird MacLeod."

She tightened her grip on the reins and sent her mare in motion again. She wasn't running away; it was simply a matter of doing what she pleased. Aye, indeed it was.

Abigail already told her what to do most of the day. Of course, it was far better than answering to a husband or to her cousin Ruth.

Her dark memories stirred again, so she leaned low

over the neck of the horse and felt the wind pulling the shorter strands of her hair from her braid. The steady beat of the mare's hooves filled her head, but there was something else too, a deeper pounding. She turned her head to find Saer MacLeod keeping pace with her, an amused grin on his lips.

She kneed her mare, urging the animal to go faster. It was an impulse that irritated her because she was letting herself be goaded. There would be no responding to Saer MacLeod.

She pulled up, the mare settling into a slow walk, tossing her head as Nareen worried her lower lip. "I'm sure ye have important things to do, Laird MacLeod."

He guided his stallion in step beside her mare. "Ensuring ye do nae get set upon by the MacKays is important. I hear they have no love for the Ross. They claim the earl killed their laird and have vowed vengeance."

"I am a Grant."

"But ye serve the earl's daughter," Saer countered. "There would be more than one man who would consider that enough to include ye in their feud."

Her heart was beating faster. She drew in a deep, slow breath to calm herself. "I do nae need yer protection." Her tone was far from smooth, further irritating her. She didn't need the man hearing how he unsettled her.

He grinned more broadly in the face of her temper, a cocksure, arrogant, full curving of his lips that sent a tingle through her belly. She was amusing him and nothing else.

"I do nae need yer permission to ensure ye come to

no harm, Nareen. Just as I did nae need yer brother's consent to let me ride along with him to deal with yer cousin Ruth."

She jerked, involuntarily pulling on the reins. The mare stopped, snorting with frustration. Saer reached out and stroked the animal's neck again. The horse quieted immediately and made a soft sound of enjoyment.

Nareen's mouth went dry at the way his touch pleased. She wondered… "Let me mare be."

Nareen tried to pull the horse away. Saer reached out and captured her hand to keep her from commanding the mare.

The contact was jarring, his warm flesh shocking her. Her own fingers were chilled from the pace of her ride, but his were warm and inviting. More than a warmth that chased away the night temperature, this was a heat that touched something deep inside her. She licked her lower lip because it was too dry, drawing his gaze to her mouth.

She jerked her hand away.

"I told ye at court, I want naught to do with ye." At last, she'd grasped enough of her composure to say what she truly needed to.

"Aye, ye did." He patted her mare's neck, stroking the velvet surface of her skin with a long motion before answering. "Look at me, Nareen Grant, and tell me if ye see a man who is easily told what to do."

His tone was soft and menacing, carrying a warning that even the mare sensed. A chill shot down Nareen's back, her gaze locking with his. She was keenly aware of him, her lips tingling with anticipation. She felt like there was something inside him that was drawing her closer, some force that reached out to stroke her, entice her to do his will.

He jerked the reins right out of her slackened grip. "What are ye doing?"

Saer didn't answer her. He held the reins, and her mare began following his stallion as he sent the beast forward. Her only option was to drop down the side of the animal while it was in motion. One look at the ground warned her against such a rash action. Moonlight illuminated the rocky ground they rode across, promising her a rough landing.

But she was still tempted, because Saer's back promised her something else. His shirtsleeves were rolled up and tied at his shoulder. She was as fascinated by his back as by his keen gaze. A long sword was strapped across his back at an angle so the pommel was behind his left shoulder and easy to reach with his right hand. There was nothing ornate about the weapon, just solid purpose. He was bastard-born and raised among the isles. The Highlanders called him a savage, and his actions proved he was exactly that.

He took what he wanted, just as he was taking her.

She looked at the ground again, but the sound of water drew her attention to where he was leading her. The noise grew until it was loud enough to drown out the steps of the horses. He guided them around a granite outcropping and down to where the moonlight shimmered off a river. It was swollen from rains farther up in the Highlands, the moonlight lighting the white peaks raised by the current.

There was a fire burning near the face of the outcropping they had just come around. It was completely hidden from the open space. Over six dozen horses and men were taking their ease near the fire, the scent of roasting rabbit floating in the air. The orange flicker from the fire showed her the colors of the MacLeod plaid in their kilts. They looked up, but turned their backs once they realized their laird had returned with a female.

"Ye would never see trouble coming, lass. The Ross have no idea we are on their land."

Saer let out a whistle, which was answered in kind. She didn't care how much truth there was in his words. He slid off his horse and handed the reins to a younger boy who had come up to serve his laird. Saer handed off the reins of her mare to another lad before dismounting.

"Will ye dismount, or shall I assist ye, lass?"

Nareen lifted her leg and slid to the ground. She did it too fast, and her ankle bent, but she recovered, welcoming the twinge of pain, because it gave her something to focus on besides his unsettling presence. Once on the ground, she battled the instinct to feel small next to Saer MacLeod.

She would not be made to feel anything by the man, and that was final.

"Ye have no authority over me, Laird MacLeod." She reached for the reins of her mare, but the lad was leading the horse away. "I'll be going where I please."

"Go into the night, and I'll follow ye." His eyes flickered with a warning. "As much as I admire the wild streak in ye, it will nae protect ye from men set on feuding. Yer brother is me friend and ally. 'Tis me duty to see ye protected." His tone was firm.

She bristled. "I do nae wish to be under yer protection," she insisted. "I've made me own place. Ye may tell me brother I absolved ye of any responsibility."

"I've clasped yer brother's wrist and called him friend. Honor is not absolved by words." He stepped closer. "But that is nae the only reason I will ride out after ye, Nareen Grant."

His voice had deepened and his tone made her knees go weak. She detested the reaction, willing herself to ignore it. Yet it persisted, turning and twisting through her like some sort of dark suggestion she couldn't ignore because it was inside her.

"I must return to me mistress."

"Ye're hiding in yer position," he accused softly. "Ye are the daughter of an ennobled laird, nae a serving lass."

"I made a place for meself when the one me noble family sent me to was sordid," she defended.

"Something ye are to be admired for." His expression changed, the hard set of his lips softening as he moved even closer. She lost the battle to ignore her response. He was too near to ignore completely; the soft night breeze carried the scent of his skin to her.

She stepped back. His lips parted, flashing his teeth as victory filled his eyes.

"Ye intrigue me, Nareen Grant. Ye are noble-born, yet ye did nae meekly accept yer plight with yer cousin."

"Of course I did nae, I am a Grant," she answered with pride. His dark eyes brightened with approval and something that looked like intent. "Do nae be intrigued." She stepped to the side, to place more space between them. "For I am nae interested in ye a bit."

One of his dark eyebrows rose. "I'm willing to wager I can change yer mind, lass."

Her eyes widened, a sickening twist of nausea shooting through her belly. "I am nae something to be made sport of."

And she couldn't bear it. The need to retch was growing as she battled the image of him taking her on the ground while his men ignored them.

There was nothing to stop him. Once more, she had only her wits, and it shamed her to know that was by her own doing. Reckless choices often delivered harsh consequences. But she was nae going to submit easily.

"Ye claim me brother is yer friend," she reminded him. "I believe he would nae care to know ye are trifling with me."

His expression hardened. "Yer cousin Ruth has paid for her deeds, but I wonder if stripping her of her freedom and placing her and her entire estate under the guardianship of a trusted man was enough. She bred a fear in ye. For that, she has nae been punished enough."

It was true, but she couldn't share such a thing with him. Not with anyone.

"Ruth no longer rules her estate?"

Saer shook his head. "Her choices are limited to what fare she might enjoy from the kitchen and what dress she may wear."

For a moment, Nareen recalled the gleam that always brightened her cousin's eyes when she was laying out her plans. The staff lived in fear of being singled out by their mistress. "Ruth thrived on control. She'll hate having none."

"Then it was well done."

His voice had a deep timbre that struck her as too familiar, too kind, too focused upon her. She recoiled from it, shaking her head because she didn't want anything about Ruth to matter to her. "I do nae care what became of her. She means naught to me."

He reached out and stroked her cheek. "'Tis a sad thing to see how hard yer feelings are. But there is naught more to fear, she'll nae have the opportunity to inflict such ills again."

Nareen jerked away from the contact. She even took a swipe at his hand, but he moved faster, withdrawing in time to avoid being struck. Someone chuckled from where his men clustered near the fires, but Saer was watching her from narrowed eyes.

"I am nae afraid of anything," she assured him.

"Is that so?" Saer inquired in a silky-smooth tone.

Nareen nodded. Satisfaction began to fill her, but it was cut short as he reached out and stroked her face again. She jumped, completely unable to control her reaction.

"Ye are making sport of me in front of yer men, like a savage."

His eyes glittered, but it wasn't with the outrage Nareen had intended to provoke. Instead, there was an unmistakable pleased looked in those dark orbs.

"I *am* a savage, Nareen." He stepped forward, placing himself within touching range again. "I do nae let words stand alone. If ye truly have no interest in me, there is no reason to avoid me touch. Stand steady and prove ye are nae moved. I have no taste for a frigid woman."

She laughed at him but stepped back again. "Then it seems we have a common ground, for I crave no man's touch."

His lips thinned. "Now that is something ye shall have to prove as well."

"I will nae. Me word should be enough on the matter, if ye truly are me brother's friend." She didn't care to hide behind her brother's name, but the circumstances offered her few alternatives.

"As ye noted, I am a savage, and I always demand proof before I believe."

This time, she was ready when he reached for her cheek. She stepped aside, avoiding him. She was just beginning to smile with her victory when he closed his hand around her wrist. He really was huge. His fingers closed easily around her smaller wrist, clasping it in an iron grip. She braced herself for pain, but there was none, only a secure hold that defied her attempt to break it.

"Release me." Her voice had risen, and she shut her mouth before revealing any more of her unsettled state.

"Prove ye are unmoved, lass, and I shall be content to accept yer dismissal." His tone had deepened, becoming something hypnotic.

"I am irritated." And remaining still was proving too difficult. She twisted her hand, trying to break his hold again.

"Aye, ye are that." He lifted her hand to his face

and pressed a kiss on the delicate skin of her inner wrist. She shuddered, the touch intensely intimate. She'd never realized her skin might be so sensitive. The simple touch of his lips unleashed a bolt of sensation that shook her all the way down to her toes. His eyes filled with satisfaction.

"But ye are also affected."

He released her, and she stumbled back a pace because she'd been resisting his hold so greatly. Laughter erupted from his men. Saer stiffened, and he crossed his arms over his chest.

"What?" she said. "Are ye trying to impress me by controlling yerself now that ye see yer men are enjoying the sport ye are making of me?"

"Aye, I am," he answered darkly. "I am nae the one who chose this setting for our meeting, Nareen. Ye should nae have refused to see me again at court. That left me no choice but to chase ye."

"Ye have no right to chase me, nor take me mare's reins."

He offered her only a slight tilt of his head. "Riding through the night hours is nae safe."

"Ye were doing it," she pointed out.

He reached back and grasped the pommel of the long sword that was strapped to his back. "I am more prepared than ye, lass."

"So ye think," she warned.

His eyes narrowed again, this time sweeping her from head to toe. He wouldn't find her dagger. At least, not until it was too late.

"I can see to meself," Nareen assured him, her confidence was high when it came to protecting herself. The knowledge restored her balance, and it was a relief.

She turned and made to go after her mare. She felt his gaze on her, but he didn't try to stop her. The young lad who had taken her mare watched as she untied the knot that secured her bridle to the other horses. No one spoke a word, but they watched her, some of the retainers stroking their beards.

Nareen mounted and turned her mare toward the path that led away from the hidden campsite. She pressed her knees into the sides of the mare to get her moving.

Saer was no longer in sight. The urge to look around for the MacLeod laird was almost irresistible, but she lifted her chin and headed up the path. Her jaw was aching by the time she gained the high ground, because she was gritting her teeth.

But she was satisfied.

She was on her way, going where she wished.

Once out of the woods, her mare picked up speed, crossing the open space that allowed the Ross fortress to see invaders coming—the site for the castle had been chosen because of the natural clearing. The gate watch made her wait while they scanned the land. She glanced behind her, looking back toward the wooded area. For a moment, something moved, and Saer emerged for just a split second.

"Open the gate," she called up.

"Ye'll wait on the captain's word," a retainer called back down. "Do nae say the Grant leave their gates open in the dark of night."

Of course they didn't. No one did. The only

reason she was allowed out was because the Ross truly did not care if she returned. A servant was replaceable, especially one from another clan. She'd taken solace in that fact, but now, she realized how foolish she had been.

Saer MacLeod could have kept her, and no one would have bothered to send out even a single rider to look for her. As much as she detested the facts of the world, she could not deny that the Grants had enemies—every clan did. Even on Ross land, she might find herself under attack from one of her brother's enemies. If Saer could find her, so could others.

It was time to think about her circumstances.

"It's clear," the captain of the watch called from the top of the corner tower.

The portcullis was raised just enough for her to enter. But the moment the gate closed behind her, she realized she was there only because Saer had allowed it. His stallion was capable of running her mare to ground.

He'd allowed her to return.

That knowledge unleashed several emotions she wanted to ignore. But as she returned her mare to her stall and rubbed her down, there was no way to hide from her own thoughts.

Saer MacLeod had allowed her to decide what she wished. His fellow Highlanders might call him a savage, but he was far more accommodating than she expected of a man.

It was what he wanted, no doubt. All men craved the same thing from women.

It was more than a word. The idea whispered

through her thoughts and along her skin, raising goose bumps. She shivered, but realized she was actually trembling. She hissed, letting her temper flare in the hopes it would burn away the memory of his touch.

Another emotion teased her, warm as a flash of temper, but it wasn't anger. She frowned as she failed to understand it. Even if she detested the man and everything about him, the memory of his lips against her wrist filled her thoughts, leaving behind a slight sting on her cheeks.

She shook her head and made her way toward her bed.

She would not think about his touch or the way it made her feel. There would be no lament over the choice she had made to reject him.

There would not be.

❧

"I'm surprised ye let her go back into that fortress," Saer's captain remarked when he joined him at the edge of the clearing. "I do nae think she'll be making it simple for ye to catch her again."

"I hope not."

Baruch chuckled. "Are ye sure ye want that one, Laird?"

Saer cut his captain a hard look. "That is what I'm here to discover. She intrigues me, and I confess I've never been impressed with a lass's strength before."

"Her brother agreed to yer suit," Baruch reminded him. "It would be a lot simpler to learn what it is ye want to know if ye had kept her."

Saer looked back at the Ross fortress. "If I did

that, she'd be able to dismiss me the same as those her cousin allowed to make sport of her." His tone betrayed his anger. "She will come to me."

"And how do ye figure to make that happen?"

Saer turned his stallion to head back to the camp. "She craves freedom. Nae the inside of that fortress."

Baruch slowly smiled. "And ye've cleverly made it so she is the one who has caged herself. Well played, Laird. Even a spitfire cannae claim ye forced her inside that gate."

"She will not," Saer confirmed. "Nareen Grant will notice exactly what I did. She is no simpleton."

Baruch let out a low whistle. "Careful, Laird, a spitfire is often more trouble than she's worth. Once the passion cools, ye'll be stuck with a harpy for a wife. One that will have the care of yer daughters."

"Or I might just have found a woman who is nae afraid of me."

Which was what he truly craved. Now that he was Laird, there were offers of brides, but he didn't have the stomach for a shivering woman in his bed. His father's bride had been one of those, a daughter offered up by her father, and white as a ghost on the day of her wedding. His father had turned to Saer's mother for passion when the years went by and his noble wife never warmed toward him.

Saer wanted nothing to do with a marriage like that.

Nareen trembled, but she also spat at him. What he really wanted to know was would she reach for him once she surrendered to passion?

It was a gamble, one that carried a large risk. Saer wasn't blind to the facts. But he also couldn't ignore the way Nareen blushed for him. Her cheeks had been hot, even in the cold night air, just as they'd been when he'd encountered her at court.

Every moment they'd shared was branded into his memory. If he was given to superstition, he'd suspect her of casting spells. Court ladies had reputations for bewitching men with their wiles.

He grinned, the burn of a challenge warming him. If Nareen had enchanted him, he was going to make sure she suffered the same fate.

"Where are ye going, Laird?" Baruch inquired.

"To introduce meself to the Earl of Ross," Saer answered without looking over his shoulder. "It would be terribly rude of me to cross his land and nae clasp his hand. Such an action might start rumors about me lack of social graces."

"Well now, we wouldn't be wanting that," Baruch agreed as he followed his laird toward the castle. "But ye know, ye do nae have to spend the night inside the fortress. The summer night is fine."

"Aye." Saer continued toward the gate.

Baruch snorted behind him and abandoned further argument. "She's under yer skin," he groused instead.

"Perhaps." Saer ignored the temptation to wait until morning to enter the castle. There was one thing he disliked more than being surrounded by stone walls, and that was ignoring a challenge. "Since I plan to claim her, it matters not."

"Aye," Baruch answered.

Whether or not Nareen was teasing him was not the reason he moved closer to her refuge. He wanted to know why she invaded his dreams. He'd stand in

her path until she faced him. The answer would be
revealed only when she stopped running.

❦

Saer MacLeod blended with the night. Where other
men braved the darkness, Saer was comfortable in its
velvet embrace. It was enticing, alluring in a way that
was sure to be wrong. How could it be anything else
when it sent such a rush of heat through her?

Nareen jerked awake, disoriented as she tried to
disengage her mind from her dream.

The image of Saer MacLeod didn't fade quickly
or easily. It lingered, keeping her from waking up
completely. She saw his dark stare, probing her eyes
and forcing her to acknowledge him.

She kicked her bedding aside and sat up.

She would ignore the man.

The sun was rising, and she could hear the bells
calling the inhabitants of the inner castle to morning
Mass. She reached for her stockings and pushed her
feet into them. Now that the summer was fully upon
them, she lamented being forced to wear so many
layers. But there were standards to be maintained.

Next she pulled her boots on and worked a lace
around the antler-horn buttons sewn along the sides,
knotting the laces in place. When she stood, her
chemise fluttered to her calves. It was creased from
sleeping in it, but no one would see the lack of iron-
ing. Not that she had time for such vanity anymore.

Nareen reached for her simple wool skirt and lifted
it over her head, using a tie to belt it at her waist.
Her bodice was unfussy, with boning sewn into it

instead of a separate corset, and it opened up the front. Nareen threaded a lace through the eyelets and tugged it tightly closed. The stiff front supported her breasts. Her sleeves attached to her bodice and were also simple in design.

There had been a time when she had been the mistress. Dressing took more time when there were more layers. Like underskirts and overskirts, inner sleeves and outer sleeves all decorated with trim and lace. She did not miss it.

Well, perhaps she missed her silk gowns from time to time. But not enough to return to her father's house.

A stab of regret pierced her heart as she brushed the tangles from her hair. Her father had not been in his right mind for many years. He'd begun losing his grip on facts, and it had only grown worse. He was Laird of the Grants, but her brother, Kael, had kept him above stairs to keep his illness from being known. As his daughter, she should be there to tend to him. But to do so, she'd have to return to where her brother was master.

Her brother had sent her to Ruth. Even if she believed Kael had done so believing Ruth would instruct her on how to run a large estate, Nareen couldn't stomach the idea of being beneath a roof where he ruled. So she stayed as Abigail's companion.

She braided her hair and grabbed a linen cap before hurrying out of the chamber. At least she didn't have to sleep in Abigail's private chambers. Many personal companions did. But Abigail was at her nastiest at sunrise, so she allowed her kinswomen to dress her in

the morning because she didn't want Nareen to leave
her service. Abigail was wise enough to know Nareen
had somewhere to go if she became displeased in her
position. So she gave concessions, such as a private
place to sleep and a stall for her mare.

Yes, a good agreement.

So why was she so full of discontentment this
morning?

Saer MacLeod.

Nareen pushed her lips into a pout. The man was
arrogant and presumptuous, so why did he continue
to fascinate her so much that he invaded her dreams?

Perhaps she was better off not knowing the answer
to that question. She'd decided she would not wed, so
it was best to avoid thinking about men at all.

The inner yard was full of maids and retainers
making their way to the small chapel inside the castle.
Off in the distance, she could hear the bell tolling in
the village church. The gate was lowered and barred,
with only a few retainers remaining on the walls to
keep watch. Everyone else made their way inside for
the morning devotion.

The priest had already begun the first prayers. She
dipped her fingers into the holy water, making the sign
of the cross over herself as she hurried to find a place in
the congregation. The other Ross serving girls shifted
to make room for her. She was just feeling relieved,
when she looked at the front of the chapel.

Saer MacLeod stood there, his dark gaze on her
instead of on the altar.

She froze, and someone bumped into her. Saer's
lips twitched as she stumbled and half fell into one of

the back pews. The priest turned around and caught her staring slack-jawed at Saer MacLeod.

The retainers manning the gate shouldn't have allowed him inside during the night.

She bit her lip as she realized how something she counted as a benefit also worked to allow Saer to torment her. Granting shelter to other clans was common. When the man in question was a new laird, and there was an unmarried daughter in the Ross family, offering him hospitality just might have rewards for both clans.

Abigail was staring at the priest, completely ignoring Saer. There was a pinched look to her lips that Nareen recognized. Her mistress was not pleased at all.

The moment the last prayer finished, Abigail jerked her skirt up and headed down the main aisle. The rest of the Rosses held still, making way for her.

"There ye are at last," Abigail grumbled.

Nareen fell into step behind her as Abigail made her way through the double doors of the chapel and into the dark entryway. Two passages led to smaller workrooms built alongside the main chapel, that were used by the priests as they worked on manuscripts—places of peace and quiet. But Abigail felt none of those things. She scowled at Nareen, her eyes bright with anger, and jerked her head toward one of the workrooms. Nareen followed, her cheeks reddening, because the Rosses were standing behind their mistress and watching the entire exchange. At least deeper in the stone passageway, she was able to hear the congregation making their way out of the sanctuary.

"I thought I told ye back at court to make sure that

savage MacLeod stopped looking at ye." Abigail sent her a stern look. "He's followed ye here."

"I doubt that," Nareen responded firmly. "No unwed laird needs to chase women. Most of the daughters in the Highlands are plotting on how to get him to wed them."

Abigail didn't care for how easily Nareen spoke her mind, but she put up with it because she didn't want one of her own clanswomen tending to her. They would tell her father anything he asked. Their loyalty was to the clan first.

"Then why is he here?" Abigail demanded.

"It is summer," Nareen offered. "It's likely the man is traveling on business."

Her cheeks heated as she recalled Saer's words from the night before. Abigail didn't miss the bright color.

"Did ye sneak out to be with him last eve?"

There was a glimmer of excitement in Abigail's eyes as she rolled her lower lip with her teeth. The raw lust was shocking, but it also brought back the odd twisting feeling in Nareen's belly. She could not lust for Saer MacLeod.

Or any man. But most especially not him.

Abigail was still watching her. She let out a little sigh. "So ye like the savage ones."

"I do nae," Nareen defended herself.

Abigail let out a husky, knowledgeable laugh. "Ye're virgin."

"Of course I am."

Abigail wasn't impressed. The woman looked at Nareen like she was a babe in need of instruction.

Abigail shrugged. "Even the Holy Mother Mary

rid herself of virginity. Ye'll see what a nuisance it is once ye grow up enough to stop worrying that God will strike ye down for enjoying yer own body. I am impressed, though. I suppose ye chose to become me servant to avoid being sold by yer cousin. Ruth did know how to please her customers. Some men like virgins above all else. She'd have gotten quite a tidy sum for ye with those plump tits ye have. I had two offers for ye last Season at court. Don't be foolish with the savage. He'll give ye nothing for yer maidenhead." Abigail offered her a sly smile. "Let me arrange a liaison at court for ye, and we'll share the gold."

Nareen was struck dumb. Abigail turned and headed toward the center of the church again. She moved confidently through the sanctuary and out the front doors without a hint of remorse for her torrid words, spoken so boldly in the very house of the Lord.

She'd known.

Known what Ruth planned and had not offered help until Nareen reached out to her. For the first time, Nareen realized it might not be so good an arrangement for her. Abigail had much in common with Ruth, it seemed.

"It appears ye have nae escaped from yer cousin Ruth's plans for ye." Saer MacLeod spoke from behind her, his tone low and edged with anger. Every muscle in Nareen's body drew tight.

"Abigail Ross is no better a mistress for ye," he said grimly. "Ye'll leave with me at dawn."

Nareen drew herself up and locked gazes with him. "I'll be going nowhere with ye. Serving the Ross is me choice."

Even if she now doubted how safe she was. But she wouldn't be reaching to Saer MacLeod for help. No, she'd fend for herself.

She made to walk away, but Saer stepped into her path. For so large a man, he moved quickly.

"Ye need counsel, Nareen. I've been in the country for only two years, and I know of Abigail's reputation. She was very serious, lass," he offered gravely.

Nareen shook her head. "I will simply make it clear that I want none of it." But she didn't care for how little confidence she had in her own words.

Saer was no fool and heard the way her voice faltered.

"She feeds only her desires. Her clan could have benefited from her marriage. Instead of doing her duty to her kin, she cannae wait to begin planning new schemes."

There was no way to ignore the truth of his words.

"I know she's selfish," Nareen confessed, "but she will nae sell me without me consent."

"Do nae be so sure," he warned.

She didn't care for the sense of vulnerability his words unleashed. It raced through her, threatening to undermine her confidence. "Abigail is pleased with me, and I with her. She will nae jeopardize our arrangement."

She hoped.

Nareen tried to go around him, but he lifted his arm and pressed his hand flat against the wall next to her head, blocking her way. Heads turned their way as the rest of the congregation passed by on their way back to their duties. Yet no one interfered.

He leaned closer and lowered his voice. "Are ye certain?"

She shivered, the reaction instant and uncontrollable.

"Ye should nae be, lass," he said. "Nae a single Ross will even stop to ensure ye are well. They have left ye here to deal with me on yer own."

"They have no reason to think ye would harm me," Nareen snapped.

"It should cross one of their minds to make certain I am nae as savage as me reputation."

"Ye are twisting things to favor yer opinion that I should leave with ye," she countered. "I will nae be changing me mind about me feelings for ye."

She propped her hand onto her hip, and his eyes narrowed. His expression gave her no hint to his thoughts, but her knees weakened as anticipation twisted her.

"I accept yer challenge," he informed her.

Her mouth went dry.

"I am nae challenging ye." But her voice had turned husky with longing.

His lips lifted in an arrogant grin. "Ye are, Nareen, and I enjoy it full well."

She shook her head, but his dark eyes flickered with determination. A moment later, he pressed his lips against hers. She gasped, recoiling, but the wall was solid behind her and gave her no room to escape. Saer cupped her nape, sending another shiver down her spine at the strength in his grip. There was something primitive about the way he controlled her, holding her in such a place.

He might snap her neck if he chose.

Instead, he kissed her.

She stiffened, rejecting him with every fiber of her

being. But he didn't smash her lips beneath his. Saer pressed a firm kiss against her lips and then another before he swept his tongue along her lower lip. One soft lap that made her notice how velvety the surface of his tongue was.

It didn't hurt.

And his fingertips weren't digging into her nape.

Surprise flashed through her, making her gasp.

Saer took advantage of her open lips, deepening the kiss. This time she couldn't help but notice how pleasant his lips felt against her own. She'd never considered that a man's lips might be soft. Saer's were.

He coaxed her with gentle pressure to kiss him back. He teased her with slow laps along the sensitive surface of her lips to open her mouth farther. When she did, he deepened the kiss and unleashed a need that twisted her insides. Heat flashed through her, making her clothing feel constricting. Her breasts felt swollen as her nipples slowly contracted behind her bodice. It was overwhelming, and she shoved against his chest, struggling to slip away from him.

When he prevented her, she reached up and slapped him.

The sound was loud and echoed inside the chapel. But there was no one to hear. Even the priest had disappeared. She was utterly abandoned.

Fear bit into her, its venom nauseating her. She shook her head, trying to stave it off, but her eyes brightened with unshed tears. Saer's keen gaze settled on her eyes, infuriating her, because she was very much afraid he saw how glassy they were.

At least anger burned away the fear, so she

welcomed it and cast aside any further attempts at being civil.

"I am nae yers," she said, but her tone lacked all strength.

He started toward her but froze at the plea in her tone. She heard him pull in a harsh breath before he gripped the wide belt holding his kilt against his lean waist.

"A kiss is nae a claim of ownership." His tone was gentler than she expected. The lack of arrogance surprised her, stilling her need to move away. But she still shook her head, unable to stop disagreeing with him.

"I did nae hurt ye. I know me strength and how to control it."

She gave a bitter bark of laughter. "All men do. Just as they all know when they no longer have to temper their will. I'll nae make the mistake of putting meself at any man's mercy."

She turned away, intent on leaving him through the back of the workroom.

"We're nae finished, Nareen."

He was so close his breath brushed her ear. Saer moved with an unnatural speed, reaching out to encircle her waist. He bound her to him, bringing their bodies into contact from shoulders to feet. Her skirts compressed, allowing her to feel his legs behind her.

"I am nae a challenge," she insisted, turning her head to make sure he heard her.

"Ye are," Saer told her in a deep whisper.

She opened her mouth to argue, and he sealed his hand over it.

"But nae in the manner ye believe, Nareen. It is nae conquest for the sake of claiming a prize that I seek."

She stretched her neck, trying to dislodge his hand. Victory was hers for a short moment, but he slid his fingers down her chin and along her neck to rest against the spot in her throat where her pulse throbbed. Shame filled her as he found the telltale proof of her racing heart. He made a soft sound of male approval that sent a shudder through her. She felt surrounded by him, and part of her enjoyed it immensely, begging her to soften and yield to his embrace.

"Ye are a challenge because ye test me control to entice ye until ye yield."

"I do nae want ye to," she claimed.

"Which is why I want to return to yer cousin's house and beat her until she gives me the names of the men who laid rough hands on ye."

She shifted, trying to ease her way out of his hold. "I do nae recall them at all."

It was a lie. The boldest one she had ever told, and she was not sorry. She was going to say it again and again until she believed it.

"I'm going to teach ye the pleasure of touch."

His voice had deepened and softened until it was like the stroke of a feather. Just barely there. She relaxed, sinking back against him to make sure she heard him.

She shouldn't. It was a weakness, one that would see her suffer at his hands once he gained what he wished.

"Once I yield, all ye will do is take. It is the nature of a man." She tried to gently push his arm away from her, but he held firm. "I lack a submissive nature, Saer.

It might amuse ye now, but ye will lose patience with me in time."

"Do ye hear the difference in me tone, Nareen?" He kissed the shell of her ear. "Listen to me and learn the difference between a man who knows pleasure should be shared, nae just taken."

He stroked lower, across skin she'd never realized was so sensitive. Beneath his fingertips, her flesh was humming with appreciation. Goose bumps spread down her torso until her nipples puckered once again.

"Ye are using words to dull me wits." She stretched her neck away from his hand. "To confuse."

"Perhaps I am trying to prove me worth." He stroked her neck again, this time all the way up to her chin, where his hand cupped her jaw. It was a slow motion, one that drew a gasp from her as sensation went thundering through her.

A pleasurable sensation, without a doubt.

There was no lying to herself.

He turned her face so she might see his eyes. "I prefer it this way, lass, for I have never been a man to be taken at merely me word." His eyes closed to mere slits. "Showing ye is going to be me pleasure." His lips curved, setting off a coil of excitement in her belly. "It will be yers too."

She jerked her face away, unable to remain still with his gaze boring into hers. He saw too much. Noticed too many things she needed to keep hidden. She might bear it, so long as no one witnessed the ugliness.

"I...cannae." The words were a plea. A tear escaped as the words made it past her resolve to remain strong. "Release me, please."

"That would be an unkind thing."

There was a solidness in his tone that made her heart accelerate. She battled the wave of panic trying to crest as he leaned over and kissed the side of her neck. The contact was jarring. She jerked, so tightly wound with anticipation. With all of her senses heightened, the impact of that gentle touch was extreme.

Her skin hummed with approval and begged for more.

Saer didn't disappoint her either. He trailed kisses along the column of her throat, making a slow progress that drove her mad with longing. She found herself stretching her neck out for him, making certain he missed none of the tender flesh where her neck and collarbone met.

"That is the way, lass…"

His voice was merely a whisper. In the darkened hallway, with the sunlight blocked by the walls of the doorway, she was almost sure she had fallen into some sort of enchantment.

Except Saer was solid behind her. Everything about him was hard, but for some reason, she found it enticing. She lowered her chin, trying to force herself to open her eyes wide.

"Nae, lass, we are just beginning."

He cupped her jaw and raised her chin until she was leaning her head back against his powerful shoulder.

"And I am eager to show ye how a man honors the trust granted to him by a lass."

"Honors?"

She didn't realize she'd spoken until his chest rumbled behind her. But it wasn't amusement. It was a deep, low growl that reminded her of just how powerful a creature he was.

"Aye," he confirmed before tracing the surface of her lower lip with his finger. She was suddenly trembling with the need to feel his kiss. The delicate surface of her lips tingled. She moved against him in purely instinctual motion.

She didn't understand it, but it felt good.

She moved again, and Saer did too. Rolling his body from side to side and pressing against her, he slid his hand over her eyes, blocking out the daylight and leaving her sinking into the sensation her body was experiencing.

"Feel, lass. Do naught but feel."

She reached for his arm, eager to do as he commanded. With his shirt tied up to the shoulders, there was nothing to separate her from his warm flesh. His forearm was hard, the definition of the muscles clear. She stroked him, trying to absorb all of his strength. It fanned the flames of need smoldering inside her.

His body hair was thicker than hers and crisp. It delighted her in a way she couldn't describe, so she merely sighed with contentment.

"That's the way, lass…"

She smiled at his praise, and he drew his hand down the side of her face. She turned her cheek until it rested against his breast so he might stroke the other side of her face. Her cheek was warm with a blush of excitement, and she wanted him to notice.

Saer made a soft circle with his fingertips over the hot spot before trailing his hand down and over the corner of her lips. Just the corner, and she let out a little sound of disappointment when he continued along the column of her neck instead of teasing her lips.

His destination became clear.

Her eyes opened wide as he smoothed over her collarbone and onto her chest.

"Close yer eyes, Nareen…" he tempted her.

She didn't, because the sight of his fingers traveling lower on her chest was too erotic to miss. It shouldn't have delighted her, but she was fascinated, unable to look away. He teased the top of her breast where her bodice pressed it up. She drew in a stiff breath and found herself holding it as delight drew its claws down her body. She felt it all along her spine, a twisting, churning delight that begged for her to arch and increase the pressure between his hand and her breast.

He pressed a kiss against her neck, this one firmer and full of hunger. One she felt inside herself as well.

Her eyes fluttered shut, and everything intensified.

She leaned her head back, and Saer boldly stroked the swell of one breast. Her nipple was still puckered, but it felt like it was drawing tighter. Nareen reached behind her, seeking his thighs through the pleated fabric of his kilt. She needed more of him, craved the feeling of his hard body.

He kissed his way up her neck and across her jawline until she was turning in his embrace, his hands guiding her until he could cover her lips with his own. He closed his embrace around her once more, and she purred with contentment. Every inch of her was humming with delight, and she reached for him, sliding her hand along the side of his face until she threaded her fingers through the strands of his hair.

He growled softly, his mouth pressing harder against hers. She opened her lips, anticipating the touch of his tongue this time. When it came, she shuddered, her entire body responding to the touch. She fisted her hand in his hair, holding him to her as she tried to mimic his motions and taste him, just as he was tasting her.

Her actions sparked a response in him that was uncontrollable. For one wild moment, he claimed her mouth like a prize. His lips played across hers with a demand that had her clitoris throbbing between the folds of her sex and her hips straining toward his.

Suddenly, he put her away from him, cupping her shoulders and setting her back a full pace. He held her there as she heard him draw in a ragged breath. His eyes glittered with hunger, and frustration needled her.

"Concede the point, Nareen." He stepped farther back and offered her his hand, the meaning unmistakable.

He wanted submission now that he'd proven her flesh was weak.

Of course he did. All men craved such from women. The kindness was over, and now the claiming would begin.

She shook her head and grabbed the front of her skirt. "I shall never concede any victory to ye."

His eyes narrowed and glittered with a promise that made her lips tingle. It was more than a look. She felt his determination as much as saw it flickering in his eyes. It stole her breath and sent her heart racing. An insane urge to bare her teeth at him surfaced, terrifying her with how intense her feelings were.

Wild…like him.

She ran.

Maybe her pride demanded she stand her ground, but there was something churning in her insides that convinced her she had no hope of prevailing against him. It was urging her back toward him, back into his embrace where she might be enchanted once again.

The blush stinging her cheeks had nothing to do with her running. She'd enjoyed his kiss and wanted more. It was a dark and wild craving, rising up from some place deep inside her, a feeling that overwhelmed logical thought, leaving her prey to her instincts.

She wouldn't be a creature of weakness. Not like Abigail, and not like those who had come to Ruth with gold in order to purchase something that they craved uncontrollably. Most of them weren't evil at their core. Lament often shone in their eyes when they were finished, but they were slaves to their needs.

No, she would not be like that.

Ever.

❧

"Me father will be at supper."

Nareen took the pot of rouge away in response. Abigail had an affection for court and its lavish ways. Even in the Highlands, she still painted her face every night. Preparing for supper took the lady a full two hours.

Except for when her father was going to be at the high table.

"I'll have to wear something boring," Abigail groused.

Nareen opened a wardrobe and sorted among the dresses. There were many made of silk, which crinkled when she moved them. Rich velvet, as well as costly brocade, was soft beneath her fingertips.

"Not the wool," Abigail instructed. "I detest it so."

Wool was the fabric of the Highlands. Abigail was a foolish brat to shun it. When it was wet, wool would still keep the body warm. No other fabric offered its wearer such an amenity, or protection from the harsh Highland climate.

Nareen selected a brocade dress with silver trim.

"I suppose I must," Abigail complained when Nareen brought it to her.

Nareen gave her no reply but got on with helping her dress. Abigail was older than she was but often reminded Nareen of a child.

❦

The Great Hall was lit with over a hundred candles. The scent of beeswax floated through the air as the Ross retainers and castle residents settled onto the long benches to enjoy the evening meal. With the sunlight gone, it was their opportunity to relax and enjoy one another's company. Only a fool wasted the daylight hours, one who would learn their lesson when they had empty bellies and leaking roofs during the winter.

The kitchens began to send in platters of hot meat pies and fresh bread. Since it was summer, there were greens and berries. Pots of fresh butter and even honey sat on the table.

The Great Hall was large and filled with long tables. At the end of the Hall was a raised platform that held the high table. The Earl of Ross presided over the evening meal from a chair that had a high back. It rose above his head and had the Ross coat of arms carved into it. From the back of the Hall, there was no missing who was master. He had a benevolent smile on his lips and looked strong enough even though his hair was gray.

Saer MacLeod sat next to the earl. He actually wore a doublet, but it was open halfway down his chest, and the sleeves were open and tied behind his back.

Nareen shivered and bit her lip to distract herself.

Did the man never feel the night air?

He'd certainly looked at home in the darkness the night before. He was at home behaving like a savage, too. Kissing in church was for those who didn't fear the wrath of the priests and their love of sentencing offenders to the stocks.

Of course, a laird didn't often suffer the same penalties as the rest of the congregation. Saer could buy his way out of a public reprimand if it came to it.

Her cheeks heated, and she aimed her gaze at Abigail's back to keep her thoughts off him. But it was not so simple to erase the memory of his kiss from her mind. She still felt the steady grip on her neck and the way she'd irrefutably enjoyed it.

That was a sin.

"There's me lass." The earl looked up from his meal. He pointed a small eating dirk at Abigail. "Ye've kept me guest waiting, Daughter."

Abigail stopped at the foot of the stairs that led up to the high table. She lowered herself, if it were possible to call the quick bob she made such a thing. It certainly lacked any sincerity. Her father frowned at her, but she flounced up the steps to take her place beside him.

"Laird MacLeod is nae here to see me, Father." Two burly retainers stepped forward to assist the lady. They pulled her chair back and waited while she fussed with her skirts before pushing it up to the table. Nareen fell into place behind her mistress's chair.

"He'll make no offer for me," Abigail said.

"What's this ye say, Daughter?"

"He was watching Nareen Grant back at court." Abigail held up her hand for her goblet. A young lad retrieved it from the cupboard and brought it to her. "And kissed her in the chapel this morning."

Nareen's cheeks burned, but she had to maintain her position behind her mistress. More than one sly look was aimed her way.

"What's this?" the earl demanded.

Abigail took a long drink, then smirked at Saer. "It is simple, Father. Laird MacLeod was raised among the isles and lacks any sort of refinement—"

"On the isles, children do nae use such tones with their parents," Saer interrupted. "If that is a lack of refinement, I am content with me rough ways."

"Ha!" The earl laughed. "What have ye to say to that, Daughter? Laird MacLeod is nae impressed with yer tart words and, unlike the last few whelps who sat at me table and tried to call themselves yer suitors, Saer MacLeod speaks plainly. That is nae a lack of refinement. It is the mark of a Highlander."

Abigail pouted. "I have no suitors any longer because ye insult them. Which is why I must return to court, to find another."

Saer's eyes narrowed. He wasn't the only man in the room who cast disapproving looks toward the highborn daughter of the house. "If a few harsh words were enough to banish them," Saer informed her, "ye are better off not wed to a coward. A Highlander should speak only the truth. If a man cannae look the father of the woman he desires in the eye, he is nae worthy of her."

"True!" The earl nodded. "I cannae stomach a man without courage." He leaned toward Saer. "I growled at her last suitor only once, and he turned white! I cannae have that sort of blood in me grandchildren."

"Yer daughter should desire better," Saer decided firmly. "The Ross are nae weaklings."

There were nods and grunts of approval from the people watching from the lower tables.

"Well, I shall nae stand for a savage instructing me on any matter." Abigail began to wave her hands at the retainers standing behind her father. "I shall sup above stairs."

"Ye'll stay, Daughter." The earl's expression tightened. The soft old man had vanished. His fingers were clenched into a fist now, his gaze sharp. "And ye'll mind that tongue of yers in front of me guest."

"Yer trust is misplaced, Father." Abigail wasn't willing to back down. "This savage kissed me companion in the church this morning. He has no sense of propriety, and I shall nae listen to him."

The earl pounded the tabletop. "Enough!" he commanded. "Where is this lass? Come around where I may see ye."

Nareen had no choice. She went around the end of the long table and lowered herself in front of the earl. He leaned forward to inspect her. His gaze was still sharp, and he made two passes up and down her length before nodding.

"I believe I'd think less of ye, Laird MacLeod, if ye didn't kiss such a fetching lass. If I were young enough to catch her, I'd do the same."

The Hall filled with laughter.

"Father, ye are being a toad!"

The earl turned and looked sternly at Abigail. "Ye need spend more time worrying about yer own sins! Ye are a gossip, and ye spend too much time thinking about what others are doing, when ye should be securing yerself a husband. A fortune has been spent on yer trips to court, and what do we have to show for it? Suitors who cannae sit through a single supper with me?" He chuckled and pulled on a gray tuft of his beard. "I am such a fearsome sight, after all. I will have me secretary sort through the offers I have for ye tomorrow, since it seems Laird MacLeod has eyes for another. I admit, I had hoped he was here to offer for ye."

Saer didn't even try to hide his disgust at the mere idea of having Abigail for wife. Behind him, his captain's expression was tight and disapproving. He even leaned slightly away from her.

Abigail's mouth hung open for a moment. She was fuming, but she closed her mouth and took a deep breath before speaking.

"I will find a better match at court," Abigail insisted in a tone that was far more respectful, even if one look in her eyes confirmed it was only a sham. "Please, Father, I beg ye to let me know what sort of man I'll wed. Proposals written on paper are so cold."

The earl drummed his fingers on the table. "What of this scandal that had ye sent home to me? The king was most displeased. The Ross do nae need the king's wrath. He sent ye home for me to deal with. Make no mistake, Daughter, I'll keep me house in order, even as old as I am."

"It was a misunderstanding only." Abigail aimed wide eyes at her sire. "I swear it upon me sweet mother's memory."

The earl instantly changed his demeanor. His gaze became soft as he became lost in his recollections. "Yer mother was a spring blossom. She never said an unkind word. Never. Her heart was so tender, I could deny her nothing."

"Ye promised her I might choose me own husband."

Her father grunted before lifting his hand for his goblet. "Only so long as the man is a good match, Daughter! Marriage is a business."

"Of course, Father, which is why I must return to court. With the king nearing the age of his majority, everyone is there to make sure they are seen."

The earl gripped his goblet and peered at his daughter over its silver rim. "Aye, that's sensible enough."

Abigail watched him take a long drink, and the corners of her mouth twitched. The earl wasn't content, and continued to drink until he'd drained his goblet.

"That's how to enjoy supper!" he declared, turning his goblet over to show one and all it was empty. The moment he handed it back to his cup boy, the lad was rushing back to the cupboard to refill it. The earl kept his hand out, his fingers opening and closing restlessly as he waited for the goblet to be returned.

"Ye are falling behind, Laird MacLeod."

Saer leaned on his elbow so he might make eye contact with the earl. "Yer daughter is correct on one account. I was raised on simple fare and find it to me taste. I have no affection for French wine, but yer cook is talented."

The earl frowned then returned to eating. "It's sad I am to hear that, but I suppose it shall leave ye clear-headed enough to nae allow me daughter too much rein tonight. She is spoilt, I confess. I should have remarried and provided her a mother. It's me failing."

Abigail was turning red, but she didn't argue. She smirked again when her father took his goblet and drank long and deep. Within an hour, he'd be senseless.

Nareen had watched it all before. The earl was not a bad man, but he still mourned his dead wife. Another goblet of wine, and he would begin telling stories of their years together. Pinned to his shoulder was a gold-framed miniature painting of her. He'd pass out right in his chair with that painting cradled in his hands. His men would carry him to his chamber, leaving Abigail to her own devices.

It was not her concern.

And yet…it was. The memory of Abigail's words needled her, undermining the trust Nareen had in her position. It might not be as safe a haven as she'd decided it was.

That didn't mean she would be taking Saer's offer.

No. The Highlander represented another danger, one that was far more personal, because she felt drawn to him. The only way to protect herself from that curse was to ensure she was nowhere near him.

Nareen stood behind her mistress, waiting for the woman to finish supper. It was her place. She didn't resent it, because she enjoyed the freedom being a servant provided. So what if she had to wait to eat until Abigail dismissed her?

It was her choice.

And that was worth everything.

Nareen shifted her gaze to Saer MacLeod without realizing it. He represented many of the reasons she was happy with her position as Abigail's servant. Saer MacLeod would likely please her brother as a match, and then she would become his servant, even her body no longer her own.

But the memory of the way Abigail's voice had filled with anticipation when she spoke of arranging a liaison returned, and it would not be banished. Perhaps Nareen couldn't allow herself to be near Saer MacLeod, but she would be a fool not to heed his advice to leave her position. She had no intention of acting the fool.

With either Abigail or Saer MacLeod.

❧

"Saer MacLeod is a beast."

Abigail was pacing the length of her receiving chamber. Beyond an arched doorway her huge bed awaited, the flicker of candles dancing over the costly cotton bedsheets.

"I cannae stomach being here any longer," Abigail wailed. "This banishment from court is intolerable!"

"It is nae forever," Nareen offered in a tone that betrayed just how little pity she had for her mistress.

Abigail turned to glare at her, but Nareen offered her no apology. "It is only a single week longer."

Abigail huffed. "Yet it is too long. The king is a child! Insisting on virtues and pious behavior. Just wait, he'll take a mistress soon enough. Just as soon as his beard comes in and his cock starts to keep him awake at night."

Abigail sat down and began to fuss with her letters. She reread them with bright eyes that glistened with unshed tears.

Nareen's belly rumbled, but Abigail was absorbed in her own concerns. It afforded Nareen the chance to slip away. Supper was long finished, and the tables cleared. Small groups of people lingered in the Hall, enjoying the warmth from the hearth. Only a few candles remained lit, allowing the night to creep across the space. She enjoyed the shadows. They offered refuge from those who might seek her out when she would rather be alone.

Along one side of the Hall, Ross retainers had pulled out their pallets for the night. These were the younger men, the ones without wives. Each one had his sword resting beside him, and the portion of his kilt that lay over his shoulder during the day raised up to cover his head. At some point during the night, they would trade places with the men standing watch on the walls.

Nareen only peeked into the Hall. The stairs ended at a junction. She could go right and be in the Great Hall or straight ahead to the armor rooms. Off to her left was the hallway that would take her to the kitchens. There were large hearths in the Hall itself for porridge and stews, but most of the cooking was done in the kitchens. They were built outside to protect the castle from fire. In the summer, it also served to keep the kitchens from becoming too hot to endure.

There were only a few lanterns left alight in the hallway to fend off the night. The gate was down, and most of the inhabitants had taken the Church's warning to shut themselves in to avoid the demons that ruled the night.

"Yer mistress is a brat."

Nareen stiffened, stepping sideways, because she just couldn't squelch the urge to put space between herself and Saer MacLeod.

"I do nae deny it."

Saer was leaning against the wall, his arms crossed over his chest and one foot lifted and set against the wall behind him. He looked remarkably at ease, but one look into his dark eyes and she realized just how sharp his focus was.

"Did someone forget to show ye to a chamber for the night, Laird MacLeod?"

He flashed a grin. "Are ye offering to see to the duty? I might just rethink me opinion of sleeping inside stone walls if it means following ye above stairs."

His tone was teasing, but her throat contracted, like a noose was knotted around it. "I am nae. If ye do nae care for stone walls, why are ye here?"

Saer studied her for a long moment, his lips settling into a firm line. "Ye do nae need to hide here, Nareen. I will escort ye to yer brother if ye wish."

It was a kind offer, one she might have considered if she trusted herself to be near him.

"I thank ye for the offer, but I am well enough on me own."

"I admire ye for being resourceful, but ye need not serve in this house. They do nae respect ye for yer diligence."

It was true, and she wasn't comfortable hearing it spoken aloud. "I am nae hiding. I have simply nae decided on where it is I wish to go from here."

He flashed a roguish grin. "Is that a fact?"

She nodded but realized too late she was letting her guard down by engaging him in conversation. With amazing ease, he had abandoned his position against the wall and blocked her path.

"I have a suggestion for ye, sweet Nareen."

She had to tip her head back to lock gazes with him. A shiver raced down her spine as she caught the flicker of determination in his eyes.

"I've heard yer idea of where I should go, and I will nae be returning to Donarch Tower and me brother's rule."

"Yer brother thought he was sending ye some place safe," Saer counseled her gravely.

There was an edge to his tone that shamed her. "I know," she whispered, the words harder to say than she'd anticipated, the sting of being banished still too fresh, but she knew she would have to forgive her brother. Kael had meant well. Ruth was the guilty one. "As I said, I have nae yet decided on where I wish to go, only that it will nae be back to me father's house."

"Ye should hear me suggestion, since ye are considering making a decision."

He moved even closer, indecently close. She shivered. Acute sensation was flooding her, numbing her wits.

"Honor demanded I offer to take ye to yer brother."

She could feel the heat from his body. She stepped away, only to collide with the wall.

"I'll confess that I'd prefer to have ye to meself, lass," he whispered.

She detested the idea. She told herself she did. But she quivered, sensation coursing through her insides and leaving her curiously elated. Just as she had been that morning.

"This morning in the chapel, ye made it clear what sort of offer ye have for me." She struggled to maintain her composure. "I've no interest in the urges of men. That is why I am here, and it is why I will nae agree to leave with ye. Ye shall nae be claiming I challenged ye, so ye have a reason yer hand at tossing me skirts once we are away and there are only yer men surrounding us."

She was being overly bold with a man who was her better, but she lifted her chin in the face of his scowl. "Do nae be so insulted. Yer men are loyal to ye. I'd be a fool no' to think on that fact. Ye deserve such words for the arrogant way ye took what ye wanted this morning. The Ross will think me a slut now. I wonder what ye would have thought of any man treating yer own sister that way."

His eyes narrowed, and he frowned.

"Yer tongue is sharp." He surprised her by speaking in an even tone. "Yet it is yer strength that draws me to ye, even when it is delivered in the form of blunt, but true, words. I was thinking only of proving ye would enjoy me touch, since I've wanted to taste ye since I saw ye at court, but it was insensitive of me to do so in public."

His words stunned her. She'd never expected such tenderness from him, much less an apology. He was a laird, set above her by God. Even the priest would tell her that.

But she didn't need to know he'd followed her from court. Something stirred inside her at such an idea. Some feeling she wasn't comfortable with, a feeling that might quickly turn into needing. Because she liked it, and she couldn't allow herself to like Saer MacLeod.

But his admission also made her feel desirable. Court was full of beautiful women, the fairest in Scotland, and she was not blind to how she compared. Her features were not too harsh, but she was no rare beauty.

"Find someone else ye crave." She lifted her chin. "'Tis disgust ye stir in me."

He'd hooked his hands into the wide belt holding his kilt around his lean waist. "Aye, that's true enough, and it makes me want to beat yer cousin to death for allowing ye to be preyed upon. There is a fire in ye, one that should nae be tempered with fear."

"I am well enough," she said and slid along the wall to escape. "Me opinion of ye has naught to do with me cousin. It is simply the way I feel."

He stepped forward, caging her with his body in one, lightning-fast motion. "Do nae lie to me. I felt ye tremble."

"I am nae—"

He lowered his head, until his lips hovered over hers. She wanted to reject him, but a soft gasp escaped her, betraying her rising excitement. Her fingers clenched in a vain attempt to grip the wall and keep herself from leaning toward him.

The urge was there, curling through her insides like a living force.

"I also felt ye gripping me hair," he whispered. "Why are ye trying to hold on to the wall behind ye? Is it to keep yer hands off me?"

There was a wicked suggestion in his tone that stoked the embers of the flames he'd brought to life inside her in the chapel. She sucked in a horrified breath, her eyes widening. She looked away, but he cupped her chin, returning her gaze to his. A shudder shook her, and his lips curved.

"That is a reaction, lass, but nae one of disgust." His voice was edged with too much confidence. "It is the reaction of a woman to a man."

He admired her. The realization set a bright glow off inside her, but it also stirred a warning. She needed to reject him, find some way to wound his pride so he would never look her way again.

For a moment, she was torn. Uncertain of what path was truly best. She searched his eyes, seeking more hints of his true nature, but only time would deliver those facts. Time and trust. If she trusted wrongly, she would suffer.

But then her belly rumbled.

His expression tightened as he bit back the desire to kiss her.

"Ye have nae eaten." He stepped back, offering her the space to precede him to the kitchens. "That damned brat let ye stand through supper without leave to fill yer belly."

"Ye do nae know that." It wasn't an outright lie, but she still cringed at how dishonest she was being. If he didn't matter to her, she had no reason to fear his knowing anything about her. Yet she was almost desperate to hide every detail about herself. But the words slipped past her lips before she realized how telling they were. "Ye cannae know what I am about during all the hours of the day."

His lips twitched with satisfaction. "I am here for ye, lass. Me attention is on ye and naught else. I know where ye have been this day and that yer mistress did nae give ye leave throughout supper. But I certainly expected she had supper for ye above stairs. Ye followed her up there several hours past."

There was a memory, a recollection of a time when she was not alone and someone else cared if she went without. She'd be a liar if she claimed she hadn't missed such a feeling.

But she'd be a fool to bask in the glow of anything Saer made her feel. He'd made his intentions plain, so she'd have to make her choice even plainer.

"I am off to the kitchens now and do nae need an escort." He was too large, both in stature and intensity. She felt overwhelmed and needed to push him away so she might catch her breath.

"Since ye have brought it to me attention that I've cast doubt on yer character, ye do," he countered.

She shook her head, every fiber of her being

denying him. Saer made a low sound that was a cross between a growl and a snarl before scooping her off her feet.

She gasped, stunned by his audacity. "Put me down!"

"Raise yer voice a bit louder, lass. It will nae bother me a bit to have us caught in a compromising position."

"I believe ye would." For there would be only one solution, to wed or face being shamed in the pillory.

She slapped his chest because she had to keep her voice low, but all the beast did was chuckle. He stole down the corridor, carrying her with an ease that was unnatural.

No man should have such strength.

No woman should enjoy it so much.

But she did.

He shouldered his way through the doors that led into the yard and then into the kitchens. The hearths were still glowing red, but the flames had died down. New wood wouldn't be added until the morning. It was stacked up nearby, but to use it during a summer night would be wasteful, as it was warm, and there was still plenty of light. Saer deposited her on a stool and looked far too pleased with his actions.

"Are ye trying to impress me with yer tender concern for me empty belly?" She sprang off the stool as though it were a spike. "Or do ye want to make sure I know ye may force me to yer will?"

She didn't care for how it made her feel, the idea that he might be darkening her name on purpose. Men used women as they pleased. It was a lesson she'd learned by witnessing what her cousin Ruth did with her charges. But part of the lesson had come from watching Ruth's customers pay so eagerly for what they wanted with no concern for those being sold.

"I plan to make sure yer belly stops rumbling. I know that pain."

He was busy looking through the bowls left on the long worktable in the center of the kitchen. They were all covered with cloths to protect the food from dust. There was always food left out for the retainers watching the castle wall. When they finished their duty, they would come to sup.

"If all I wanted was a rough tumble, Nareen, I'd have had it last night before ye even saw me face." He sent her a hard look. "I wouldn't have taken ye to yer brother, but carried ye into a church and declared the truth. If forcing ye to be me wife was what I wished, it would be done."

His words were blunt. But true.

He looked back at her. "I'm telling ye so there is no misunderstanding between us. I admire strength, for I know how painful it is to build. Many fold rather than grow stronger." His eyes flashed with admiration. "Ye did nae fold. Breaking ye is nae what I crave."

As far as compliments went, it was far different than what she had been raised to desire from a man. Yet it pleased her in a way no comparison to a summer rose might have.

She sat down, her anger deflating. He slid a plate onto the table in front of her. Just the sight of the food drew a low rumble from her empty belly. Her last meal had been so long ago, her mouth began to water, and her fingers shook as she reached for the food.

Saer missed none of it, but she saw a look of bitter experience emerging past the controlled expression he so often hid behind.

"There were times me mother could nae provide for me. She had been turned out by me father because he had a wife who cared naught for a reminder that another woman had given him a son when she had naught but a tiny daughter. The land he banished her to was difficult to cultivate. I was chasing rabbits for our supper as far back as I can recall. I have hard thoughts for me father when I remember just how grateful me mother was when I brought one home. But now that I am grown, I wonder if he did it to make sure I would grow up strong, since he would not be able to see to it himself."

"That is a hard way to grow up."

She tore a piece of bread in half. She could smell its nutty aroma, in spite of the fact that it was cold. Her fingers shook as she stuffed some into her mouth. To her starved body, the taste was intense.

"That brat has no grasp of how many hours she makes ye go without food. Just as me laird father did nae know how many times I went to bed hungry before I grew strong enough to catch those rabbits. But maybe he wanted me to know what those born beneath me position felt like, so I would nae be like Abigail."

He filled a goblet with fresh milk from the night milking and sat it near her.

Once she was able to control the urge to keep shoving food into her mouth, she asked, "Yet yer father must have paid for yer sword training. Such training is nae given for naught."

"He did. Yet it was made plain to me that every day might be me last if his legitimate wife produced a living son." Satisfaction glowed in his eyes. "I trained longer and harder than any other lad. I could best them all by the time I was growing me first beard. Of course, me master pit me only against those older than me to make sure I did nae grow arrogant."

"I am nae sure that worked." She spoke with soft amusement.

He shrugged. "Yet I earned what I am."

"True." For a moment, it was easy conversing with him, a sense of common understanding growing between them. He had often been spoken of at court, for no one knew much about him, and against the odds, he was laird of the MacLeods.

Little wonder he was as massive and hard as he was. Her gaze slid over his face, finding the details of his harsh life. It was there in the scar on his left cheek and the bump in the center of his nose. Another scar ran through his right eyebrow, and there were several on his bared forearms.

"That is a harsh way to live," she whispered.

His dark gaze locked with hers. "As difficult as lying down in yer bed and knowing yer own kin might be selling yer body?"

Nareen looked away, unable to share that pain with him. It was too deep, too personal, too intimate.

"We all endure what we must," she countered. "Only babes think life is fair."

"Aye. As I endure being inside these walls to be near ye."

He was leaning against the wall again. There was a

hint of discomfort in his expression, and she realized it was because he truly did not care for the walls surrounding him.

It was another thing they had in common.

She shook off the feeling. He inspired too many emotions in her. She finished her meal and took the plate to a bucket used for dirty tableware. They'd be taken outside in the morning for washing.

"Good night, Laird MacLeod."

He remained leaning against the wall, arms folded across his chest. Even with night fully fallen, his shirtsleeves were still tied up to the shoulder to bare his arms.

"Good night, Nareen Grant, may yer rest be peaceful."

There was something too calm about his words. She hesitated in the kitchen doorway, trying to deduce what it was.

"As for meself, I am wide awake," he continued, lowering the foot he'd had braced against the kitchen wall. "Would ye care to ride with me?"

The impulse to nod was too strong, and she was already lowering her head before she realized what she was doing.

"I cannae."

He chuckled and rolled his shoulders before stretching his neck and casting her a devilish look.

"But would ye dare to, Nareen?" He moved toward the door that led out into the yard. He turned and offered her his hand. "That's what I really want to know. Are ye going to waste yer free time or find the boldness to enjoy it?"

"I do nae need to accept yer invitation to do as I

please, now that Abigail is finished with me for the night." She walked past him to prove it. The night air was cool and fresh, making her smile. With her belly full, her energy returned. She made her way to the stables, and her mare let out a sound of greeting.

But Saer was the one who fit the bridle over the mare's muzzle. He rubbed her head gently too, showing he had a care for her feelings.

"I am nae riding with ye," Nareen insisted.

"I'm sorry ye lack the courage to be in me company."

She stiffened and faced him. "It is nae about courage."

Saer turned, his kilt flaring out as he slid a hand around her waist and pulled her against his body. She pressed her hands against his chest, but lost the urge to push him away when she felt how hard his body was beneath his shirt.

"Ye should wear a doublet."

He cupped her nape and leaned his head to the side so she felt his breath against the skin of her neck.

"And miss the feeling of yer hands against me skin? Nae, lass. I came here for ye. It is yer touch I was determined to feel."

She trembled. "Have ye no shame?"

It was a foolish question, considering their position. He lifted his head and locked gazes with her.

"What I have, is no use for pretense. Clothing is for keeping warm. I am nae cold, but ye can feel that, cannae ye, lass?"

She could, and it pleased her in a way she had never thought of before. The urge to slide her hand along the ridges of hard muscles covering his chest was gaining strength, undermining her determination to remain unmoved. In another few moments, she'd be nothing but a servant of her cravings.

"Fine. I'll ride with ye."

His eyes narrowed, and the grip on her nape tightened just a bit.

"So release me, and I'll accept yer invitation."

He grunted, frustration clear in his expression. But he complied, opening his embrace to allow her free.

"I think ye are toying with me, Nareen."

She grasped her mare's bridle and began to lead her from the stable. "No more than ye are with me, Laird MacLeod."

She was sure truer words had never been spoken.

He chuckled, sending a blush onto her cheeks. "Which only proves what a fine match we'd be."

It only proved how well he could find her weaknesses. She should turn around. It would be the sensible thing to do, but she didn't. The night was warm enough and the air so fresh. A smile curved her lips, and she simply didn't have the strength to turn her back on the freedom she'd find in a night ride.

At least riding was a weakness she might indulge in.

But she would have to make certain it was the only weakness she allowed to be fed tonight.

❧

Nareen didn't wait for him.

She made her way through the yard as Saer readied his stallion to ride. He might have caught up to her easily, but he trailed behind her. Perhaps stalk was a better word, for it fit his feelings better.

She was going to use his name before the dawn.

It was a possessive thought, one he really had no business thinking. Nareen didn't belong to him, and she was a virtuous woman. Although riding out in the dark of night didn't fit the ideals of virtue. At least not for the more civilized—which he was not.

Yet neither was Nareen.

Saer made his way through the open gate and swung up onto his stallion's back. Beyond the walls of the castle was the village, but Nareen didn't ride toward the flickering lights. She headed into the dark, where the starlight reflected off the stones.

He enjoyed the surge of anticipation warming his blood and grinned.

Savage. Aye, he was that. But Nareen Grant was wild, which made her his match. He was looking forward to running her to ground, and the lass was going to enjoy it. That was his solemn vow.

Two

FOR A BRIEF MOMENT, NAREEN WAS ABLE TO IGNORE everything. She was immersed in the feeling of the horse moving beneath her and the way the wind ripped at her hair, making her smile.

But she heard Saer closing the distance between them.

His stallion had heavier steps, and her mare let out a shrill cry before moving faster. Nareen leaned low, hugging the sides of the horse with her thighs and moving in unison with her.

The sounds of the stallion came closer. Anticipation tingled along her nape, raising the tiny hairs and rippling down her spine. She'd never realized she might feel so much sensation from just knowing a man was near.

With Saer, she felt his presence keenly. The darkness seemed to be intensifying the connection between them. The urge to look behind her was impossible to ignore. She turned her head and caught a glimpse of him.

He was magnificent. Like some legend from eras past. His hair was held back with a thin braid along the left side of his face, telling one and all he'd been born outside the bonds of matrimony.

It suited him.

There was nothing about him that fit into the model of what civilization lived by.

She drank in the details of his rugged physique. Strength radiated from him, hitting her like a gust of wind. He surged past, taking the lead. In the night, stallion and master were like living shadows. He rode hard, out across Ross land, until the fortress was out of sight. Nareen never ventured so far, but she had no fear tonight. In fact, she felt freer than she could recall ever feeling. Saer slowed and shook his head, letting the stallion rear up and paw at the night sky.

She laughed, the sound silvery and refreshing. Her mare slowed, her strength spent as she covered the last few paces to where Saer's stallion was prancing in a small circle. Saer kept the beast under control, his bare knees pressed into its sides to keep himself firmly in the saddle, but he didn't force the animal to stand still.

He clearly understood the creature's nature. In fact, she was sure he shared it. Both were powerful and unsatisfied by stillness.

"Come, lass, let's rinse the ride off our skin."

His words confused her until she realized the roaring she heard was the sound of water nearby. She suddenly became aware of how sweaty she was, and the idea of bathing was pleasing. At least it was until she looked up to see Saer leading the way.

Her mare was already in motion, following the stallion. Saer never looked back. She watched the moonlight turn him silver as he sat strong and proud in the saddle.

She tightened her hands on the reins, beginning to pull up. The mare let out a disgruntled nicker, making it clear she wanted to follow the stallion.

The reason was plain.

Nareen found herself envying the mare. The animal had far more freedom than she did. For the horses, the instinct to touch was not wicked, yet it was for her.

Or was it?

The question was a valid one. There was no one about to stop her from doing whatever she wished. Saer MacLeod might be a savage, but he was also one of the few men she didn't have to worry about running home to her brother with tales of her behavior and how it didn't fit what society expected of her. Besides, she did not even have to fear the loss of her reputation—no one thought her a maiden any longer, even though she was.

Freedom. Wasn't that what she craved? Saer was offering it.

That much was also true. He wanted something as well. Still, she was as tempted by him as she was weary of pretenses. So weary. Saer offered her the one thing she craved above all others, the opportunity simply to be as she liked.

Now that was true freedom. It was an offer she'd never had from another human being, except for her brother, Kael, when they were young. The memory shimmered, gleaming with the allure of a time when she was the happiest she had ever been.

Saer tempted her in more ways than she'd ever imagined possible.

The water was spilling over a large outcropping of boulders. It cascaded down into a pool that was several dozen feet across, before flowing down the side of the valley. The moon was half hidden behind the clouds, but the faint silver light still turned the surface of the water into a mirror. Ripples disturbed its surface as the water continued to pound down.

Saer took a moment to survey the entire area, scanning the far shore of the small pond and the top of the waterfall. Once he was satisfied they were alone, he dismounted near the water's edge, smoothing his hand along his stallion's neck, then removing the bridle. The animal shook its head, making its mane bounce, then lowered its head to graze.

Saer pulled off his sword and leaned it against a rock. The trees had thinned out near the shoreline. He leaned against a boulder and began to unlace one of his knee-high boots. Nareen slid from the back of her mare and removed the bridle so the mare might graze as well. The horses moved off, slowly nibbling at the grass.

Saer's second boot hit the ground, and he reached for the tail of his wide belt.

He opened the belt holding his kilt around his waist and caught the length of pleated fabric with a practiced hand. He draped it over the boulder.

"There is a tub in the kitchen."

He shook his head and pulled his shirt off. Her mouth went dry as the starlight washed over every hard inch of him. All of the strength she'd felt through the layers of their clothing was there to behold.

"I'm not a babe to be washed in a tub like a dirty dish."

He certainly wasn't.

Every bit of him was molded and chiseled. Her gaze roamed along his shoulders and chest, and farther down, to his flat belly.

She jerked her attention away. "Ye have no shame," she accused, but she was breathless.

"What I have is no use for nonsense, preached by those who have always been fortunate enough to have a bathing tub. It's simple enough for them to tell ye it is a sin to make use of what nature provides. The way I see it, God created this world, so wouldn't it be a sin to shun what he has crafted?" Saer pulled something from the surface of the rock and started walking toward the water. "I'll clean me body here, nae sitting in me own filth. All I need is this bar of soap."

He lifted his hand holding the soap, and continued on into the water.

"Ye had no right to have me follow ye here, when ye planned all the time to…to…"

He stepped into the water, wading until he dove straight into the pool. His body glided through the water smoothly, making her skin itch to enjoy the same thing.

He surfaced and began to rub the bar of soap along his body. "Ye can turn around if yer gentle sensibilities are too bruised, Nareen."

"Do nae be ridiculous." The words just slipped out, earning a chuckle from him.

"As I thought, ye are concerned only because ye are tempted to join me."

He stood waist deep in the water, the dark liquid hiding the part of him she'd shied away from looking at. She regretted that now. It was easier to fear the unknown.

She'd learned that under her cousin's rule.

"Are ye trying yer hand at gentling me?" Suspicion coated her words. "Bringing me along and allowing me to see ye in yer private moments so I'll become more accustomed to ye?"

He shrugged, drawing her gaze to his powerful shoulders again.

"Ye're a woman fully grown, lass... What I want to know is what sort of woman do ye plan to be? One who lives her life squeezing her eyes shut, or one who dances into the shadows simply because they are there. I suppose there is some truth in yer words, but consider this. What other man would care to put ye at ease when all he need do is gain yer brother's approval to have ye?"

"Why did ye no'?"

He stared at her, and she felt the connection just as keenly as she would have his touch. "Me sire's wife was a cringing coward. I remember her weeping in the hallways, unable to look her husband in the eye."

"She was English."

"Aye." He nodded. "And she never adjusted to being wed to a Highlander. All she gave him was one fae-like daughter, but at least me sister, Daphne, has her father's spirit. The MacLeod deserve better than another mistress who cannae stand with her chin held high."

It was on the tip of her tongue to tell him she did not want to be his wife.

But she quelled the urge. To insult him for the sake of

arguing was childish. He deserved more than that from her. Aye, he was arrogant, but he was not a brute. At least he hadn't proved to be yet. But her brother could have contracted her to him without a single word from her on the matter. As a laird's daughter, she'd been raised to expect to wed for her clan's benefit. Saer claimed to have permission to court her, and she had been foolish enough not to question what else Kael had agreed to.

Leaving the Ross castle so far behind suddenly seemed a poor choice.

Suspicion flooded her, and she looked at him.

He was working the soap along his chest, and she found herself wanting to do the chore for him. The brief moments she'd felt his hard chest seemed too long ago. She craved another opportunity to discover what his skin was like when in contact with her own.

He looked up, holding her gaze, and grinned. She paused, a memory surfacing of leering faces peering down at her. Her fingers froze as her cousin's voice invaded the moment.

Nareen shuddered, a horrified gasp escaping her lips. Even now, it felt like their gazes had left a dirty smear on her skin. She was caught in the memory, feeling the way she'd felt trapped in her tiny cell-like chamber. The moments feeling endless until her cousin guided her clients away to look at another girl because they declined to pay the price her cousin put on Nareen's maidenhead.

A girl less fortunate than Nareen had been that night.

But she still heard the bar being shoved down on the other side of the chamber door to make sure she was there when another buyer arrived.

A wet hand cupped her chin, bringing her attention back to the moment.

"Stay here with me, lass. The past belongs where it is."

The feeling of his skin was firm and exactly what she needed. The past was a ghost, one she refused to be chained to.

"Aye." She yanked the lace that held her bodice closed free with more force than was necessary, pulling the knot up so that she might loosen it. She needed to prove she would not be ruled by Ruth or any of her bad memories.

But she still shied away from disrobing facing Saer. She turned her back on him and forced herself to continue disrobing.

He'd seen a woman's form before.

She was the same as other women.

Her arguments didn't really reinforce her confidence. Hearing him step back into the water did. The tiny splashing sound gave her enough courage to pull free the lace that held her bodice closed. The moment she did, the fronts sagged beneath the weight of her breasts. They felt swollen, her nipples tingling as they drew tight. She tossed her bodice aside and opened her skirts. Her dress was simpler than Abigail's, with only one set of skirts secured to a single waistband. Once it was open, she untied the small, padded bolster that went around her hips to save her back from the weight of the wool, and it all dropped down to her ankles.

When she stepped free, her chemise fluttered in the breeze. She shivered, but it had nothing to do with the temperature. The heat rising inside her was wild and uncontrollable, but it also bolstered her courage.

"The water is refreshing, Nareen…" His voice was edged with temptation. She reached for her braid and delayed turning around as she worked the strands free. A few years ago, she'd dreamed of meeting her groom with her hair flowing as proof of her virginity. Of course, that was before her reputation was tarnished.

So it didn't matter what she did tonight. At least not to anyone except herself and Saer.

Besides, if he ravished her, she could at last stop fearing it. That thought filled her with courage. Or maybe it was desperation. But the idea of being free of fear was enough to shed the last of her reservations.

She turned and found him submerged to his chin. The moonlight flashed off his eyes as he watched her. But instead of making her self-conscious, his gaze made her bold. He was the definition of strength, and she was not going to cringe in his sight.

The first touch of the water sent a chill up her leg. She stifled a giggle before plunging her foot all the way in. It was cold only for the first moment. She hurried deeper in and began to swim to accustom herself to the temperature. Within moments, she was comfortable, the cool water soothing. She ducked beneath the surface to wet her hair and smiled when she came up. Until she opened her eyes to find Saer right in front of her.

The smile faded from her lips as their gazes locked. She felt the challenge coming from him and stared straight back. She lifted her chin.

"Are ye satisfied, Laird MacLeod?"

Her tone had turned sultry, stunning her with how wanton she sounded.

"Aye…" He closed the distance between them. "And yet, nae."

He offered her the bar of soap. Anticipation tingled in her belly as she eyed it. There wasn't enough light to judge his expression, but she felt he was testing her. She reached out for the soap, curling her fingers around its slippery surface, but he didn't release immediately. For a moment, their fingers mingled, the soap coating their skin.

She shook her head, not trusting her voice. Being near him was unleashing something untamed inside her that was drawing her closer to him and his unabashed ways. With him, there were no rules to cage her. But that was dangerous.

She tugged on the soap, and he released it.

Dangerous because there was nothing to bind them to each other. Part of her reveled in that idea, but there was still a whisper of caution holding her back. Women who fell from grace did not meet good ends. She swam closer to the shore where she could touch the bottom, and began to wash herself.

"Admit it, Nareen, no tub of well water would please ye so much."

He'd followed her, standing the same distance from her.

"Ye're testing me." She'd stopped short of exposing her breasts to him completely, but the water made it difficult to move quickly. It was both comforting and confining.

"Aye, I am," he admitted freely.

She turned to eye him, her hand stilling on her arm as she became more focused on his words than her bath. "Why?"

"Strength begets strength."

She was mesmerized by the way he moved closer and stopped just a foot away from her. She'd never been so completely bare in the presence of a man before, but it was more than their lack of clothing. Saer saw more than most. He stripped away her words and stared at the raw wounds still open across her soul.

"Ye are a survivor." He plucked the forgotten soap bar from her hand and cupped her shoulder. "So am I." He turned her away from him and swept her hair over her shoulder before applying the soap to her back. She shivered, the knowledge that she was nude becoming almost overwhelming. "Ye care not for the rules because ye did nae receive the security they promised when ye were compliant."

"Some would say I am simply making excuses to do as I please. I think they may be partially right," she warned him. "I am nae obedient."

But a queer sort of compliance was taking hold of her, a rationale that made it acceptable, because he was also bare. In that moment, they were simply the same, neither more exposed than the other. Both of them being more honest than they might be otherwise.

"Ye are making yer way, in whatever fashion ye might." He smoothed the soap over her shoulders with slow motions. "Doing the best ye can for yerself. That is nae an excuse, it is being resourceful."

She grunted softly. "Be careful, ye'll have the Church

after ye for nae telling me to accept me place as a woman."

"I prefer ye being strong enough to face me without shivering." He was rubbing the soap into her hair. "The place for me woman is standing firmly at me side."

She heard a soft sound of male approval from behind her.

"I am nae conceding anything to ye, Laird MacLeod."

He snorted. "Insist on laying the sharp side of yer tongue on me, lass, and ye'll have to forfeit the rest of yer bath."

She whipped around, the water splashing up into her face. "Do nae instruct me, Laird—"

The bar of soap went flying toward the shore, and he had his hand curled around her nape before she heard it land.

"Saer."

His teeth were bared at her, and his face was only a few inches from her own. The warmth of his breath against her lips made them tremble and yearn for another kiss.

"If I want to let me title impress a lass, I do nae have to suffer sitting inside the Earl of Ross's castle."

"Well, do nae do so for me." She shoved at him but ended up with her hands flattened against his hard chest.

He was going to kiss her.

But he didn't.

She pushed against him again, but he didn't give even a tiny amount of space. Instead, he held her nape, keeping her in place as their gazes held.

"What do ye want?" she demanded, unable to remain silent. It felt like she was coming apart inside.

"I want to know why I am drawn to ye." His fingers gently massaged her nape, sending a tingle down her spine. He moved closer, so close she felt his body heat through the water. "I see yer face in me dreams."

But she couldn't admit it. She shook her head, fighting against his grip until he tightened it.

"Do nae lie." He bit out the three words. "Insult me. Slice me with yer words, but never lie."

She lifted her chin, trying to break his hold on her neck. With a soft snort, he let her go. She dove into the water, swimming away, escaping. But her lungs burned, and she had to surface at last. When she did, Saer was nowhere, the surface of the water giving her no hint as to where he was.

He surged up from beneath the surface of the water beside her. For a moment, she was stunned by the sight of his powerful body erupting from the water like some sort of pagan god of centuries past. He shook his head, water flying off the ends of his hair before he opened his eyes and looked at her.

"I'm going to teach ye how to enjoy yer own body…"

His warning hadn't even sunk completely into her senses when he reached for her. Saer proved his strength again as he plucked her from the water and tossed her over his shoulder. Water streamed off both their bodies as he walked up to where they had left their clothing. He grabbed his kilt and shook it out with one hand. The fabric fluttered to the ground, the edges still rippling as he laid her out on it.

"What ye are doing is proving ye are no different than any other man I have ever met."

He followed her down but didn't trap her beneath his body. She felt no less pinned though, for he settled beside her, his elbow on the ground and his head resting in his hand. He laid his leg over hers, keeping her on her back.

A soft moan escaped her, as she bit into her lower lip to keep herself from voicing how exposed she felt. She would never let him hear her cry.

"I will nae rape ye, Nareen, I promised ye that already."

He had, and that strange sense of complacency moved through her. She refused to consider it trust, because she would never trust any man.

"I wish to rise."

He stroked the side of her face, his fingers delightfully warm. "Say me name."

Her eyes widened, and she struck out and slapped him before being able to control the impulse. That made no sense; an open hand would do little harm. So she tightened her fingers into a fist, but he closed his hand around it.

"I prefer yer feminine claws, nae the skills ye learned from watching yer brother train."

She tried to break his hold, her heart pounding with the effort. "He did more than let me watch."

She'd meant it as a warning, a secret about herself that would prove she lacked a submissive nature, but Saer responded with a deep, husky growl of approval.

"I wondered at the reason ye are so bold, lass."

"Well do nae," she said. "Because I do nae want ye thinking about me at all."

"Humm…" He released her hand, and she jerked it away, but her triumph was short-lived. A moment later, his attention had dropped to her bare breasts as he cupped one gently.

"That leaves me naught but action…" He held the tender mound with a gentle grip that sent a shaft of pleasure through her. "Yet I will confess to enjoying action far more than talking. Ye are more beautiful than a fae princess…"

He stroked her breast, running his fingers all the way around it before brushing the puckered nipple with his thumb. She jerked, unable to remain still as sensation overwhelmed her. Never once had she imagined her breast might be so sensitive or such a point of pleasure.

"Saer—"

"Ah… I enjoy it when me name crosses yer lips." He closed his hand around her breast, holding her gaze. "I believe I understand the means necessary to claim what I want from ye now, Nareen."

Something flashed in his eyes. She felt it as much as saw it. He lowered his head, his warm breath teasing the tip of her nipple a single time before he lapped the hardened peak with his tongue.

"Saer!"

She arched in a crazy need to move, because she couldn't remain still. It felt like lightening had struck her.

"Even better…" he purred deeply—darkly.

He leaned over her, trapping her right shoulder with his own, and licked her nipple again. This time, he teased the entire areola with his velvet tongue before closing his lips around the puckered tip and sucking it into his mouth.

She grabbed a fistful of his hair, but that pleased her too, and she moaned softly as her eyes slid closed. She didn't need to see. The contact between their bodies was unleashing a torrent of pleasure that washed over her, and she didn't care to fight it.

He sucked harder, and she arched up to offer her flesh to him. But it wasn't enough; she wasn't close enough to him. The need to press herself against him was too great to ignore. She rolled toward him.

"Slowly, lass…"

He released her breast and stroked her belly. Her eyes opened wide at the boldness of the touch.

"No one—"

He silenced her with a soft kiss.

"That is the only reason yer cousin is still alive." He rubbed the flat plane of her abdomen, sending a hundred little bolts of enjoyment through her. But his expression had hardened. "If she'd allowed ye to be used without yer consent, I would have hung her before coming after ye."

His tone was rich with protectiveness, and it washed over her, soothing the wounds she thought would never be comforted.

"Do ye mean ye would have accepted me without me virtue?" She scoffed at him softly. "I doubt it. Men enjoy dallying, but demand purity in their brides."

"I value strength in a woman, and such will never be found in one who does nae admit her own nature. If ye'd had a lover, I would have made sure I surpassed his memory."

He teased her belly again with a warm brush of his hand. He leaned down and placed a kiss against her chin, and then another farther up her jawline, and yet a third just below her earlobe. She trembled, the tenderness of his touch undeniable. He had the strength to take whatever he wished, yet he controlled it. That was true honor.

"Ye captivate me, Nareen," he whispered against her ear, then inhaled the scent of her hair. "And I know ye are fascinated by me."

"I've said no such thing." Yet she had felt it.

He lifted his head and flattened his hand on her belly. "Yet ye lay here with me, without flinching. Why? Ye are no wanton. If ye were, ye would have found plenty of lovers to satisfy ye at court."

Her lips twisted with distaste, drawing a pleased growl from him.

"I saw that in yer eyes at court"—he captured her breast again, the hold striking her as possessive—"and it made me want to impress ye."

"I do nae—"

"Aye, ye do, lass." He pressed a hard kiss against her lips, stilling her argument with his mouth. It was demanding, and it stirred the flames he unleashed inside her.

She reached for him, seeking to touch what she'd been drawn to. His arms were covered in smooth, warm skin, but the muscle was firm and hard. She stroked him, up toward his shoulders and along the planes of his chest.

"Open yer mouth, Nareen…"

He cupped her nape, raising her face toward his.

She slid her hands into his hair again, gripping hand-fuls of it to keep his mouth against hers. The need to kiss him was strong, overriding every other thought. There was only impulse and action left in her.

He swept her lower lip with his tongue, setting off a riot of excitement. She stretched her tongue out to mingle with his. For a moment, they stroked each other before he boldly thrust his deep inside her mouth.

She gasped, stunned and excited by the invasion. Her body arched, pressing against his. It was necessary to move, absolutely vital for her to strain toward him. His body pleased her along every point of contact. Even where her thigh pressed against his hard member.

She wanted to take his weight on top of her, even pulled at his shoulder, but he kept her on her back with one large hand pressed flat on top of her belly.

"I'm going to introduce ye to passion, lass."

There was a promise in his tone, an arrogant one, but it struck a chord inside her that unleashed a surge of anticipation.

He sent his hand lower, venturing into the curls that crowned her sex.

"Sacr   "

"I made ye a promise, Nareen."

His fingers slid closer to the little nub throbbing at the top of her sex, and her lips went dry. "What… what was that?"

"To teach ye how to enjoy yer body…"

He pressed his lips against the side of her throat. Her eyes fluttered shut.

But she jerked when he stroked her slit.

"Ye cannae...touch me...there," she exclaimed, her eyes popping open.

"I am," he assured her and sent his fingers back along the folds guarding her passage. "And I intend to do much, much more."

"But it must be...sinful."

But it felt delightful, and she closed her eyes again. True ecstasy rolled through her as he stroked the sensitive folds between her thighs. The skin was slick with her juices, intensifying even the slightest touch.

"There was a time when a warrior had to prove his worth to a woman by bringing her to climax without his cock. Only then would she pledge herself to him."

She opened her eyes and found him watching her face. She felt exposed and helpless. "I cannae do this..."

"All ye must do is trust me."

Trust. The word "trust" broke through the intoxication holding her spellbound.

"No. I refuse to trust." She felt empty as she faced the harsh, cold reality of her feelings. "I cannae trust."

His expression tightened. "Ye will, Nareen. Ye shall trust me."

He crushed her retort beneath a kiss. His mouth took command of her lips, pressing them apart. When she surrendered, he thrust his tongue deeply inside her mouth and sent his finger between the folds of her sex.

Together, the twin points of contact were mind shattering.

Her hips lifted toward his hand, her clitoris sending an intense amount of pleasure through her passage and into her womb. She gasped, breaking their kiss because her lungs were starving for breath. Her heart was pounding, and so was the little nub between the folds of her sex.

Saer rubbed it, sending her hips into a frantic bucking that she had no will to check. There was only the need churning inside her and the delight his finger produced with every stroke. She held on to him with a desperate grip as her need tightened into a knot. When it broke, pleasure swept over her in a rush, stealing every last thought from her mind as she cried out. It twisted through her, wringing her like a rag and dropping her in a panting, spent heap beneath Saer's probing gaze. His dark eyes were full of savage hunger. He did nothing to disguise it, and for several long moments, she was too exhausted to move.

In that moment, she was helpless.

But what made it intolerable was the fact that she had allowed him to reduce her to such a state. She couldn't, wouldn't, allow herself to be so exposed.

"I will never trust ye."

He growled at her, but she pushed against him.

"Ye just did, Nareen." His teeth were bared, and his cock hard against her belly. "There is no denying that ye enjoyed it, too. Pleasure awaits ye in me bed."

He pushed himself up and off her. The night air rushed in to steal the heat his body had shared with her. He reached down and grasped her biceps, easily pulling her to her feet.

"But ye'll never truly trust me if I take ye tonight. Allowing me to touch ye was but a beginning."

He found her chemise and tossed it to her. He truly was at home in the dark, because she hadn't been able to differentiate between her garments. Saer found what she needed first before pulling his shirt off a rock and shrugging into it.

Her fingers shook, but it wasn't from the chill. It took her three tries to get her hands pushed into the sleeves of the garment. When it slid into place, she found Saer watching her. His shirt did little to disguise the hunger that was pulsing through him.

It was tormenting her as well. Twisting and clawing at her insides like a living force with its own will. She craved something more, something deeper, and she was old enough to know it was his cock deep inside her.

"I cannae be…give ye what ye want…" She was stammering, her emotions a breath away from boiling over. "Ye should seek another."

"It is ye I crave."

His tone was firm and full of promise. She shook her head, but he only tossed her skirt to her before he turned and pulled his kilt from the ground and started pleating it on the top of a rock. She busied herself with putting her skirt on and kept her gaze away from his.

He was so confident, it grated on her nerves. To his way of thinking, it was all decided, but it couldn't be. She had to make it clear to him.

"I refuse any arrangement with ye, Laird MacLeod."

She heard a soft crunch of gravel before he cupped her chin and raised her face.

"Yer brother has already agreed to me suit," he admitted.

"Then why toy with me this way? To torment me with how little choice I have?"

He shook his head, the moonlight illuminating a frown. "I came to prove me worth to ye. Once we are on MacLeod land, I will nae be able to allow ye so much freedom. I have demands on me time, and they are numerous."

The breath froze in her chest. It was far more than he had to give her, yet it was everything she'd feared. "I am nae going to MacLeod land."

She jerked away from him, hurrying over to grab her bodice and put it on. But she felt his gaze on her and couldn't hide from the truth that she was acting the coward. Even if it was his pride talking, there was a sense of honor in him she could not dismiss.

"I belong to meself." She steadied herself and looked back at him. "Ye've proven me flesh is weak, but me will is strong. I will nae trust any man. Such is a weakness, and I've found me salvation in strength." Her voice was close to pleading. "Ye need to understand, Saer, I know me nature and would nae have ye disappointed."

His lips parted to show his teeth. She wouldn't call it a grin, because the expression was far more primal. She felt it down to her toes.

"Which is what makes ye such a prize, Nareen. One I plan to claim. Our sons will have that strength in them, and I will never have to worry that ye fear me. I want no unproven lass birthing me babes. Ye'll give them yer spirit and raise them to face what life brings without flinching." He offered her his hand. "Come home with me…let us see what else we have in common…trust takes time to grow, give it a chance."

It was tempting.

Her body yearned for it, craved his in a way she could not understand. But the look in his eyes made her deny it. He was so certain of his effect on her. So sure of his ability to give her what she needed.

She couldn't admit how correct he was. It was submission. Admission of defeat. She would not do it.

Ever.

"I am going back to the castle."

He grunted. "To Abigail?"

She nodded, defeated by her own doubts.

"Why?" he demanded.

She drew in a long, deep breath and tasted bitter defeat. What lay between them were her own failings. "Because I will nae submit to yer will, Saer."

He folded his arms over his chest and contemplated her. He finally made a noise that was part frustration, part admiration. "I never thought I'd be pleased to hear ye sticking to yer position, yet I find the idea of submission from ye distasteful."

He gathered their horses, leaving her grateful he didn't see the tear that escaped her eye. She'd made her choice and must accept the result.

He was accepting it at last.

She should have been pleased.

Yet she was not.

◆

"Ye were out quite late last eve."

Nareen wasn't in the mood to deal with Abigail, but her mistress smiled and drew her fingers under her own eyes before looking at the dark circles beneath Nareen's eyes knowingly.

"Aye, I went riding."

"One of the stable lads told me Saer MacLeod followed ye." Abigail looked around to make sure no one else was close enough to overhear. "Did ye let him have ye?"

Nareen felt her cheeks heat. "Nae."

"Oh do nae be such a prude. I hear ye kissed him back in the chapel." Abigail smiled slyly. "The blush staining yer cheeks says he kissed ye again last night."

"It does nae matter," Nareen said, dismissing the topic, "since ye shall be returning to court soon. Saer MacLeod has no liking for court."

Abigail refused to be silenced. "I've had one or two like him." She leaned closer and licked her lower lip. "There is something very pleasing about their hard bodies when they are riding ye. Even their arrogance can be enjoyed, since ye know ye do nae have to suffer it forever, like a wife."

Nareen grabbed a gown and took it to the wardrobe to get her out of Abigail's range. Her mistress laughed softly and brought the matching underskirt along.

"Maybe ye should let him rid ye of yer maidenhead. No one thinks ye have it anymore anyway," Abigail whispered. "So there is no need to deny yerself."

Oh, there was a need, but there was no way to explain it to her shallow mistress. Truthfully, she'd have to understand it completely herself, and when it came to Saer, Nareen was discovering a great deal of confusion. And frustration. And need.

Someone knocked on the outer chamber door.

"At last!" Abigail exclaimed with glee. One of the maids in the outer chamber opened the door.

Two Ross retainers pulled on the corner of their caps before turning and lifting a trunk. They carried it inside and set it down. Once they'd deposited it, they left, their kilts swinging behind them. Another pair followed with a second trunk, and then a third and fourth.

"We are going to pack, Nareen," Abigail declared. "I am returning to court immediately, now that me father has agreed."

It should have pleased her. Instead, Nareen discovered disappointment clawing at her. There was no sense in her feelings; however, at least that was something familiar. When it came to Saer MacLeod, her emotions had no sense either.

"I cannae wait to be back at court."

Abigail sounded like a girl. She hummed a little tune as she twirled around and around in circles. The silk dress she adored rose up as she danced, showing off her stockings with their embroidery. It was a waste to wear such costly things in her private chambers, but Abigail refused to be practical.

"I am going to me father's steward before me sire rises," Abigail announced. "I must have silver for new gowns and other comforts."

She skipped away, leaving Nareen and the maids to pack.

Saer had said it plainly and truthfully. Not that Nareen needed him to tell her what she already knew.

She shivered, recalling even the deep timbre of his voice.

There was no denying she had enjoyed it. In fact, she'd woken up with a hunger in her passage for something deeper.

Nareen froze, her thoughts bothering her.

Why would she wish to deny it? There would be only one reason, and that would be to argue with Saer. To quarrel simply for the sake of winning, no matter the truth of the matter, was foolish. And childish.

It was a good question, one she wanted to know the answer to herself.

Saer MacLeod would be there, in the shadows. She was sure of it.

A ripple of sensation moved down her back, leaving a trail of heat in its wake.

"What should we do?"

One of the maids had spoken up. She and her companion were always banished to the receiving chamber when Abigail was present. Even now, they stood at the arched doorway that separated the receiving chamber from the dressing area. Another doorway behind Nareen led to the bedchamber. Abigail certainly liked to maintain herself in noble style and insisted that she have servants for each area. Nareen was the only one who might cross all three doorways without permission.

Pretentious.

"Come in, let us fill this trunk before she returns and makes simple tasks difficult."

The two Ross women smiled knowingly, indulging themselves by showing their emotions since Abigail wasn't there to reprimand them. Nareen fit a key into the locks on the wardrobes and opened them wide. There was the rustle of silk as underskirts and overskirts were lifted and folded carefully. Elaborately decorated headdresses were gently tucked inside of

wooden boxes made especially for them, then placed
into the trunks. Nareen busied herself with making
sure all the smaller items necessary to a wardrobe were
not left behind.

Things like chemises and stockings. Shoes and jew-
elry. She included veils and even hawking gauntlets,
along with making sure a travel writing desk was well
stocked with parchment, quills, and ink.

She knew what was needed, because she had been
raised to know how to dress to represent her family.
But she had never made her possessions so important.
Abigail was quick to slap if any of her precious silk
was marred. All of the maids tried to stay out of their
mistress's reach. Nareen was the only one Abigail held
her hand with. Likely because she was afraid Nareen
would slap her right back. Such actions would get her
dismissed, but Nareen had a home to go to.

She didn't want to be like Abigail, but she knew she
was hiding behind her mistress. It was a hard truth, but
one she needed to thank Saer for forcing her to see.
No matter how frustrating she found his presence, she
had to acknowledge the good he meant.

It was time to leave Abigail's service. The decision
felt good, relieving some of the uncertainty that had
been lingering in her thoughts. But that left her with
the choice of where to go.

Saer's offer rose in her memory.

She had to stifle a dry laugh behind her hand before
the other maids turned to investigate. Nareen didn't
need them seeing her bright cheeks.

Why did she blush for a man who was nowhere near?
She wasn't really sure she wanted to know the answer.

But she had to face the fact that Saer fascinated her. In mind and body, but when she was close to him, all she wanted to do was feed her fascination with his body. Was she wanton? Possibly. The Church certainly warned that women who cast off submissiveness became prey to all forms of sinfulness. But she didn't feel shame over it. She'd felt a great many things the night before, but the only time shame had risen to torment her was when Saer pointed out that she was hiding. That was cowardly.

She drew in a deep breath. There would be no more hiding. She was a Grant and born of Highlander stock. She would follow Abigail back to court and find her father's envoy there to arrange escort home. And she would make sure her brother knew there would be no matches for her.

For a moment, she lamented the invitation she'd declined from Saer. It would haunt her, that opportunity she had refused to take. But there was nothing left to do about it.

Saer MacLeod was not a man to forgive such a slight. She did not expect to see him again.

❧

"I insist," the Earl of Ross said with a flourish of his hand. "And do nae be looking at me as though hearing those words are akin to being challenged to a death match. I was yer age once too, lad, and remember the burn of pride very well. No man such as ye enjoys being told an old man wants his company for the day."

Saer choked out a single chuckle in response.

The earl grinned. "Yet, I think it will be in yer favor. Ye see, I heard ye are building up yer land."

"Aye," Saer confirmed. "The MacLeod suffered being raided after me sire rode with the king at Sauchieburn." His voice hardened. "It will nae happen again."

"A worthy reason to be spending yer coin on building." The earl gestured at his retainers to pull his chair out, cringing as they did so. "Me knees complain bitterly these days. Wine soothes the pain, but I want to show ye me quarry, which means I must leave the wine for later."

He made his way slowly down the steps until he stood next to Saer. "I lost the will to build when me sweet wife died." For a moment, he was lost in his memories.

"Yet ye have an active stone quarry?" Saer asked to gain the man's attention again.

The earl stiffened. "Aye. Aye! Ye see, there are men working there who are the sons of men who served me father. So ye see, I could nae cut off their wages. Now I know ye have stone aplenty, but I have a stockpile of stones that are cut and ready to be laid. Is that something ye'd like to see?"

"It is indeed."

"Exactly what I thought ye might say and why I wanted to demand yer attention today." The earl chuckled. "I sell off the cut stone to balance the books, but it has been a while since I had me a customer. They are just stacked up, waiting."

He patted Saer on the shoulder. "Mind ye, if ye were here to court me daughter, that stone might have found itself attached to her dowry."

"If I wanted to wed for gain, I did nae have to leave me land, but would have sent me secretary to sort out the details and fetch me a bride."

"Are ye so sure I would have given me daughter into the keeping of a man who will nae look me in the eye?" The earl responded with a touch of vigor that hinted at the young man he must have once been.

Saer hooked his hands into the wide belt holding his kilt around his waist. "I'd expect ye to understand that I am very new to being laird of the MacLeod. They deserve a man who will nae ride off without good purpose, especially when the castle has been proven ineffective against attack."

The earl seemed to slump, his eyes growing cloudy. "'Tis truly a shame that ye are nae drawn to Abigail. That lass needs a man with a sure hand, and I would see her with one who wants more than what I can dower her with."

But he brightened and waved Saer forward. "I've plenty of stone and will make ye a better deal than anyone else."

Saer felt a momentary tug of warning, but there was nothing out of place. He realized it was the fact that he hadn't seen Nareen yet. Both she and her mistress had missed services.

He did need the stone, and the sooner he had it, the sooner he might depart for MacLeod land.

With Nareen.

He refused to consider any other outcome. She would be his, if he had to use the savage side of his nature to haul her home.

❧

"We are leaving now."

Nareen looked up as Abigail burst back into her

chambers. Her face was flushed and her eyes bright with excitement. In her hands, she had a small chest with a lock on it that looked heavy, but she kept her grip tight on the handles.

"Good," Abigail said as she looked at the trunks Nareen had been filling. "Close them up, I've already instructed that the horses and escort be readied."

"I did nae realize we would leave quite so soon."

Abigail smiled slyly and moved closer to Nareen. "Me father has taken Saer MacLeod off to the quarry. It's the perfect time for both of us to take our flight."

So he hadn't left...

"But the king's order for ye to be gone from court has nae yet reached its time."

Abigail shrugged and put the smaller chest inside one of the larger ones. "The king will nae have time to notice I have returned a week or two early. I shall stay out of his sight and he'll not even know I am there."

Nareen doubted it. Abigail didn't know how to avoid drawing notice to herself. "Hurry, Nareen. We must be well away before me father returns. Now that Saer MacLeod has had a taste of ye, I doubt he'll think very long on riding after us if he thinks he can catch us."

A memory of Saer on his black stallion surfaced. A ripple of sensation traveled along her spine and left her fighting back regret. But she'd made her decision, one that did not include Saer MacLeod in her life. She couldn't worry too much about him. In fact, seeing him again would only grant her fickle emotions another opportunity to soften toward him. He made it appealing to change her mind.

But trust was too much. More than one bride had discovered her groom's kindness evaporated after the wedding vows were spoken. Perhaps Abigail wasn't so spoiled after all. It was possible the woman was no fool and had decided to enjoy the ease of being courted over the duty of being a wife.

Aye, there was a price for everything. Saer MacLeod's offer to take her home with him would be no different. He'd already told her what he'd expect. Sons. And if she didn't conceive quickly, or produced a daughter, his temper would rise. It was the way things were. Her only choice would be to not wed him.

"I am coming," Nareen replied. Abigail laughed merrily as she rummaged through one of the open wardrobes for a dress suitable for traveling. Her smile didn't even fade when she pulled out a wool dress.

"Do nae be so pensive, Nareen."

Abigail brought the dress over and carelessly tossed it onto the bed.

"I'll find ye plenty of lovers at court to take yer thoughts away from that savage."

"I do nae wish ye to do so."

Nareen was busy unlacing Abigail's gown. Abigail let out a long sigh.

"Ye really should mature, Nareen. There is much pleasure to be had if ye will stop being such a child."

Nareen slid the bodice off Abigail and began to help her with her overskirt. Abigail stood still, waiting to be disrobed.

"I know who is a good lover at court," Abigail continued. "The Earl of Matheson's sons are quite vigorous, and they do nae mind sharing."

"I am nae interested," Nareen maintained.

Abigail simply clicked her tongue. "There is naught like having two men to please ye at the same time. Men are often easily spent, leaving a woman unsatisfied."

Nareen locked gazes with Abigail, sending her a stern look.

"As ye like," Abigail groused.

Nareen finished dressing her and turned to making herself ready. Unlike Abigail, Nareen took time to be certain she had a dagger strapped to her thigh and another one tucked into her boot. Those were the things that mattered when one was riding across open land.

"Hurry, Nareen…" Abigail sang out cheerfully. The retainers had returned to take the trunks, and Abigail was hot on their heels.

Nareen took a moment longer to put on an arisaid. The length of plaid was falling out of fashion with many, but she'd been raised farther up in the Highlands, where tradition remained firm.

She was a Grant and would wear the colors proudly.

She used a belt to secure it around her waist. The wool fabric draped down her back, covering part of her skirt. She'd belted it at the three-quarters point, which allowed her to pull the end of it up and secure it on her right shoulder with a broach of silver, with her father's crest. Fabric draped across her shoulders so she might raise it to cover her head and protect her from rain. Abigail would insist on a hooded cloak, but Nareen preferred her arisaid.

She slid a dagger between her belt and back before leaving. The drape of the arisaid hid it somewhat.

There would be hell to pay if it was spotted, to be sure. But she wasn't going onto the road unarmed. Her brother, Kael, might have agreed to Saer's suit, but he'd also taught her to defend herself in spite of the Church's teachings.

So she'd forgive Kael, just as soon as she made it clear to her brother that there would be no matches for her.

Her mind was set.

❧

It was a fine day for traveling. The sun was warm, and there was no sign of rain. But the Ross retainers were not happy with their mistress's order to ride out.

"It would be best if ye waited on yer father to return, mistress."

The captain of the guard met Abigail at the top of the stairs that led out of the tower and into the yard. His tone was respectful but firm. He blocked Abigail's path to the yard, gripping the wide leather belt holding his kilt around his waist.

"I do nae wish to wait," Abigail informed him with her nose in the air. She swished her hand, but the captain remained firmly planted in her path.

"Yer father took a large escort with him," the captain continued. "I have only limited numbers of men to provide ye as escort. On the morrow, I will have the proper number to ensure yer safety."

The horses were standing ready, along with a wagon holding Abigail's trunks. She gazed longingly at them, but Nareen focused on the six Ross retainers. They held their expressions tight, but there was no missing the look in their eyes that told of their misgivings. Six was not enough if they encountered trouble.

"We should wait," Nareen counseled Abigail.

"I do nae wish to wait," Abigail whined.

Nareen shared a frustrated glance with the captain. He had his hands settled on his belt, which reminded her of Saer.

"Mistress, I would prefer nae to send ye out so poorly attended. The MacKays—"

"Have nae raided in months!" Abigail cried. "I am going back to court. No one will trifle with me. They will fear I have the ear of the king."

Abigail started down the steps. Nareen grabbed Abigail's wrist. "It's an unnecessary risk. Ye need to consider those six men. Two are only lads. If there is trouble, they will suffer for yer choice."

Abigail's eyes widened with outrage. "How dare ye tell me what to do. Ye are me—" She shook off Nareen's grip. "If ye do nae do as I bid ye, I shall tell me father I am finished with ye, and to give ye to that savage."

She grabbed the front of her skirt and stomped down the steps toward her mare.

"Brat," the captain muttered under his breath.

"I was thinking selfish fool," Nareen answered softly.

The captain grunted and nodded. "That as well." He stepped partially into Abigail's path and leveled a hard look at her. "I advise ye to stay here, lass. I know Laird MacLeod will nae be happy to hear ye have departed, much less so when he hears that ye ride without proper escort. The MacKays have vowed vengeance on the Ross with just cause, I'm sorry to say."

It was a foolish risk. She knew better.

"Well, Nareen?" Abigail called from atop her mare. "Are ye attending me, or shall I make sure me father knows he owes ye not a single crust of bread? He is me sire, so do nae be thinking he'll have ye beneath his roof without me good word."

"Laird MacLeod would want ye to be here when he returns," the captain pressed quietly.

"Which is why I must go," Nareen replied. "I know ye are right, but I cannae accept his suit. So I cannae make any demands on him. That would nae be right. I'm going home to me father from court."

"At least ye are nae going to continue serving her."

It was a bold thing to say about the earl's daughter, but the captain was a Highlander. Just as Saer was. They were men who kept their own minds and didn't bend their knees to the undeserving.

"Nareen…" Abigail whined again.

"Good luck to ye, Mistress Grant." The captain stepped aside.

"Thank ye," Nareen replied.

Her belly was knotted, and she worried that she was going to need that luck.

A great deal of it.

❧

Saer discovered himself happy to see the walls of the Ross fortress that evening. It wasn't the sturdy walls that warmed his heart, even though he had spent the day selecting stone to build up his own. No. He craved Nareen. It was more than a need to ease his lust. He longed for her smile and the way she looked him straight in the eye when she had something to tell him.

His grin broadened.

And he liked the way she resisted him. Propping her hand onto her hip. He doubted she realized how much that pose pushed her breasts up. He might just tell her, for the sake of seeing her reaction. She'd spit fire at him, but he liked that facet of her character.

And hoped marriage would never change her.

But the captain of the guard met them in the yard, and the news he carried was grim.

"Ye allowed them to depart with only six retainers?" Saer exploded before the earl had a chance to respond. "Are ye a half-wit?"

The captain's eyes narrowed, and he directed his answer to the earl. "I warned them of the dangers. Mistress Grant even tried to hold yer daughter back, but there was no stopping her."

"She's half yer size, man," Saer growled. "Ye should have locked her in the damned stocks and left her there until she gained some sense."

The earl waved his hands in the air. "Me daughter is strong-willed." His body was trembling, and he licked his lips repeatedly. "They will be well enough." The earl dismissed the news as he began to climb the stairs. His gillie was already waiting at the top with his master's goblet. The earl reached for the drinking vessel like a starving babe, gulping down mouthfuls of the wine so fast, it trickled down the sides of his chin and stained the collar of his shirt.

Saer turned away in disgust, eyeing the captain again.

"The mistress was right nasty to Mistress Grant."

Saer forced himself to hear the man out. It took effort, because all he wanted to do was get moving after Nareen.

"She threatened to dismiss her and have her father give her to ye."

"That's the drivel of a spoiled brat," Saer snarled. "The earl has no say in Nareen's fate."

"He is the master here," the captain replied. "The lass would have no one to guard her back, and that much is true. It would also be true on yer land, for one who is nae yer own clan."

"The hell it would be," Saer snapped. "Any man wearing me colors will have integrity or find somewhere else to lay his head. Innocents will nae fear being attacked in me hallways. I'll turn out any man who acts so savagely."

"I can only wish things were so here," the captain said with a jerk of his head. Saer looked up the steps to see the earl finishing off his second goblet of wine. He was out of breath because he'd been drinking so quickly. He smiled with relief as he stumbled into the keep.

It was sickening. He had once been a Highlander, but no more.

"The man's sons need to know of his state," the captain muttered. "Yet the pair of them seem to have more interest in serving at court."

Saer looked back at the captain. "I am more concerned with retrieving Nareen Grant. If ye're worthy of yer position, find a way yerself, or live with the consequences. A coward deserves his fate."

That was a law of the isles and those who tried to make their way there.

Saer whistled, and his men grinned. They refastened straps they'd begun to undo and made their horses ready to ride again. They were sixty strong and would not have to fear anything on the open road.

"So we're off at last?" Baruch asked with a twinkle in his eyes.

"Aye," Saer responded as he swung up onto the back of his stallion. "There is naught here to interest me any longer."

The sun was setting quickly, and Saer rode through the gate without a backward glance.

&

"It is lumpy," Abigail complained as she poked a finger into the pallet Nareen laid out for her.

Nareen didn't spare Abigail even a smile.

"Ye should nae be sulking," Abigail admonished. "It is me right to remind ye of yer place."

Nareen finished transforming the bed of the wagon into a sleeping pallet for Abigail. With the trunks removed, there was ample space to lay out a padded cushion. It was stuffed with carded wool and would make a fine place to spend the night, since there were no inns nearby.

Of course, only Abigail would enjoy such luxury. The rest of her escort would be making do with the ground, but that didn't stop Abigail from pushing her fingers into the pad and wrinkling her nose with distaste.

Nareen turned to look at her. "I am the daughter of a laird and yer companion."

Abigail's eyes widened. "Ye cannae say what ye are to me!"

"I can and will," Nareen answered firmly.

Abigail's face contorted with anger. "I'll put ye out right here."

"Do as ye like," Nareen replied. "The mare is mine, and I'll make me way very well. I do nae need others to see to me needs, but ye will have no one to dress ye come morning if I am gone."

It was a bold statement. She'd have to cross four different clan lands before making it back to Grant territory. It would be a dangerous endeavor.

"Yet it was me father who paid for the feed for the mare. I'll nae allow ye to take her with ye."

"And ye, who left with only six retainers," Nareen reminded her. "Are ye truly so foolish as to waste their attention on watching me and me mare?"

"That is outrageous!"

Nareen stared straight at her. "As much so as ye threatening to have yer father give me to Saer MacLeod."

Abigail snapped her mouth shut and looked at the ground like a naughty child. "It was nae very kind of me, I know, and I will nae do such a thing again."

"Ye do nae understand the concept of kindness, and I shall no longer serve ye, for ye do nae value me dedication."

"Oh...but I do, Nareen," Abigail argued. "Did I nae rescue ye from yer cousin's home?"

"Aye," Nareen said. "But ye committed the same sin Ruth did when ye threatened to give me to Saer MacLeod. I have always made it clear to ye that I shall not be owned. Ye will find a new companion at court."

"It will nae be difficult," Abigail snapped.

"I am glad we are in agreement." Nareen jumped down from the cart, leaving Abigail behind.

"Nareen—"

"Hush!" Nareen scolded her as she realized something was wrong. The horses were dancing and fighting to break free. Their ears had perked up, and they began to jerk their heads against the bridles holding them to some nearby trees. The Ross retainers stopped talking by the fire they'd built to cook supper, and turned to face the darkness beyond them.

"But…" Abigail whined.

"There is trouble here." Nareen grabbed the dagger she had secured to her belt.

Abigail's eyes widened as the firelight flashed off the blade of the dagger. With a muffled squeal, she scooted back into the wagon like a frightened child.

The attack came swiftly. There was a cry the night wind carried before the camp was overrun.

Abigail screamed and didn't stop.

Nareen cursed the woman while trying to defend herself. She raised the dagger and turned to face the man who tried to lock his arms around her from behind. She slashed across his forearm, drawing a vicious growl from him.

"So ye have claws…do ye?"

"I've no wish to kill ye," she warned, backing away as the screams of the Ross retainers filled the night.

He lowered himself and opened his arms wide. "Ye're nae going to be the end of me, lass…"

Her stomach tightened, and sweat began to coat her palm. But she tightened her grip and moved away from the wagon to give herself more room. The warrior launched himself at her, but she twisted and moved out of his path. He stumbled past her, turning at the last second when he realized she was in motion, and clamping a hard hand onto the wrist in which she held her dagger.

He snickered. "Well now, that was nae—"

Nareen shoved her fist up, into the soft spot beneath his jaw. He snarled and jerked backward out of reflex. She stumbled away, regaining her footing as more men came toward her.

"What have we here? Colm?"

The man she'd struck jumped to his feet and spit before wiping his mouth across his forearm. "She's mine," he barked.

His comrades chuckled. "It does nae look that way from here," one taunted.

Colm began closing the distance between them. Nareen turned to face him, allowing the firelight to illuminate her arisaid.

"Hold, Colm, she's a Grant."

"I do nae give a shit. She cut me, and I'm going to take that little toy away from her."

With her attention on Colm, Nareen missed the men coming up behind her. The night was full of them, at least thirty or more. One grabbed the dagger and pulled her back against his body with an arm around her chest. He ripped the weapon from her grip with a soft snort.

"She's lost her toy, so calm yerself, Colm."

Nareen twisted, ducking her head beneath the arm that held her as Kael had taught her. She broke free and heard Colm chuckle.

"Ye see?" Colm muttered as he pointed at her. "This one is trouble."

Someone yanked Abigail out of the cart. She was whimpering, the firelight shining off trails of tears wetting her face.

"I'll gladly trade ye this one for that one," the man hauling Abigail said to his comrades. "At least that one does nae scream like a babe."

"How dare ye!" Abigail exploded. "I am the daughter of the Earl of Ross! She is naught but the castoff of the Grants."

Colm stopped inspecting the cut on his forearm and peered at Abigail. "Are ye now? Well, lads, it seems we've found the means to justice tonight. Laird MacKay will be right displeased to know we found a prize and he was nae along."

Nareen's stomach was knotted. There was no way to fight them all off. Still, she turned one way and then another as she searched for an escape. Someone clamped their arms around her, lifting her right off her feet to the amusement of the MacKays. One of the men watching grabbed one of her ankles and began tying a rope around it. She snarled and kicked out at him. Her foot connected with his head, making a dull thud. He rolled back, head over heels, before righting himself.

"Bitch!" he cursed her.

But the man holding her only laughed. "I'm thinking the laird is going to enjoy this one more than the other."

He began squeezing her until she couldn't fill her lungs.

"Vengeance is cold, but this little spitfire is plenty warm."

Unable to breathe, Nareen's vision began to blur. Her muscles lost their strength, and she sagged. Helplessness rushed over her, filling her with terror as she struggled to maintain consciousness. All her fight gained her was one last look at the satisfied smirks on the faces of her captors.

And the knowledge that she was completely at their mercy.

Three

NAREEN WOKE WITH HER HEAD HANGING OVER HER MARE. Her belly hurt from the saddle pressing into it, but she was tied tight, unable to do anything more than endure.

The MacKay had left the campsite behind and were now stopped in the shadow of a ridge where the moonlight didn't penetrate. Water rushed by, helping to mask the sound of the men and horses. A fire was burning near the ridge, to keep the light from being seen by the Ross.

They were experienced raiders, and the realization sent a chill through her.

"So ye're done sleeping, eh?"

Colm appeared beside her and pulled her off the back of the mare. Nareen snorted in disgust, but she had little choice with her hands bound.

"Cut me loose, so I do nae have to suffer yer hands upon me."

Colm shook his head. "Ye are far too handy with a dagger, lass, and me wife would likely nae appreciate me having to handle ye any more than I already have, for ye are a fine-looking woman."

He locked a firm hand around her upper arm and began to guide her toward the center of the group. Abigail let out a wail from somewhere in front of them. Nareen turned to see her mistress collapsed in a heap. The MacKay retainers dealing with her left her where she'd fallen. But a whistle from Colm, and they reached down to haul Abigail up.

"Me father will gut ye all for this!" Her nose was red, and tears had made dirty smears down her cheeks.

"Thank Christ ye are nae such a weakling," Colm muttered to Nareen. "I know the Earl of Ross to be a man without honor, but I'm still shocked to see the whelp he's allowed his daughter to become."

Colm pushed her forward until she faced a man whose bonnet had three feathers standing up on its side. The pommel of his sword was visible over his left shoulder like the rest of his men, but it had a gleam the others lacked.

"Laird MacKay?" she asked boldly—maybe too boldly, given she was bound and surrounded, but Nareen lifted her chin and faced off with him.

He frowned, his gaze settling on her as his eyes narrowed. Somehow, she got the feeling he was not pleased with his men, but that was likely wishful thinking on her part. Whatever his feelings, he controlled his expression.

"Ye're a handsome woman."

Nareen held her chin steady. She resisted the urge to test her bonds again. She could feel the rope biting into her wrists, and knew they were firm. So she would stand steady.

"I am Bastian MacKay."

"Ye are a man who preys on women, and naught else about ye interests me," Nareen informed him. She was being brazen, and for certain there were plenty who would call her foolish, for Bastian was a large man in his prime. His hair was golden brown, and his eyes the color of a summer sky. He looked like a Viking, but the kilt strapped to his lean waist proclaimed him a Highlander.

He grinned at her. "Ye are nothing like yer mistress."

Abigail was still whimpering in a heap where the MacKay retainers had left her.

"I am a Grant."

His lips parted in a grin. "Ye are Nareen Grant, Laird Grant's only daughter, which accounts for the boldness in ye." His expression settled into a stony one. "I know who me men have brought me, but if I did nae, yer mistress there was happy to tell me."

Of course. Abigail lacked sense as well as self-discipline.

"Excellent," Nareen replied calmly, as though her hands were not bound. "That will make it much easier for me. I wish to make it plain to ye that it is in yer best interests to send a message to me brother, stating yer ransom demands."

His lips curved again, this time reminding her too much of Saer.

"I believe I might enjoy explaining me demands to ye instead."

Nareen scoffed at him. "Forgive me, I mistook ye for a Highlander. Nae a common thief who has no concept of honor."

"He understands honor, Nareen."

The MacKay parted, many of the retainers jumping

around and pulling their swords before they realized Saer MacLeod was at the top of the ridge. He jumped down, landing perfectly before making his path toward her with a purposeful stride.

She closed her eyes and opened them again, but he was still there. A crazy twist of relief went through her, until she realized there just might be a bloodbath. Saer's retainers were following him with determined expressions, and she felt the tension tightening as they came down the ridge.

She couldn't live with blood on her skirts. It was her fault for leaving without a proper escort. She knew better. A laird's daughter owed her people the respect of not placing them in the position of needing to fight for her.

But Saer pointed at Bastian, making it clear who he wanted to see.

The MacKay laird grunted and waved Saer forward. The MacKay retainers parted, but their expressions were grim.

"I am Saer MacLeod."

"And ye're off yer land," Bastian remarked.

"So are ye." Saer stepped up, squaring off with him. He set his retainers back with a firm motion of his hand. "This one belongs to me."

Nareen opened her mouth, but shut it when Bastian looked her way. The MacKay laird burst into laughter.

"Seems she does nae agree with ye."

Saer sent her a narrow-eyed look before returning his attention to Bastian. "Yer feud with the MacKays does nae need the Grants becoming involved." Saer spoke clear and loud enough for the men watching to hear.

Bastian tilted his head to one side. "Now I think that is a matter of what side they become involved on. If I were to wed this fiery lass, the Grants would have to support me."

"They would nae," Nareen said. "And I am nae wedding ye."

Bastian winked at her. "Ye'll get accustomed to me, lass, as all lasses do. And ye would nae be wanting to see yer babe bastard-born." His expression tightened. "Ye'll wed if I take ye home with me."

"She belongs to me." Saer's voice was menacing. Nareen shivered.

"It looks like she was running away from ye, MacLeod," Bastian taunted.

"At least I know how to run her down, and do nae need to tie her up."

The MacLeod retainers chuckled.

"Well now, Colm there is a married man." Bastian pulled a dagger from his belt and slit the leather knotted around Nareen's wrists. "He couldn't be holding on to her, now could he?"

Nareen rubbed her wrists, trying to restore feeling to her hands.

"Laird MacLeod, ye must take me back to me father," Abigail wailed.

Bastian's lips twitched. "I'd be happy to give ye that one."

"Why don't ye wed her and end yer feud?" Saer suggested.

The MacKay retainers groaned. Abigail's eyes widened, a hurt expression emerging on her face.

"Because I was hoping to have a wife who was

more mature than the babes she'll give me," Bastian explained. "There is no comparing the two lasses, and ye are here because ye know it."

The teasing mood vanished. Bastian faced off with Saer, the two men equally powerful. They had the same number of retainers, and Nareen felt her mouth go dry as she recognized how dire her circumstances were. Either Saer would fight for her or leave her to her fate.

"Then we have business," Saer decided. He reached up and lifted his sword belt over his head and handed it to Baruch. He tossed his bonnet aside too, and flexed his fingers.

Bastian watched him from beneath hooded eyes. The MacKay laird turned and raked her from head to toe with his gaze.

"Aye, we've got business. She's a prize worth fighting to keep," Bastian declared as he looked straight into her eyes.

"Ye will nae fight over me!" Her blood chilled, and not just from the thought of them fighting. Bastian was every bit as powerful as Saer. Dread nauseated her.

Bastian stepped in front of her, so Saer had to go through him to get her. "I'm nae giving her up."

"And I'm nae leaving without her," Saer confirmed menacingly.

Someone reached out and pulled her back by the belt securing her arisaid. The men also moved until they circled the two combatants. Fear knotted her insides. She clamped her mouth shut and curled her fingers into the fabric of her skirt to control herself.

She couldn't distract Saer.

The thought entered her mind and refused to leave. It was a protective idea, one she couldn't ignore. There was no denying that she cared what happened to him.

They circled each other in slow, crouched paces. Saer watched for an opening, weighing his opponent's strengths as Bastian studied Saer with the same critical look.

When they clashed, Nareen flinched.

There was the harsh sound of flesh hitting flesh, and the raw groans of men colliding. Bastian went low in an attempt to lift Saer off his feet, but Saer was ready for him, cutting to the side as he drove his fist into Bastian's jaw.

The MacKay laird stumbled back but shook his head and chuckled. "Me sister hits harder."

"Is that who taught ye to fight then?" Saer asked.

The men clustered around them were laying out wagers. Saer launched himself at Bastian, grabbing him by the hair and slipping behind him to lock his arm around his neck. Bastian dropped to the ground, tossing Saer over his shoulder. They rolled, and their spectators made way. Bastian tried to use his legs to trap Saer as the two wrestled like a pair of bears.

It was brutal and savage. More blows landed, and blood began to trickle down both their faces. Bastian had a split lip, while Saer's nose had taken a hard hit. They were breathing harshly, their chests laboring to draw in enough breath to support their battle. The retainers cheered on their laird, but Bastian and Saer had their attention only on each other.

It was a horrifying display, one that drove home

how helpless Nareen was. Tears strung the corners of her eyes as she watched. The hard sound of flesh hitting flesh was sickening.

The MacLeod let out a cheer as Saer succeeded in getting a solid lock around Bastian's neck. They were both grappling on the ground, but the MacKay laird was struggling to breathe. Saer leaned over the man, digging his feet into the dirt to add his body weight to the hold. Bastian clawed at him but lost his strength at last, going limp.

Saer released him before he passed out, jumping back to a low crouch in case the man wasn't ready to admit defeat. Bastian rolled over and snarled as he adopted the same position. But he was still blinking his eyes as his head cleared.

"Damn it all," he cursed while easing his stance and standing up. He was furious but nodding. "'Tis done."

Bastian extended his hand. Saer straightened up and took a long moment studying his opponent's hand.

"I'm a man of honor, MacLeod. The woman is yers," Bastian clarified. "Although I'm thinking about returning her dagger to her without telling ye."

Saer took his hand, clasping his wrist. "Another reason why she's worth fighting for. She is nae helpless."

"She'll give ye fierce sons." Bastian wiped the blood off his chin with his shirtsleeve. "And putting them in her belly is a chore I envy ye."

Her cheeks turned scarlet as the men around them cheered.

Bastian looked back at her and jerked his head toward Saer. Someone gave her a push from behind, gaining another chuckle from the men watching.

She didn't make eye contact with Saer. She couldn't.

Her emotions were just a breath away from spilling over. She wanted to weep, and she wanted to rail against being given to him. But she didn't want to stay with Bastian, and it was all churning inside her like a storm making ready to burst.

So she walked to her mare and mounted. Snickers followed her as the MacLeod all mounted.

"Nareen… Ye cannae leave me!" Abigail wailed.

Saer wiped the sweat from his face but didn't move. He remained squared off with Bastian.

"Do nae worry, Saer MacLeod. I do nae plan to settle me differences with Laird Ross through a woman."

"Then what do ye plan to do with her?" Saer asked.

"I'll use her to draw him out of his fortress," Bastian replied. "The man hides there, refusing to face me. He killed me father during a game of dice."

"The earl is addicted to wine. He nearly buckled for being deprived of it for a single day. Hardly a worthy opponent. It will bring ye no satisfaction to fight him."

"If it was yer father's blood on his hands, would that excuse be enough to make ye forget the matter without so much as a meeting?"

The tension built around them again, the MacKay retainers glaring at Saer to see what sort of man he was. Saer finally shook his head.

"It would not."

Bastian nodded with approval.

"But I still cannae leave her in uncertain circumstances. Her father's sins are nae hers." Saer made his point clear.

"I'm here because I heard he'd gone out. Nae to raid." Bastian growled in frustration. "A few hours more sunlight, and I might have caught him. But I have his daughter now, and if he wants her back, he'll have to face me."

Bastian lifted his chin, making it clear he wouldn't be changing his position.

"Ye cannae leave me with this savage, Laird MacLeod!"

Saer looked at Abigail, and she gasped before covering her mouth with her hands. "Do nae hold the fact that I called ye savage against me, I was just—"

"Being a brat," Saer confirmed.

Bastian nodded. "She is that."

Saer looked back at him. "Her father is in no condition to face ye. Look what he has let his daughter become."

Bastian looked at Abigail, but he shook his head. "She'll nae be harmed." He locked gazes with Saer. "Even if she whines otherwise. I give ye me word on that. But her father will face me if he wants her back."

Saer lifted an eyebrow. "And if he leaves her with ye?"

Bastian grunted. "Do nae rub me face in yer victory. I was just thinking I like ye, man. How can ye wish such a fate upon me?"

Saer nodded before turning toward his men.

"No… No!"

Abigail cried, but no one paid her any attention. When they ignored her, she closed her mouth and looked confused.

Nareen couldn't help but pity her. She was a creation

of her father's lack of self-discipline. Coddling her when she was a child had brought her to where she was. Maybe she would be better off when this was over.

Nareen only wished she might feel the same for her own fate.

But Saer stopped by her mare, looking up at her with a glitter of victory in his eyes. There was something else, too, and it sent a shiver down her spine. When she looked away, he boldly cupped her knee to bring her attention back to his face.

"I promised ye, Nareen, when ye run, I will follow."

His tone was low and edged with a promise. Excitement began to pulse inside her passage, the memory of the pleasure he'd delivered to her making her hungry for more of his touch.

"I should thank ye…for coming to me aid." She locked gazes with him and felt like he was seeing her thoughts. "But the truth is, I do nae want to."

He threw back his head and laughed. When he finished, he looked back into her eyes. "Ye're a spitfire, and it pleases me that ye are nae a liar."

"Ye may no' always be so pleased with me spirit. Think on that before ye insist on taking me to yer land. I will nae obey ye or any man. Why do ye think I do nae seek marriage?"

His lips pressed into a hard line. "Trust takes time. Ye'll wed me once ye trust me."

She shook her head, but he moved past her to his stallion, mounting the creature in one powerful motion. His kilt swished with his actions, flashing her a brief glance at the perfection of his thighs and backside.

Every inch of him was hard, and she liked it far too

much. Like some dark need that lived deep inside her. It stunned her with its intensity.

Saer lifted his hand, and his men rode out on his order. They swept her up in their columns, moving her away from Bastian MacKay.

She just wished she didn't feel such a dread for what was to come. Saer was a good man, and she knew without a doubt she was going to have to disappoint him.

That fact gave her no happiness at all.

∝∾

Before the moon hit its highest point, Baruch insisted, "The horses need rest."

"Aye," Saer agreed. "Even if it's the last thing I want to do."

He yearned for his own land. But he headed toward a forested area, guiding his horse into the tree line to gain cover.

"Only until dawn."

The men near him nodded. It wasn't a submissive acknowledgment of his order; it was more of an agreement. He preferred his lairdship to be one of mutual respect, and his men knew he'd never ask them to do something he would not himself do.

"Yer lass is wandering again," Baruch informed him.

Saer looked up to catch the last hint of Nareen's arisaid as she made her way away from his men.

"I'll see to her. Set a watch and make sure everyone gets some rest."

"Aye, Laird."

Saer hurried through rubbing his horse down, but the animal was more interested in resting, turning away before Saer had finished. He offered him a last pat before indulging his personal desire to follow Nareen.

⤜⤛

She heard him approaching.

There was a soft crack of dry leaves, nothing else. She was tense, and her senses were heightened. She would have sworn she felt Saer closing the distance between them.

It had to be a curse, the way she felt him.

"So ye've run me down." She forced the words past her lips. "What do ye expect I am doing after so long in the saddle? I needed a moment of privacy."

He'd planted his feet in a wide stance and crossed his arms over his chest. His hands rested on his forearms as he contemplated her.

"Would ye have preferred Bastian in yer bed?"

She stiffened, the MacKay laird's declaration still ringing in her ears, but what really held her attention was the tension on Saer's face.

"No. I meant what I said, Saer, I will nae wed, because I have no wish to see ye looking at me with anger when I cannae settle into the role of a wife. Ye need to listen to me. I know me mind. What amuses ye now, will irritate ye in the future."

He reached up and tapped the side of his face that was blackened from one of Bastian's fists.

"Ye owe me thanks for freeing ye."

It was too dark to judge his expression, but she moved closer, trying to get a good look into his eyes. All she gained was a tightening in her belly as she neared him. Once more, she was keenly aware of him.

"I do." He confused her, distorting the logical decisions she'd made and leaving her questioning her reasoning.

"Does the idea of being with me truly frighten ye so much that ye would leave without protection?"

There was tightly controlled rage in his tone, and it shamed her, but her pride flared up. "Ye unsettle me." She backed away from him. "Which is different than frighten, I'll have ye know. But when ye are near, me thoughts become muddled."

He grunted softly in response.

"I wouldn't expect ye to understand," she sighed. "For I do nae understand the effect ye have on me."

He uncrossed his arms and crooked his finger. "Come here."

She shook her head.

"Ye enjoy me touch." He stepped toward her, and she retreated.

"A light skirt does as well, so I've been told. It does nae mean she enjoys the position of being used."

"I will nae be using ye, Nareen."

He came closer, his strides longer than hers, making it a challenge for her to maintain the distance between them.

"And yet ye have already begun to make it clear what yer demands are. Sons. That's what ye want of me."

He stopped, tilting his head to one side. "Do ye nae care for children?"

"I—" She snapped her mouth shut when she

realized she was back to arguing just for the sake of fighting with him. "Like them well enough."

"Then there is no difficulty."

"No…there is," she said with hesitation.

He reached out and caught a handful of her skirt, jerking her to a halt. Excitement rippled across her skin as she trembled.

"Is what, lass? Ye want to tell me no, and naught but no." He leaned down until she felt his warm breath teasing her ear. "No matter how much sense I am making?"

She locked gazes with him, but in the dark his eyes were only glassy pools. "It is nae about making sense. 'Tis how I feel. Until ye are close, and then…naught makes sense." She flattened her hand on his chest. A feeble attempt to ward him off, but she used a gentle touch, hoping to touch the tender part of his character. "Ye must find another, Saer."

His eyes narrowed, and his lips softened. "The sound of me name on yer lips is sweet, lass."

She sighed. "Ye are nae listening, and I truly do nae want to be a harpy."

"At last, agreement between us." He reached out and closed his hand around her wrist. "I do nae care for the slicing side of yer tongue either."

"Liar." She could have bitten her tongue in half for letting the word out.

Saer had begun tugging her through the trees, but he stopped and turned to look at her.

"Ye thrive on challenge," she said. "If I were meek and sweetly obedient to yer will, ye'd nae be anywhere near me."

He grinned. "And that is exactly why I am here, Nareen. Ye understand me."

"Ye're arrogant…"

But he resumed pulling her along behind him. The sound of moving water increased until he tugged her through a few last trees to the edge of a stream.

"I've earned it," he informed her confidently as he sat down on a large rock. "I have nothing I have nae earned or proven meself able to hold. Including ye."

The memory of the fight rose up in vivid color, twisting her insides again.

"Ye should nae have had to fight for me."

He reached into his doublet and pulled out a length of fabric. "Life is nae fair, Nareen. Ye should have stayed in the Ross fortress, but ye did nae."

"It was foolish, I know."

He nodded approvingly at her admission.

"Tend to me."

She wasn't sure of his meaning. He offered her the length of fabric. There was something not quite right about the way he remained perched on the rock.

"Ye're trying to lull me into a sense of ease," she said.

One of his eyebrows arched. "I'm asking ye to tend to the bruises I endured to keep ye from becoming Bastian MacKay's prize."

She owed it to him. But reaching for that cloth took more effort than it should have. She stepped closer to him, her heart accelerated, and she was conscious of how extremely sensitive her skin felt. She bent her knees and plunged the cloth into the water. It was cold and refreshing, carrying the dust away from her fingers. She squeezed the excess water out of the cloth and stood up.

Her mouth went dry as she managed to step forward. Power radiated from him, wrapping around her when she was standing close enough to touch him.

But he waited. Waited for her to reach for him.

Her hand trembled when she did, and her breath felt like it was frozen in her lungs.

"Is it so hard to touch me, lass?"

His voice was a soft whisper mingling with the breeze that rustled the leaves on the trees around them. It was like he was part of the night, reaching out to fold her into an embrace that would take her beyond reality.

"Ye unsettle me."

She knelt down to rinse the cloth, shuddering at the temperature difference between the water and his skin. When she stood back up and smoothed the cloth along his jaw, he caught her wrist and carried her hand to his chest, where he pressed it over his heart.

"Ye do the same to me."

The cloth pressed water into his shirt, but he didn't seem to care. She felt the steady beat of his heart and realized it matched the tempo of her own.

"This cannae be right," she whispered, but her fingers smoothed over the wet patch of shirt that separated her skin from his.

"What is wrong with taking the enjoyment we can when it is before us?" He stood up, abandoning his relaxed demeanor. She felt the change instantly. The power she'd noticed so often in him washed over her in a wave that went all the way down to her toes.

"I crave ye, Nareen." He slid his arm around her, cupping her hip and easing forward to press against her. "And ye are nae unmoved by me. I feel ye trembling."

"But—"

He sealed her protest beneath his lips, pressing his mouth over hers as she shuddered. This time, it was even more intense, the cravings inside of her jumping at the opportunity to be appeased. She reached for him, slipping her hand into his hair and gripping the inky strands. Hunger flared up inside her, and she kissed him back, seeking a deeper taste of him. She wasn't close enough, wasn't kissing him hard enough.

Saer groaned, and she felt him changing. It was as if his control had shredded. His kiss turned fierce, demanding she open her mouth and allow his tongue to sweep inside. It was an invasion, an act of domination that thrilled her so much she moaned. He cupped the back of her head and smoothed his hand away from her hip to grip one side of her bottom. Her bud was throbbing between the folds of her sex, begging for her to lift her leg and lock it around his waist.

But he suddenly set her back.

It felt like she was ripped away from him, and frustration prickled along her nerve endings.

"Nae here," he growled, but she wasn't sure if he was telling her or himself. His breath was ragged, and his nostrils flared. He pointed one thick finger at her. "Nae here."

She wrapped her arms around herself, the certainty of just how much he affected her ripping through her. She had no control, no ability to think once he touched her. It was undermining her confidence.

"I'll have ye in me bed, on me land. No' on the ground like a savage." He was on the edge; she could hear it in his voice. It fanned the flames of recklessness licking at her insides.

"Go back to camp, Nareen, before I forget what I know ye deserve from me in favor of what I see ye craving in yer eyes. But do nae forget that it would serve me to see the matter settled here. I'll earn yer trust, lass."

She turned and made her way back to his camp. At least the darkness hid the tears glistening in her eyes. Tears she'd sworn never to shed again. But they eased from the corners of her eyes anyway.

Cruel little droplets of proof that she was helpless against Saer MacLeod.

There was nothing she detested more.

Which was why she had to escape him before he grew to detest her.

❦

Saer woke them before dawn.

Nareen rolled over and rubbed her eyes. They were burning from the salt her tears had left behind. The MacLeod retainers were efficient as they readied their horses. They were all well on their way before the horizon turned pink.

They ate oatcakes that had been stored in leather pouches. Some had dried fruits mixed in to make them sweet. Water was always plentiful in the Highlands, and the farther north they traveled, the more streams they had to cross. By dusk, Ross land was far behind, and they were well into MacNicols territory. Nareen breathed a sigh of relief when they stopped for the night and made camp.

Nareen's cheeks heated with shame as she admitted to herself that she didn't have the willpower to resist Saer. She was drawn to him.

At least out in the open, she didn't have to worry about being alone with him someplace where her passion might overrule her senses. In fact, by the end of the day, she was very, very sure she needed to make certain she was never alone with him again.

She knew what she wanted from life, and it was not to be a wife. In no way might she reconcile herself to obedience. Saer MacLeod was master of his clan and would certainly expect to be the same over his wife.

So she would have to leave him before she committed a greater sin by disappointing him. She was sure she couldn't bear to see resentment or scorn in his eyes when he looked at her.

A gillie came and took her mare. The young lad guided the horse along the side of a stream until a floodplain stretched out with plenty of grazing. The other horses were already nibbling at the shoots, their saddles laid over large rocks for the night.

The MacLeod retainers were starting fires and cleaning rabbits they had shot from the road with arrows in the last hours. The air was soon full of the scent of roasting meat. Saer was leaning over a flat rack with two of his captains, studying a map with the last of the day's light. Nareen took the opportunity to slip off into the woods for some privacy.

She had to force herself to return.

The urge to run was strong, but she knew Saer

would only come after her. Success lie in making sure he was sleeping when she made her run for Deigh Tower. Broen MacNicols would grant her shelter and an escort to her brother. It was a foolish risk, to venture out alone again, but she felt it a greater risk to stay. It was only a day's ride to Deigh Tower. She focused on that and held firm in her decision.

She drank deeply from the water bag, knowing she'd wake in the early morning hours to relieve herself. Then she settled down to sleep, forcing herself to ignore the rabbit in favor of sleeping while Saer was awake.

It was the best solution, really. She wanted no master, and would make sure she didn't have the chance to lose her resolve again.

It was certainly better than watching him grow dissatisfied with her.

∾

"Ye wore the lass out," Baruch remarked. "She did nae even wait for supper."

Saer looked up, taking a moment to drink in the sight of Nareen. She'd curled up beside a large cluster of rocks with her arisaid wrapped around her.

Pride moved through him. She was strong, sleeping out on the trail without any complaint over the lack of comforts.

"That brat she was serving ran her to exhaustion," he informed his captains. They turned the conversation back to planning the route home.

It was much later when Saer was able to move toward Nareen. Her breathing was slow and steady.

He watched her for a long moment, studying her face. He still didn't understand his need for her. It defied logic, even sense.

But it was her face he saw when he closed his eyes, so he stretched out beside her and enjoyed the soft sound of her breathing until he fell asleep.

For the first time in the many months since he'd first seen her at court, he felt a lack of urgency. Peace settled over him, and it was far sweeter than he'd ever imagined.

❧

Nareen smelled Saer before she opened her eyes. The scent of his skin, which she'd somehow memorized from the times she'd been in his embrace, intoxicated her and undermined her resolve to deny her hunger for him.

She opened her eyes and saw him sleeping next to her. He'd raised the portion of his kilt that draped over his back to cover his head, but the rest of the wool was still secured around his waist. In the distance, she could see his men completely wrapped in the kilts they had taken off before lying down.

Not Saer. He slept, ready to be on his feet in a moment. Laid out between them was his sword. It was even pulled from the scabbard, in case he needed to defend himself. He didn't trust the world any more than she did.

For a moment, she was torn. Again.

It seemed to be the way he affected her.

The only way to be free of the turmoil was to leave. She turned her head slowly and looked across camp.

Two retainers were still awake. They were poking at the fire as they spoke in low tones. Off in the distance, the horses were dark shapes.

But fate was kind. There was a thick forest between her and the animals. She took a last look at Saer and rolled up and onto her feet. He didn't move, and she kept her paces slow as she made her way into the forest. The urge to move faster needled her, but she forced herself to take her time.

Her mare was smaller than the other horses and had drifted off by herself. Nareen cooed softly to her, watching as her ears perked up.

Retrieving the saddle would be too great a risk, so she eased the bridle into place and led her mare away from the others. Each moment seemed to be longer than normal, and her steps sounded too loud, but the other horses remained quiet as she made her way.

She used a rock to mount and held tight with her thighs as the horse began to carry her away from the camp. Nareen let her set the pace, moving in unison with the animal. The sky was clear, allowing her to see the constellations and guide them toward the MacNicols stronghold. When she looked up, she saw just the faintest outline of one of the towers in the distance. With luck, she'd make it by dawn.

But there was a blur of motion beside her before a hard arm reached across and snagged her off the back of her mare. Nareen let out a screech as Saer clamped her against his chest and used his knees to steer his stallion.

"Let me go!"

He pulled her to the ground and planted himself

between her and her mare. He was furious, his brows lowered and his lips pressed into a hard line. He pointed one thick finger at her.

"Why, Nareen?" he demanded in a rough tone. "Tell me the name of the man ye are intent on returning to."

"Kael Grant," she snapped. "I'm going to make sure me brother knows I want no master. And certainly nae ye!"

He drew in a harsh breath. "Ye want me, Nareen."

She shook her head. "I refuse to be any man's."

He chuckled darkly, moving toward her. She backed up and realized she was moving into the forest. The limbs of the trees blocked out the moon's bright light.

"That is nae what yer actions were saying when ye entangled yer hand in me hair and stroked me tongue with yer own."

"I'm saying it to ye now," she insisted as she tried to hedge around him and back into the light. He blended with the night too well, and she had no defense against the urges that came out when she was with him.

He hooked her around the waist and pressed her back against the solid trunk of a tree. His body was huge and impossible to move, but the worst part was the way she shuddered with delight.

"Ye'll have to prove it, Nareen. Refuse me kiss and stand unmoved in me embrace, and I will let ye go."

"See if I don't bite ye," she warned.

He stepped back, surprising her. And disappointing her too.

She stood in shocked amazement as she tried to decide what to do.

But she'd misunderstood his action, and that was a mistake. He reached out and pulled free the cord that held her bodice closed. With a hard tug, the knot opened, and he used one finger to drag the cord free of the first few eyelets. The weight of her breasts opened the bodice, giving him room to plunge his hands inside the loose neck of her chemise and cup both tender mounds.

She gasped, arching back against the trunk of the tree. He massaged the tender globes, brushing her puckered nipples with his thumbs.

"Tell me ye do nae like me hands on ye, Nareen."

She clamped her mouth shut and closed her eyes. He tugged on her nipples, drawing a heated moan from her lips. Never once had she thought her breasts might feel so good. Saer held them, massaging them, and it felt like they grew heavier.

"Put yer hands on me."

It was a rough command, and she curled her hands into the bark of the tree to deny herself the feeling of him.

He swept his hand through the front of her bodice, opening it completely before leaning over and licking one hard nipple.

"Oh, Christ!" She shoved her hands into his hair, gripping the smooth strands as he arched her toward him.

Liquid fire was flowing down to her sex. He didn't stop at licking, but opened his mouth and sucked on her nipple like he was starving.

She was starving too. Starving for him.

All the need that had been threatening to burst,

exploded. She lost the will to think, to consider, or even identify what she was doing. There were only her cravings and the fact that he was there to sate her. She leaned over, seeking some of his warm skin to kiss. She wanted to taste him, wanted to drive him as insane as he was making her.

Her mouth connected with his jaw, and she kissed her way along it until he lifted his head away from her breast to allow her to kiss him.

It was a hungry merging of lips and tongue. There was nothing tender about it. He demanded and she matched him motion for motion. She clawed at his shirt, hating the fabric, but his sword was still resting on his back, making it impossible to strip the garment from him. She settled for grasping his biceps, where his sleeves were tied up to the shoulders. A moan of rapture passed her lips as she connected with his skin. She shoved her hands farther beneath his shirt, to feel his shoulders.

"That's the way…" He encouraged her in a rough voice. "Touch me, Nareen, enjoy me as much as I enjoy ye…"

He pressed a hard kiss against the side of her neck, and then another before yanking her skirt up. The night air was a relief, carrying away some of the heat. But she still felt like she might boil alive when he slid his hand up her thigh.

He chuckled when he discovered the dagger strapped there. "Bastian might have gotten a nasty surprise when he tried to bed ye."

"I wouldn't have let him…" Her thoughts began to clear when she opened her eyes and locked gazes with him. "I'm not letting ye—"

He cupped her mons, grazing the center of her folds with a fingertip. She choked on what she'd been saying, her body drawing taut.

"Agreed." He plunged his finger between the folds of her sex and stroked his way from the entrance of her passage to her throbbing clitoris. "Ye are nae letting me bed ye, lass, ye are trysting with me."

He rubbed the center of her pleasure, his voice like a spell drawing her into a realm of dark enchantment. The scent of his skin filled her senses, somehow conveying strength. She arched toward him, seeking release from the hunger driving her mad, but he didn't give it to her. He slid his finger down to tease the opening of her body, then thrust up inside her passage.

She was slick, and she opened her eyes wide with shock as pleasure tore through her. It was deeper than what he'd given her before, the walls of her passage incredibly sensitive. And needy.

She felt empty, his finger not nearly enough to satisfy her.

"When I do bed ye, Nareen, I am going to suck ye until ye scream."

"What?" Her voice was a ghost of a whisper. She blinked, trying to understand what he meant. Her cheeks flamed when she made sense of it. Court was a swirling haze of sexual liaisons.

"But nae tonight." There was a hard purpose in his voice. He pulled his hand free and hooked her knee. "Tonight, I am going to claim ye."

"I'll not—"

He sealed her denial beneath a hard kiss. She wanted to refuse, but he thrust his tongue deep inside her mouth, and her passage clamored for attention too. How could a kiss be so overwhelming? A moment after he sealed her lips beneath his, she was opening her mouth and licking his lower lip. She craved him, every bit of him.

He lifted her up, spreading her thighs wide with his body. "Claw me…"

It shouldn't have sounded like a good idea, but her fingers curled into talons, her nails sinking into his skin. She was desperate for a deeper contact with him.

Saer didn't grant it to her immediately.

He pinned her to the tree, his wide chest pressing her against it. He stroked her folds a few more times before introducing the harder touch of his cock. She gasped as pleasure rolled through her. It was just a ripple—the next wave was deeper as he fit the head of his member against the opening of her passage.

It felt too large, but she was empty and aching for his hardness. He grasped her thighs and held her still, controlling his entry completely. The first thrust was only an inch. Her body stretched to accommodate him before he withdrew.

"Just do it," she urged.

"No." His tone was rigid. She opened her eyes and witnessed the strain on his face. A muscle was ticking along his jaw as he slowly pressed deeper into her.

This time there was pain. It snaked through her quickly, and he withdrew again. His cock was sliding against her bud, sending renewed need through her, so by the time he'd removed his length, she was craving it again.

"Ye claimed ye admired me strength…" She sank

her fingernails into the thick muscles of his shoulders. "So do nae coddle me now."

His nostrils flared. Raw hunger smoldered in his eyes. He offered her a single nod and began thrusting slowly into her spread body. Her passage resisted, feeling too tight, but it gave way. She was slick and wet, allowing his rigid length to burrow deeper and deeper until it felt like he was touching her womb.

She hissed and felt blood beneath her fingernails. With a gasp, she pulled her hands off him.

"Draw yer share of blood, lass…" he encouraged darkly and pulled free before thrusting straight and true back into her. "For I've matched ye measure for measure…"

The pain subsided into a dull ache. "Ye dinnae hurt me at all."

He brushed her lips with a kiss. It was the lightest, most tender of touches, surprising her, because he was so hard. Both in nature and form.

"I'll make it worth yer courage now," he promised in a dark, raspy voice.

Her eyelids felt heavy, but she lifted them and gazed at him. His features were drawn tight with need, his nostrils flaring with unsatisfied hunger. The sight drove her need up, whipping the flames into a frenzy.

"I'll make it very much worth yer courage…"

He flexed his hips, thrusting against her. The tree was solid behind her back, but her skirt gave her enough padding. By the second thrust, she was sure she wouldn't have noticed bark digging into her anyway. There was too much delight coming from the motions of his cock. She arched toward him, seeking more pressure against her clitoris. Pleasure was gathering in her belly, tightening with every thrust. She strained against him, needing it to burst. She felt like she might die if she didn't strain toward him.

Saer didn't disappoint her. He worked against her until rapture shattered inside her. It was blindingly bright, ripping through her and sending her spinning into a vortex of sensation. He growled as she cried out, increasing his speed and driving himself into her with hard, fierce motions. She opened her eyes when he shouted, the sound savage but full of satisfaction. Deep inside her passage, she felt the first spurt of his seed, hot and searing against her insides. His member jerked as it delivered the last of its offering, and she felt like her body was tightening around him, trying to milk the last drops.

He buried his face against her neck, his breath coming in soft pants. Every muscle she had quivered, satisfaction settling over her like a thick cloud. She leaned her head on his shoulder, the need to quarrel finally at rest. There was only the beating of his heart against hers.

When he moved, she made a soft sound of protest.

"Aye, but we need to return in case Bastian has set out after us."

Her skirts fell down to cover her thighs, and she felt her virgin's blood sticky on them. Saer walked back to the water's edge and retrieved the cloth. He plunged it into the water then brought it back to her.

She snatched the cloth, mortified to know he understood what she needed, and made her way back to the edge of the stream. But he stood watching her. "Well…"

He crossed his arms over his chest and frowned at her. "Well what, woman?"

"Turn around."

"Ye're shy now?" he asked incredulously.

She bit her lip because she was afraid her voice would betray just how vulnerable she felt. It was practically unbearable, and she looked away instead of meeting his gaze.

He let out a snort and whipped around so fast the longer lengths of wool at the back of his kilt flared out. Relief surged through her as she made quick work of cleaning herself.

"Ye make no sense, Nareen."

He reached for the cloth when she was finished. She turned her back when he lifted his kilt and ended up twisting her ankle because she wasn't paying attention to where she put her feet.

"So at last ye understand we are not well matched," she said.

She heard him rinsing the rag before he appeared in front of her. He cupped her chin, raising it so their eyes met.

"I will chase ye down as many times as it takes for ye to admit how perfectly matched we are."

She shook off his grip. "I am nae yers."

She expected him to be annoyed with her. Instead, his lips parted and he stroked the side of her cheek. She jerked her head away.

"Ye will be, if I have to tie ye around me waist tomorrow to get ye onto me land."

"Ye wouldn't." The words had barely left her mouth when she realized how foolish they were.

She knew he was not a man to ignore a challenge. "Never doubt the savage side of me nature. I'm rather fond of it."

His tone was arrogant, which inflamed her temper.

"Get on yer mare, or I'll drag ye back across me stallion's back." His tone had grown hard. She would have liked to argue, but there was no disputing the fact that he was strong enough—and savage enough—to see his threat through. Both thoughts left her in despair. She took a last look toward Deigh Tower. It was just beyond the edge of the forest but might as well have been a hundred miles away.

She'd failed, and it was bitter knowledge.

But it was also spurring her on, encouraging her to think of another way to evade Saer. The pleasure he'd filled her with only intensified her need to escape. If she stayed, she'd lose herself completely and become another conquest. Once that happened, he'd grow tired of her lack of submission and grow to hate her. More than one man had chased a strong-willed woman only to find the attraction dulling after the wedding. Those women became known as harpies and scorned wives who did not know their place. She couldn't live with such a fate.

For seeing hatred in Saer's eyes was something she was certain would kill her.

❧

Dawn was gloomy.

The gray clouds and rain suited her mood. Nareen pulled her arisaid up to cover her head. It was the fabric of the Highlands for a reason. When it rained, wool could still be relied upon to keep the wearer warm.

Nareen was sure her shame could do just as well.

The MacLeod retainers had changed. From the moment she awoke, they watched her. When Saer went to talk with his captains, another retainer planted himself ten paces from her and did not turn his back on her except for when she sought privacy farther back in the woods. Even then, he followed her, granting her only twenty feet of separation.

She'd been raised under the watchful eye of Grant retainers, but she'd forgotten how it felt to have them always near. When she returned to the camp, the men who made eye contact with her reached up to tug on the edges of their knitted bonnets in respect.

For the first time.

In their minds, it was all decided. She belonged to Saer.

Her mare was saddled and waiting for her. Saer pulled away from his captains and moved toward her to help her mount. With a toss of her head she pulled her mare closer to a rock and used it to mount instead. The horse sidestepped, getting used to her weight. Saer calmed her with one sure hand against her neck. He muttered softly to the mare in Gaelic, but Nareen felt like he was really intending his words for her.

He aimed a hard stare at her, but she refused to meet his gaze. She felt him battling the urge to force the issue, but his men were mounting all around them, waiting on their laird. He gave a short snort, then boldly stroked her thigh.

She hissed at him, meeting his eyes as she shot him

a glare. Victory sparkled in his jet eyes as his lips rose into a satisfied curve.

"A challenge I shall be happy to meet tonight, Nareen. Ignore me as long as ye can, lass. I'm looking forward to our clashes."

❧

The war room of the Ross castle hadn't seen use in a long time. The servants kept it clean enough, but the earl had to fight the urge to admit he was unsure as to where everything was kept. His memory was unclear, but he faced his captains and spoke in a clear voice.

"Saer MacLeod abandoned me daughter," the Earl of Ross growled again. But he'd done it so often, no one really paid him any mind. He frowned as he took in the glazed-over looks of his men. When had he stopped being respected?

He tried to straighten up and puff out his chest, but his body was lax and too heavy.

"By Christ! I'll nae have it!"

He flattened his hand on the tabletop, but the only attention it gained was that of his gillie, who brought his goblet to him. He stared at the dark liquid, feeling the need to consume it. His lower lip was so dry, he licked it. A movement caught his eye, and he looked across the table to see two of his captains exchanging a look. One of revulsion.

He smacked the goblet aside, roaring as the wine went splashing across the floor and men guarding his back.

Betrayal! He'd betrayed himself by becoming a slave to the wine. For a moment, everything was clear, every moment since his wife had died until the moment Bastian MacKay had sent him a ransom note for his daughter.

Saer MacLeod had left his daughter in the hands of his enemy! It wasn't to be borne. And it wouldn't pass without being avenged.

But it meant facing Bastian MacKay. He shied away from that action, focusing his wrath on Saer.

"Draw up a ransom for the MacKays," he instructed his secretary. The man sat at a tiny writing desk behind the main table where the captains were.

"MacKay doesn't want money."

"Ha!" The earl snorted. "We'll send him an offer and see if the greedy man declines it. I doubt it."

He stuck his finger out. "And I'll be making sure Saer MacLeod regrets leaving me daughter with Bastian MacKay. No one crosses a Ross!"

‿✦‿

Nareen was sore.

When Saer finally called an end to their travel, she slid off the back of the mare and winced as her legs took her weight. That wasn't the only part of her that was tender.

Her cheeks should have brightened with a blush, but she was honestly too tired to even be embarrassed. At least the rain had stopped halfway through the day. She'd taken off her arisaid to make sure it had the chance to dry before the sun set. Only a few damp places remained in the deeper folds of her skirt.

She dearly wanted to take her boots off.

But Saer had bypassed Deigh Tower and left

MacNicols land behind—not that she was surprised; she'd always known him to be a man who was comfortable in the outdoors. Her belly was cramped with hunger, but she considered just curling up instead of waiting for supper to cook. The lack of sleep the night before was taking its toll, along with the grueling pace Saer set.

"I cry yer pardon, miss."

Nareen lifted her head, not really sure when she'd sat down. Yet she had, and she'd lowered her head to rest on her crossed arms that were propped on her raised knees. One of Saer's men stood before her. When she looked at him, he grinned and tugged on his bonnet. He showed off a chunk of soap, held securely in his hand.

"The laird told me to take ye upstream a bit, so ye might have some privacy while the meat is roasting."

So polite, and yet it was a clear order for her to stay awake until she ate. He was right, but it still chafed.

Saer MacLeod was driving her insane. Before long, she'd be ready for Bedlam or the back room of a convent where the devoted brides of Christ could see to her.

"Miss?" the retainer urged.

"Aye." She rose and looked at him. The man stood confused for a moment before Nareen opened her hands and gestured for him to show her the way.

"Aye," he chirped. "Just this way."

At least her toes were no longer numb.

❧

Saer looked upstream where Nareen had gone. His man stood just at the top of the rise, so Saer could see him looking back toward camp and not at his future mistress.

Baruch interrupted Saer's fascination with Nareen. "I do nae know why ye set someone else to dealing with her if all ye were going to do was watch her."

Saer turned back to consider Baruch, but his captain didn't even blink in the face of his displeasure.

"Sure ye do nae want to reconsider Bastian MacKay's offer of the Ross girl? I'm guessing ye'll have an easier time of dismissing her."

"Aye," Saer agreed. "And it will be ye who will have to deal with her whining when I've had enough."

Baruch tilted his head to one side. "Now that ye mention it, I'm rather sure the Ross lass is nae to yer taste."

"Thank ye for making sure I know that."

Baruch sniffed and nodded. "Well now, I'd be a poor captain if I did nae speak up when I notice important matters."

Saer offered him a half grin before turning and following Nareen. For certain, there would be plenty who would tell him to ignore her, but he didn't care. Something pulled him toward her, and bedding her hadn't dimmed it.

Was he spellbound?

Perhaps.

But he had to admit he wasn't wholly dismayed by the idea. Part of being laird would be making sure he had a strong son to follow him. The MacLeods had had enough of lairds who left the clan in uncertainty when they died. He had to wed, and soon. Better it be to a woman he was interested in than a stranger who arrived with nothing but duty warming her eyes.

He saw many things in Nareen's eyes, and none of them were the sedate flames of duty.

He made his way along the river's edge. The retainer he'd sent with Nareen saw him, pleasing Saer. The lad was young but not unworthy of the position he held. With a jerk of his head, Saer sent the lad back toward the fire. But the retainer shook his head and held his position.

Saer stopped in front of him, but the man only reached up and tugged on the corner of his bonnet. "I cannae take me ease while yer back is exposed, Laird."

"I can see to meself."

"Aye, in many cases I would agree, but here ye will be distracted."

The retainer didn't wait for Saer to answer. He moved a little farther away, just enough so the sound of the flowing water would mask any conversation Nareen and Saer had.

It chafed, but not nearly as much as it pleased him to know Nareen was protected. There was a satisfaction in that knowledge that rivaled everything he'd ever enjoyed before. A sense of rightness that swept away any misgivings he had. She belonged to him.

She had to, because he was certain he'd never feel whole without her.

❧

At least she'd gotten her wish to wash her feet.

It was amazing how much relief came with the action. The water was cold, and the night air was too. Her toes were chilled, but she smiled and left her boots off. Just another few moments before returning to the confinement of reality. Boots or Saer and his retainers, both represented the end of her freedom.

She'd been raised to expect no less, and still she rebelled. Perhaps she was unnatural, as the Church preached might happen when a woman took charge of her own fate. But she couldn't bring herself to regret not obeying her cousin.

With a sigh, she began to put her boots back on, working a length of leather through the antler-horn buttons that were sewn on the side from the top to the sole.

"I imagine Abigail wrinkled her fine nose at those boots."

Nareen jerked, the sound of Saer's voice startling her. Of course, everything about the man roused her.

He stood nearby, watching her with his midnight eyes. Sensation rippled across her skin, making her aware of the power in his body. It radiated off him, even when her toes were chilled.

"Abigail and I had an understanding that I would nae be changing meself to please her."

Nareen finished and started to stand. Saer offered her a hand. She stared at it for a long moment.

"Do nae be stubborn, Nareen."

She grabbed her skirt and made sure the fabric was out of the way before she stood on her own. "I am being sensible."

One of his dark eyebrows rose. "Ye're challenging me, woman, but I am nae complaining."

"Stop it," she said. "I am nae a challenge, at least nae any longer."

His expression tightened. "Because I had ye?" He clicked his tongue and stepped toward her. "Only a selfish man would think he'd had ye. There is much, much more to be shared between us. I am looking forward to being inside a bedchamber for the first time in me life, because it means I'll be free to explore yer body."

His tone deepened, unleashing a flicker of need inside her. It was like her body was awakening, stretching toward his and humming with anticipation.

But it also allowed another feeling. It nauseated her, because she could see the need to possess her gleaming in his eyes. She felt like a noose was being knotted around her neck.

"Ye do nae understand," she told him. "I cannae stomach the things ye make me feel."

He caught her chin. It was so simple a touch, that it surprised her. "Are ye sure ye understand yerself, Nareen? Because I'll admit I do nae comprehend what is between us. But I know it is a rare thing."

"Lust is nae rare," she countered as she lifted her chin out of his grip.

"Was it lust that had ye baring yerself to me?" He reached out and caught a handful of her skirt to keep her close. "I did nae force yer hand, Nareen. Ye bared yerself…for me."

She shook her head. "No, I did it to prove that I will do what I please. I wanted ye to know what sort of rebellion burns inside me. Ye should heed me warning."

His face lit until his eyes fairly glowed. He tossed his head back and laughed.

She slapped at his hand. "Ye were nae supposed to find that amusing. What sort of a man enjoys knowing a woman will do what she pleases no matter what the rest of the world thinks?"

"A savage." His lips were split in a wide smile. He pulled her closer, until his heat wrapped around her. Was it his body heat or the strength inside him she felt? She honestly didn't know.

"Ye shouldn't enjoy it," she answered, appalled by how easily she responded to him. He wasn't even touching her, only holding on to a handful of her skirts and keeping her close. "Ye are a laird now."

"So I shouldn't enjoy seeing the spirit in ye? Should I become a liar now that I have a title?" Saer demanded softly. "Do nae be so unkind, lass. I told ye yer strength draws me to ye."

"But...it should nae."

"Because the Church will nae approve?" he asked. She nodded.

His expression became menacing. "The Church has never approved of me. Nae since the day I was conceived without their blessing, until the moment when me father's clan sent for me because they had no one else to turn to and nae a single barrel of barley left to fill their bellies. The good servants of the Church were starving right along with the rest of the MacLeods, and all of them look to me to provide for them, so they will take me as I am."

Pain laced his words and flickered in his eyes. For a brief moment, she realized how alone he really felt.

She laid her hand along his jaw. He stiffened, his eyes narrowing as his eyes glittered.

"So do nae be telling me to judge what woman I desire by what the Church and society says is right." He pulled her closer so his breath teased her lips. "'Tis ye who makes me hard. It's deeper than lust, for I've known that sin well enough in me life." He leaned down and inhaled the scent of her hair, his chest rumbling with a sound of male appreciation. "I want more than to fuck ye."

"What more is there?"

He lifted his head and locked gazes with her. "I do nae know, for ye are the only woman who has stirred such a longing in me."

She pulled back, and there was a pop as one of the stitches holding her skirt to the waistband broke. He gave a snort of disapproval.

"Stand steady, Nareen, ye are no coward."

"I think maybe I am." The words escaped before she could bite her lip to keep the admission hidden. "At least with ye."

"I do nae want yer pity."

"Ye do nae have it." Saer released her skirt. "But ye do have me challenge, Nareen. The question is, do ye want to slay yer demons or live with them choking ye?"

He crooked his finger at her. "Come here."

"Ye'd enjoy that."

"Aye," he cooed. "Yer touch drives me mad."

It was an admission to match hers. But it was also a challenge. Only this time, he was issuing the challenge to her. That idea filled her with boldness, and with it came a relief from her fears.

"I've dreamed of ye since I met ye at court. Why else do ye think I've left the other offers I've had for marriage laying on me secretary's desk?"

"Ye have me brother's permission."

He nodded. "I've no wish to fight with Kael, but I'd be here even if he'd refused me."

She believed him. It was clear in his tone and on his face. "I—"

"Do nae," he snapped, with one thick finger pointing at her. "Do nae issue that challenge. I need to let ye be tonight, since ye were virgin, but say ye do nae want me, and we'll end up against another tree as I prove how much ye enjoy me touch."

Excitement twisted inside her, needling her to do exactly what he warned her against simply because she knew she'd be pushing him too far.

She nodded, and his eyebrow rose.

"Do nae be surprised, Saer. I've sense enough to realize when I'm fighting with ye, just to absolve meself of responsibility for what happens when I push ye too far."

He offered her his hand again, but she shook her head.

"Ye are nae listening, Saer. Trust is something I cannae give ye, and I think neither of us will be happy without it. Ye should send me home to me brother, for I will never take vows that will make me yer property."

"By law, yer brother is yer master, lass. Ye gain nothing by returning home."

"Kael gave me his word years ago never to force me to wed." Disappointment was filling her, as though she didn't want to convince him. "I have a place on

Grant land, and that is what I wish. If ye insist on taking me to yer land, it will nae change me feelings. I will never change them."

She passed him by, walking back toward camp. But she felt him behind her, felt his gaze on her back. It fanned the flames smoldering in her body, making her more aware of the sway of her hips.

Her cheeks burned, but what shamed her was how little it bothered her to know she liked Saer's attention. She was a wanton. But even that label didn't concern her overmuch.

One of the retainers met her with a thin length of steel that had chunks of roasted rabbit on it. Steam rose from the meat, and the scent earned a rumble from her stomach. But once she'd consumed it, she felt the cold even more. She pulled her arisaid up and over her head before lying down, but her skirts were still damp. There was a fire, but she stayed well away from it. The night was a shield she needed; being too near Saer's men was unbearable. They looked her way from time to time, proving she was not completely out of their notice.

She shivered, her teeth chattering.

"Perhaps this form of touching will be more to yer liking, lass."

There was a flutter of fabric, and the length of his kilt settled on top of her. Saer pressed up behind her, instantly warming her chilled body.

"But—"

She started to lift her head, and he sent his arm beneath it before locking her against him with his other arm. The man even trapped her ankles between his. The moment he joined her, his men turned their backs completely on them, even moving farther away.

A Highlander shared his colors only with his woman. It was tradition.

Saer tucked the wool around her, and she was helpless to hold back the sigh of relief that escaped her lips. With his body behind her and his kilt on top of her, the night was no longer cold.

"I'll nae see ye shiver, Nareen." He kissed her temple and rubbed her hip with a slow motion that chased the chill away. "Ye'll learn to trust that I will see to yer needs."

"I do nae want ye to."

He kissed her temple. "I understand that feeling too, lass. The last thing I ever wanted was to provide for the clan that shunned me and me mother. Me father was a royalist and died at Sauchieburn, along with a large number of his retainers. The loss left MacLeod land unprotected, and it was raided."

"Even if ye had been raised on MacLeod land, ye would have followed yer father to Sauchieburn. MacLeod land would still have been raided."

He grunted. "Perhaps." He stroked her hip in an unhurried motion. "I'm grateful for me past, for it's shown me that there is more to life than the pain we suffer. Ye'll see that truth, Nareen, once we've had time together. Ye're stronger for yer trials, and it will make ye value what ye have, because ye know what it is like to survive with less."

"As ye do?"

"Aye." He nuzzled against her hair. "We are well matched. The MacLeod do nae need a mistress who arrives with the notion that she should be waited upon the whole day through. Ye are no longer a girl but a woman, and that is what will make ye see the rightness of our union. Ye will nae be content to live out yer days as a spinster who will have to serve whomever yer brother weds. Return to yer father's house, and that will be yer lot. As me wife, ye can be proud of yer day's work."

A shiver moved through her, because she was close to believing him. The man radiated strength and purpose. She knew it was foolish to dismiss his promise. Just as she would be foolish to forget he expected obedience in return.

For certain there was something she should say in response, but all she was interested in was falling asleep now that she was warm. Saer was warm enough to keep the night from biting into her. That made his embrace right.

So very right. It was nae going to be easy.

Saer smoothed a hand along Nareen's shoulder and felt her shift in her sleep.

Uncertainty wasn't something he was a stranger to, but with Nareen, it unsettled him. She had been such a strong force in his mind since he'd met her, that it felt as though their relationship was already firmly rooted.

Her resistance was catching him off guard.

He was tired but didn't want to waste his moments with her in sleep. He wanted to feel her against him, listen to the sound of her breathing, and savor the scent of her hair. There was something mystical about her. Something that went beyond enticing.

He stroked her cheek, and she turned toward him.

No matter how much he'd enjoyed the memory of her, the reality was far, far better.

"Nae, lass, there will be no going back to yer father's land to live in a cold tower room."

Because she belonged with him.

❧

Saer felt good.

At least in her dreams she didn't have to worry about how she reacted to him.

Nareen slid her hands along his chest, marveling at the sculpted ridges. The scent of his skin affected her strangely. Filling her with some deep understanding of just how strong he was.

She wanted to taste him.

So she kissed his skin and felt his crisp hair tease her nose before he moved, threading his fingers through her hair. She hadn't braided it before going to sleep, and it was a fine, soft cloud around her shoulders now.

Her eyes flew open and widened with horror. She was not dreaming.

Saer didn't give her a chance to wiggle away from him. He cupped her nape and angled his head so he might fit his lips against hers.

A tiny moan escaped her lips as she kissed him back. Teasing his lips with little touches of her tongue. She needed to touch him, not just be held in position for his kiss. All of the need she'd suppressed the night before was loose, sleep having robbed her of her self-discipline.

He groaned, his grip tightening before he rubbed

his hand down her back. She arched, her spine needing to release all the sensation he was unleashing. Remaining still was impossible.

She craved him.

Darkness still cloaked them, making her bold. She pulled on a tie that kept his doublet closed. His shirt was already open at the neck, allowing her to bury her face against the bare skin of his neck. He cupped her bottom, kneading and massaging each cheek.

Need spiked through her. Intense and red-hot. Her passage felt empty, and she thrust toward him.

His cock was hard.

She purred with that knowledge, pressing her belly against him as desire threatened to numb her wits completely.

He stroked the swells of her breast, pushing his fingers inside her bodice to tease her nipples. Her breasts strained against the tight confines of her clothing. He found the lace holding her top closed and opened the knot with a sharp tug.

"I'm going to keep ye bare for a month." He leaned over, nuzzling into her open bodice and kissing the side of her breast. She shuddered, arousal jolting through her like an explosion. He teased the delicate skin, seeking out one nipple. When he closed his lips around it, she arched, offering it to him.

He suckled it like a treat, swiping his tongue around the puckered tip and finally across the hard top. She needed the contact as much as he seemed to, slipping her hands into his hair and gripping the strands.

He rolled farther onto her, reaching down to pull her skirt up. It was a blunt action, but she was desperate to be in contact with him. She reached for him, seeking what she craved. Slipping her hand across his chest and down to where his shirttail lay over what she desired.

He lifted his head as she slid her hand lower, to the edge of his shirt. A little sigh of satisfaction passed her lips when she encountered the firm surface of his thigh.

"Touch what ye crave, lass."

His voice was so low, it might have been an echo from her own thoughts. Except the deep, rich timbre sent a shiver across her skin. He teased her cheek with his fingers, making her aware of just how good his skin felt against her own.

She wanted more though, and she reached for it, slipping her hand along the inside of his thigh until she found his hip. He sucked in a breath, which stilled her motions as trepidation flashed through her.

"Do nae stop." He bared his teeth at her. "Sweet Christ, I think I'm ready to beg ye nae to stop."

"I've known that same madness."

He opened his eyes, locking gazes with her as understanding flowed between them. She'd never comprehended intimacy in such a way before, never felt truly connected to another soul as she did just then.

But he was still too powerful, holding her down as he leaned over her. She could feel his strength, had to acknowledge how simple it would be for him to take her. So she moved her hand up and stroked his length.

They both gasped. Nareen was fascinated by the raw enjoyment displayed on his face. His control was gone, the mask he so often presented ripped away. It left her staring at the delight her touch sparked. She wrapped her hand around his staff, marveling at how smooth the skin was. The organ was hard but covered in silken skin that begged to be petted. She toyed with it, stunned to feel just how thick it was, because it defied her logic to know she'd taken it.

"Ye'll unman me…" he growled through gritted teeth.

"I hope so." She circled the crown and teased the slit, carrying away a drop of fluid. "I seem to recall ye enjoying driving me daft with yer fingers."

His lips curved up with satisfaction. "Wait until I have ye stripped again and a solid door to ensure our privacy, lass." He cupped her bare breast and massaged it until she whimpered. "I plan to enjoy the sound of yer screams, but me men are too close for that tonight."

Disappointment needled her, and he chuckled before releasing her breast and tugging her skirt the rest of the way up her body. His kilt still covered her, but he flattened his hand against her belly and leaned down to bite her earlobe.

"Worry not, lass, I'll nae leave ye wanting."

He teased the curls crowning her mons. Tugging on the soft, silken strands before stroking the lips guarding her sex. She jerked away, the level of sensation too great. It felt like she might burst from just that single touch.

But she was pinned. He pressed his knee between her thighs, making room for his hand.

"Saer…"

"Shhh…our voices will carry…"

He sealed her protest beneath his lips before stroking her again. This time, he began at the entrance of her passage. Dipping his fingers into the cream collecting there, he drew it along the seam of her slit, sending pleasure shooting through her. But he didn't give her what she truly craved. The little button throbbing for attention at the top of her sex went untouched. She twisted with the need to gain pressure against it, lifting her hips, but he'd already moved his hand back to the entrance of her body.

He lingered there. Teasing the opening with only a single fingertip while he finished kissing her. When he lifted his head, he hovered over her, his breath hitting her wet lips.

He was propped on his elbow and toying with her cheek. His fingers moved to touch the corner of her lips before he trust his digit inside her passage.

She moaned, and he clasped his hand over her mouth to contain the sound. All that escaped was a muffled groan. Need tormented her, the hard presence of his cock against her thigh was driving her mad. She opened her legs wider as her eyes slid shut.

She sank down into the swirling madness his fingers were creating. He teased her opening and then the seam of her slit. Up and down and then back up to the top where the wet folds opened completely to bare her bud. He didn't ignore it this time. Little sounds of pleasure made their way around the hand over her mouth as he teased and fingered the little nub. She strained toward him, needing relief from the twisting pleasure tightening in her belly. It was deep inside her, in that place only his cock could satisfy.

She opened her eyes and glared at him. He was watching her, his dark eyes pools of hunger. His face tightened with determination when their gazes locked. He rolled completely over her, settling between her thighs. His weight pleased her, but with the first touch of his cock, she arched upward, seeking the fullness he could give her. He stretched her with his first thrust, sliding smoothly with the aid of the cream coating her sex.

He muffled another groan with his fingers, but she felt his chest vibrating with an answering one.

"Sweet Christ, Nareen, be still or I'll be finished before we begin."

She purred softly, accepting his challenge.

Boldness took hold of her. There was no pain tonight, just the fullness she'd desired. She tightened her thighs around him and lifted her bottom off the ground to drive him even deeper.

"Witch…" he growled softly.

She opened her jaw and sank her teeth into his finger. Just enough to make him move. He pulled free, the length of his cock sliding along her sensitive button. She groaned, biting into his finger without meaning to.

He chuckled.

And she reached down to cup both sides of his ass.

"Christ!"

He thrust back into her with more force, sending a jolt of pleasure through her body. It stole her breath, leaving her panting, but she moved with him, lifting her hips so he slid completely into her. There was no shame, only need and the building pleasure tightening in her core.

She kneaded his backside and lifted her chest so her bared breasts brushed his chest.

"Too fast…" he snarled. "But I cannae stop…"

He thrust into her. Once, twice, and rolled his hips once he was buried deep inside her. The motion unleashed a whole new set of sensations, and she felt rapture breaking apart inside her. It surprised her, how suddenly it burst, and pleasure flooded her.

"Yes…yes, Nareen…that's what I will always give ye…"

She would have screamed—and not cared who heard her—if he hadn't covered her mouth. In that moment, her need for him was greater than anything else.

When she opened her eyes, his attention was on her face, triumph shimmering in his eyes.

"I will pleasure ye and make ye glad to be in me bed."

There was a promise in his voice that made her shudder. Her passage actually tightened around his cock, and he groaned. It was the sort of pure reaction she was beginning to become used to happening with him. But she wasn't willing to submit.

She lifted her hips and tightened her muscles so her passage contracted around his cock again.

He bared his teeth at her. "Yes…"

He flexed and thrust into her. His powerful body moving hers as he thrust and retreated in a motion that drove the breath from her body.

She dug her fingers into his cheeks and matched his rhythm.

His eyes slid shut as he lost the battle to maintain his control. He arched his head back, the muscles cording along the thick column of his neck. He was breathing hard, and his member felt like it was swelling even more. Two more hard thrusts, and she felt him erupt. His seed began to flow deep inside her. She tightened her core muscles again, pulling it from his length.

His eyes opened wide, and he gripped her hair as he settled his face an inch above hers.

His cock finished emptying, but he held her beneath him, smoothing her hair back with gentle touches.

"Mine," he repeated softly. She shook her head, denying his claim, but he laid a kiss against her lips, pressing them open and tasting her.

A moment later, he stood up and pulled her up with him. Her skirts fell down to cover her as he scooped up his kilt.

Somehow, she'd missed the brightening of the horizon. The sun wasn't really visible, but the night was losing its hold on the world. "We'll touch MacLeod land today."

"I want to go to Grant land."

Saer looked like he had the first time she saw him. Immovable. His stance powerful and unyielding. His seed was hot inside her, marking her like a possession, and she shook her head.

"Ye said ye would take me to me brother."

"When ye were a maiden, I would have," Saer countered swiftly.

"I hold ye to no agreement."

He cupped her chin and captured her bicep when she tried to jerk away. "Honor is a personal duty, Nareen. Me seed is in yer belly, and I'll nae see any child of mine bastard-born."

"Then ye should stay away from me."

His lips split into a grin that was menacing, promising a fight. "Ye clung to me…"

She pulled back, but he held her steady and continued. "And milked me…"

She snarled at him, but he wasn't finished.

"And I will take ye home with me, Nareen Grant, for ye are a prize far greater than I could ever have wished for."

He let her go, his stance still unwavering. The first rays of sun broke the horizon behind him, illuminating the hard certainty on his face.

"Ye have a few minutes of privacy, no more."

His gillie had come up and taken the length of MacLeod plaid from the ground and was pleating it on a large rock. Saer turned and let the lad help him dress.

He was just proving his authority.

She knew it because it was the first time she'd ever seen him let the lad serve him. The youth had even hesitated for a moment before jumping forward.

She wasn't his. She wasn't.

Four

SAER GAVE A ROAR WHEN THEY REACHED MACLEOD land. He sounded primitive and savage, and his men lifted their voices to match his.

It was the last straw for Nareen.

When they had left that morning, the MacLeod retainers had formed around her the moment she mounted her mare. They kept her in their midst as they rode hard for the MacLeod land.

Saer led them, looking too full of authority to suit her mood. His sword was strapped to his back, driving home the fact that he would defend his will if necessary.

She felt the noose tightening.

Looking past the men riding near her, she glanced toward her father's land. She couldn't see it, of course, but it felt as if it was calling to her.

One of the retainers' horses tried to nip her mare, because Nareen had started pulling the horse in the direction she gazed. The stallion snorted, and his rider growled something in Gaelic before she was able to bring the mare back into the center of the road. But she couldn't resist one last look toward Grant land.

The retainer riding along the opposite side of her peeled away in a fluid motion as Saer guided his stallion into step beside her. She had only a moment to register his appearance before he reached across and scooped her off her mare.

She squealed as she felt herself passing between the animals. It was a dangerous place to be with the rest of the retainers behind them. If she fell, she'd be trampled.

Saer hauled her in front of him and turned his stallion away from the other horses.

"Are ye mad?" she demanded as she tried to push away from him, but with the horse in motion, it was impossible. He clamped a solid arm around her, binding her against his hard body.

She'd forgotten she enjoyed the way his skin smelled.

"Put me back on me mare!" she insisted.

One short, solid word was his response. "No." His tone was clipped and unyielding.

"Ye're a spitfire at times, Nareen."

He stopped his horse, and his men pulled up as well. Dust swirled in the air and the animals snorted.

"But ye're my spitfire," he informed her smugly.

"I am nae," she argued.

Determination flickered in his eyes, making her mouth go dry. The savage side of his nature was showing through. She recognized it now.

"We'll see," he promised softly. "But for that, ye'll have to be coming home with me."

She opened her mouth to argue, but he wrapped something around her arm. He started knotting a strip of his tartan around her wrist.

"Ye cut yer kilt?"

It was such a waste, and most Highlanders considered it an insult. Saer chuckled darkly.

"There is no better way to bind ye to me and ensure everyone knows exactly what I intend."

His meaning eluded her, until he grabbed her belt and slipped her around behind him. She swung her leg over the horse frantically, to keep herself from sliding, and grabbed his belt to steady herself.

Saer captured her free wrist and tugged her forward until she was flush against his back.

She sputtered, fighting against him, but he had too much strength.

"Savage!"

"Aye." He looped the tartan around her free wrist and tied another knot. "I am that. Remember it the next time ye want to test me."

He'd left only enough space between her hands so the tartan wasn't biting into her wrists and the girth of his body wasn't straining her arms.

But she was pressed against him. There was no way even to move her hips away from his firm backside. She had to lean against his right shoulder to avoid his sword.

His men sent up another cheer when he rode back up to join them.

She grumbled against him and bit back a curse.

Saer moved in motion with the stallion, and she had to as well. Other travelers on the road looked up and stared at her in bewilderment. A few of them gave Saer wicked grins, making her grind her teeth.

The fields to the side of the road were full of crops. Even angry, she couldn't help but admire the barley stocks that were beginning to turn gold. Saer had inherited a striped land. Those clans who had ridden with the young king James IV had taken their pay from the lands of those defeated at the battle of Sauchieburn by raiding the MacLeod and carrying off everything of value.

The MacLeod had suffered more than one raid, and there had been little left behind two years ago. Yet they passed a village, with round homes built from stone and crowned with peat-moss roofs. There were cattle and other animals, even flocks of sheep being grazed on the land that was not suitable for farming.

But the real achievement was revealed when the MacLeod towers came into view. The sun was beginning to set, but she could still hear the sound of the stonemasons, the steady clip, clip, clip of their chisels against solid stone. The old towers stood inside a massive construction site. New, taller towers were being built, as well as walls to enclose it all. Stones were being lifted to the towers by several large wooden wheels, which were operated by men walking inside them. Fires burned in the yard as mortar was mixed and then put into baskets tied to the sides of ponies that walked up narrow ramps to where stone was being laid. A loch stretched out behind the site, adding even more security to it, because no one could attack from that side.

Saer pulled up and turned his stallion so she might see the entire castle.

"We'll nae be raided again," he promised ominously.

"But where did ye get the silver for so many workmen?"

He rubbed her hand gently. "Worried I am interested only in yer dowry, lass?"

"It would explain why ye have tied me around ye like some raiding prize," she bit back.

"Me sister had a fortune for dowry."

"I heard the rumor, but wasn't it taken?" she asked.

"The dowry had been transferred to the Sutherland coffers before Sauchieburn."

"But yer sister Daphne wed Norris Sutherland," Nareen said, still confused by the cattle and sheep. They could not have been replaced without coin.

"Me in-laws were willing to negotiate a bit on the amount."

"That is unheard of," Nareen exclaimed.

"The Sutherland enjoy a good reputation," Saer explained. "I may have mentioned that the MacLeod would think more kindly toward them if they didn't take every last bit of that dowry, seeing as the MacLeod had so little at the time. It would be rather simple for the MacLeod to view Norris Sutherland as another raider, for he did come down and insist on taking Daphne."

"Aye, I can see that." Nareen then pulled on the wool binding her wrists. "Have ye given any thought to what sort of reputation ye'll be enjoying if ye persist in riding into yer castle with me tied around ye?"

Someone began to ring a bell on the top of the old section of wall. Another bell joined it, and soon there were over twenty, ringing out to gain the attention of those working.

"Ye and I are fighting a personal battle, lass." He angled his head back so he might see her face. "That is why ye are bound."

"Ye're humiliating me."

"I am also making a point."

He rode forward as his people waved and cheered. They came out of everywhere, wearing aprons and with sweat on their foreheads. Saer rode through what would become the new gate to a new tower that rose four stories into the air.

"Ye built that in a single year?"

She couldn't help but be astonished.

He rode up to the base of the new tower and stopped his stallion.

"Aye." He pointed up to the top of it. "Our chambers are there."

"*Yer* chambers," she corrected.

He reached down and pulled a dagger from his boot. The last of the sun's rays flashed off the blade before he used it to slice through the strip of tartan binding her. He lifted his leg over the head of the horse and slid to the ground while she was stretching her back.

He reached up, grasped her waist, and lifted her off the animal.

"They will be *ours*, Nareen."

He winked at her before bending over and throwing her over his shoulder. She let out an outraged screech that only brought laughter from those watching. Many whistled in encouragement as Saer took the stairs two at a time and then entered the keep through a wide double doorway.

Nareen only had a glimpse of women lined up to greet the laird, before Saer mounted the stairs and carried her away. But she still heard the giggles.

She fumed. But what bothered her most was that she had to fight off the urge to cry. She'd not weep.

At least the satisfied smirk on Saer's face when he set her down ignited her temper. She snarled at him, but in response, he only closed the doors he'd carried her through.

When he turned around, she froze, recognizing the look of desire in his black eyes. He was impossibly handsome. Every inch of him hard and sculpted. She enjoyed looking at him and challenging him.

It was damned frustrating the way the sight of him distracted her from what she'd decided she wanted.

"Do nae stop sputtering now that I've got ye alone."

Nareen propped her hand onto her hip and lifted her chin. "So ye need me irritated, do ye?"

He shrugged and offered her a grin. "No' at all, lass. Although I'll admit to enjoying the fire in ye." He moved closer, and she ordered herself to stand still. She heard him make a short, gruff sound of approval as he closed the space between them completely. He stroked her cheek with the back of his hand.

She shuddered, the contact instantly awakening a hunger. Her body wasn't slow to respond, because she already knew what satisfaction might be hers.

If she yielded.

"Well…I will nae," she stated firmly as she stepped away from him.

She half-expected him to reach for her, but he cast her a questioning look and held his position.

"Ye will nae…what?" he asked.

Her cheeks heated as she realized she'd spoken aloud.

Saer took a step after her, the privacy of the chambers allowing her to hear the soles of his boots making contact with the stone floor.

"Will nae…what, Nareen?"

She had to tip her head back to make eye contact. She felt him near her, like the heat coming from a hearth on a cold night. Her flesh welcomed it.

"I will nae wed ye." She forced the words past her lips, but her temper had deserted her, leaving her trying to convince him of the rightness of her words. "That is what ye crave, in the end, and I cannae grant it to ye. Tying me about ye and forcing me to come here only makes me more certain. I will nae promise to obey ye as a wife must."

He crossed his arms over his chest. It looked like he was forcing himself to keep his hands off her and think on her words. It struck her as tender, and kept her in place as she waited to hear his reply. What they both needed was rational thought.

But that didn't explain why she felt disappointed to see him thinking though her argument.

He sighed. "I suppose I should nae have bound ye, nae when I know yer cousin treated ye much the same way."

"I do nae wish to speak of her." Nareen turned away.

Saer reached out and captured her wrist. But he didn't pull her into his embrace; he merely kept her from walking away.

"I ask only that ye allow us the chance to know each other."

She faced him and tried to shake off his hold. His lips pressed into a hard line before he snorted and released her wrist.

"Ye have dragged me into yer personal chambers after arriving with me tied around ye. That is nae asking for anything."

"Ye closed yer hand around me cock and demanded satisfaction once I was inside ye, Nareen."

Her cheeks burned, and her jaw dropped. "That has naught to do with—"

He moved toward her, pressing her backward across the wide expanse of open floor. She needed to look behind her, but knew turning her gaze away would be the fatal mistake he was waiting for her to make.

"It has everything to do with why ye are here, Nareen."

Something caught her eye, and she realized she'd backed right into a huge bed. Saer closed his hands around her waist and sent her onto its wide expanse. The bed ropes creaked and then groaned as Saer lunged after her.

He pinned her down, capturing her wrists and pressing them to the surface of the bed.

"Let me loose," she demanded. But her voice had grown raspy.

"Are yer nipples tightening, Nareen?"

"Get off me."

His lips twitched. "Ye were a maiden."

"Aye, and I wanted to remain one."

He leaned down and kissed the side of her neck. "No ye did nae." Sensation rippled down her body, and her nipples did indeed begin to tighten. "Ye wanted to choose who ye let become yer lover, and that was me."

She chewed on her lower lip.

He nodded confidently. "I understand ye, and I dare ye to argue against that."

"It does nae mean it is right for me to be here. Have ye thought what me brother will make of it?" She twisted her wrists, and Saer rolled onto his back with a disgusted grunt.

She stumbled to her feet, irritated by how clumsy her steps were. The man had set her knees to feeling weak again.

"Kael gave me his permission to chase ye."

Saer sat up, but was in no hurry to follow her. The chamber doors were closed.

"Did he grant ye leave to lock me in yer private chambers and post yer retainers at the doors to keep me with ye?"

Saer shrugged and stood up. "I did nae sit down and compare courtship details with him."

"Courtship?" She laughed.

Saer lifted one dark eyebrow. "Have I nae been attentive to ye, lass?" He stalked her across the floor. "Did I nae move ye to ecstasy with me fingers before—"

"Enough." Her cheeks were heating.

He smirked at her. "No, I agree that fingering was nae enough. Nae for ye or me."

"I do nae wish to discuss this."

She bumped into the closed doors, and he flattened his hands on either side of her flushed face.

"No?"

"No." Her voice was only a squeak.

"Good." He nodded. "I prefer action meself."

He leaned forward, and she covered his mouth with her hand. It was a desperate move to keep him from kissing her.

She'd lose her senses if he did.

"I'm trying to make ye see reason, Saer."

He lifted his chin, dislodging her hand. "So am I,

lass. Life is hard enough without it being lonely. Fate can be very fickle when it comes to bestowing the sort of heat that is between us. I have no intention of letting ye turn yer back on me before we've given each other a fair chance."

His tone was gentle, but determination glittered in his eyes. He lifted one hand, granting her an escape route. Once she'd bolted out of the embrace, he took up a solid stance in front of the chamber doors.

"Welcome to me new tower, Nareen. I hope ye find it pleasing."

A change in topic was welcome—a relief really. But that shamed her because she was being a coward again.

She looked at him and he raised an eyebrow. "If ye do nae want to wash…"

"With ye here?"

He shrugged and opened the doublet he'd worn since they'd left Ross land. It was leather, lined with sturdy wool. It closed with a leather cord laced through worked eyelets. Practical, not fancy. He obviously invested all of his coin in the castle.

"I never believed the rumors about how grand Daphne's dowry was, but it must have been for ye to afford this much construction."

He finished unlacing the jerkin and laid it aside. "Me father had me trained and educated. I made sure to put those skills to use."

"But this…" She turned around and was struck dumb.

The chamber was open to the night. She should have realized it. She could feel the night breeze and smell the ripening barley in the fields. The air lacked the stale scent that was common in towers. It was something everyone bore because of the need for study walls to protect them from raiders.

But Saer's chambers had only arched doorways along the far side of the chamber. She moved past the large hearth to stand in one, and looked out. There was a portion of flooring that extended past the arches for another twenty feet until a half wall rose up around it all. Columns were placed at the same intervals as the arches to support a roof. She realized the flooring covered a chamber below them. Logic dictated that there should have been walls all around the area, because towers rose up in columns, but not Saer's tower. She turned to find him trailing her, patiently waiting for her to inspect his chambers.

"What is it?" she asked in awe.

"The Italians call them *terrazzino*." Saer moved out into the evening air. He tipped his head back and inhaled. "I call it a very necessary part of me personal chambers. It keeps me in the castle at night, which I'm sure you'll agree is me place, since I am laird."

He opened his eyes and looked toward her. "There is naught I detest more than being shut inside a chamber at night. In Italy, the weather is warmer, so they do nae wall off all the chambers."

"Ye've been to Italy?" she asked incredulously.

Saer shook his head. "I've met men who have and seen the sketches they made of the homes there. While strong, they also offer the inhabitants fresh air."

She had to admit the chamber smelled far more inviting than she would have thought possible.

"What of the rain or snow?"

He smiled and pointed at something sitting outside

the main chamber. "Here, lass, there are doors to shut the snow out, but the roof will keep it from the main chamber unless it is blowing."

He pulled a door from the outside that covered half the arched doorway space. He reached out again and pulled the other side into position before lowering a solid latch.

"It's remarkable, but what if there is an attack?" She ran a hand over the wood door. It was solid and thick.

"This will keep out even crossbow arrows. The *terrazzino* faces the inner yard. If both curtain walls are breached, there is no reason to worry about the lack of stone here. The castle will have fallen."

He surveyed the door before opening it again. "But do nae worry, lass. I'm nae going to allow the MacLeod to suffer being raided again."

Nareen walked out onto the *terrazzino*, enjoying the fresh air. "It is hard to believe yer sister had a dowry large enough to allow ye the coin for so many stonemasons."

The workers covered the walls, and the lower yard was full. Everyone was working at a steady pace. Saer joined her.

"I offered them a place where each man would be judged on his work, nae the actions of his father." Saer braced his hands on the half wall and leaned out to get a better view of the workers toiling on the half-completed inner curtain wall. "The isles are full of bastard-born men who are told they are less than other men because of the stigma of their birth. That will no' be the way it is here."

"Ye are paying them in respect." Something many

of those men could never hope to gain anywhere else. The Church preached that a child was stained with the sins of its parents. Being bastard-born held merits only if the sire was a nobleman. Like Saer.

"More than that. I'm offering them a clan," he informed her with the unmistakable ring of pride in his tone. "Any man who labors here for five full seasons will be allowed to call himself a MacLeod and wear his colors proudly."

She marveled at his plan. Below, hundreds of men and women were working. Only the king would have had enough coin to pay them all, but Saer had found another way. Much like the Church did. The Church demanded labor in exchange for blessings, and Saer had discovered a means of offering something the men below them could find nowhere else. As the light began to fade, they started to make their way down from their work places to long tables set up for their supper.

"There are so many, the Hall cannae accommodate them," he added. "But once the stonework is done, they will set to work on their own homes."

"Ye are an amazement, Saer MacLeod," she whispered as she watched the men make their way to long troughs full of water. They washed and even dunked their heads before sitting down at the tables. Women were already serving the evening meal, the scent drifting up. "Ye invite the shunned and are rebuilding yer clan with men who have nowhere else to go. Yer neighbors had best take care, for the MacLeod numbers will be something to be reckoned with."

"More important, men who have nowhere else to go

will defend what they have like no other men on earth."
He pointed past the half-finished inner wall. "Out there
is where me retainers are being trained. They are the
half-grown sons of these men and women."

"Ye offer sword training?" Her eyes widened.

"Do nae be alarmed, Nareen," he soothed. "I have
known most of those men for years. I would never
train men whose honor was in question." He pointed
at the tables below them. "But these stonemasons will
wed, and their sons will be born MacLeods."

She'd be a fool not to be impressed. Nowhere else
in the Highlands was there a place for the unwanted.
Saer was rebuilding his clan far faster than anyone
would have thought possible.

But the kindness of it threatened to send tears down
her cheeks. "Ye are a good man."

He turned to look at her, but she wasn't sure she
could stand letting him see how his actions affected
her. Men often said many things but still did exactly
as they pleased.

But when she turned, she stopped, because there
was something else on the *terrazzino* she'd never
seen before.

"Ah yes, ye've yet to see where ye may wash the
dust from yer skin."

Saer passed her by and walked to the far end of
the *terrazzino*. The hearth was set into the far wall
of the chamber, and there was a four-foot section
of wall before the first arch opening. There was
another smaller section of wall, just two feet high,
and above it was a chain with slim buckets attached
at regular intervals.

"This, Nareen, is how we get the loch water to the *terrazzino*." He stripped off his clothing and grinned when she looked away.

But when she heard a splash, she just couldn't keep her eyes averted.

The man was magnificent. Her mouth went dry, and she couldn't help but feast on the sight of his bare body. Every inch was hard and pleasing. She felt the urge to strip and forget every reason she had for arguing against what he wanted. It would be a blatant lie to claim part of her wasn't very interested in belonging to him.

But once she surrendered, there would be no dictating to him what she wanted. Muffled conversation drifted up from the yard, reminding her of how kind he was, but her memory was quick to offer up the demands he'd already revealed.

The man was building a strong clan, and it would be her duty to provide sons. Quickly. No matter how kind he was, he was still ruthless when it came to what he wanted from life. Those laboring below would not be getting a warm welcome into the MacLeod clan without hard work. Nothing in life was free. And certainly not when it came from a man like Saer MacLeod. He was laird and would no doubt use his savage nature to defend his position.

Only a fool would forget it.

He shook the water from his eyes.

Saer turned a handle that moved a gear above his head. Its teeth caught in the links of the chain. She moved closer to get a better view of the complexity of the design. The buckets rose from the loch below, all the way up three stories to the edge of the *terrazzino*. A wheel above his head moved the chain over a large, flat stone, dumping the water over it. The edge of the stone was worked with a lip that had indentations in it. The water split into a hundred little streams that flowed down over Saer.

She moved closer, amazed. The floor beneath Saer's feet was slanted slightly, and there was a stone missing in the outer half wall that let the used water flow right down the side of the tower and back onto the shore of the loch.

"Amazing," she whispered in awe. "Whoever thought of such a thing?"

"The Romans had heated water," he answered as he turned the gear some more, rinsing himself again. He'd lathered up with a chunk of soap and now cleaned it off his skin. "At Hayden's wall, there are ruins of bathhouses. But I've yet to find someone with the courage to try building one."

"This is a marvel in itself."

She might be clean whenever she wished. The hearth was only a few steps away to warm her, even in the dead of winter.

Saer finished and dried himself on a length of linen hanging from a nearby hook. "As ye see, lass, I've made sure to be able to keep ye well."

"Keeping me here is..." She fought to keep her tone even, because the moment she gave into passion, he'd be happy to take advantage of it.

She caught sight of the bed and noted the size of it. Fit for a laird, it had bed curtains and plump pillows.

"Is what?" he demanded.

"Well, it's nae courting," she finished, too agitated for her comfort. Her gaze slipped to the bed again.

It was so close. And likely more comfortable than a tree.

"I see." Saer moved around until he was looking at the bed too. "So I've made an error."

"Aye." She turned her back on the bed.

"In that case, I should amend me ways immediately."

Disappointment stabbed at her, but she nodded. "Ye should."

His eyes flickered with wicked intent. "I'll change me wording. This is nae a courtship, but a claiming, which means it's time for me to get to ravishing ye."

"Saer," she sputtered and jumped away from him. The only problem was, she was moving toward his bed. And he was still completely bare. The cold water hadn't affected his cock at all—it stood rigid, promising her all the passion he'd already shown her and more, now that they were in private.

He arched an eyebrow. "Does that mean ye prefer courting, sweet Nareen? I'm a bit confused. Perhaps ye could clarify which method ye would like."

"For what?" she questioned.

He took one slow, long step toward her.

She wanted to stand her ground, but she could feel the passion radiating off him. It was kindling the coals of her own desire, and she knew it would flare up with just one kiss.

"Courtship or claiming?" He took another step. "Name yer desire."

"With ye, there is no difference."

His expression hardened with determination. "There is, lass."

He reached out and grasped a handful of her skirt to hold her. His teasing demeanor evaporated, leaving nothing but hard purpose.

"Ye can enjoy washing the road dust from yer skin, and I promise to awaken yer desire with soft touches as I did the first night I touched ye..."

She licked her lower lip. His gaze narrowed, a muscle beginning to tick along his jaw.

"Or I will strip ye down and ravish ye as any claiming should be done."

She shuddered, frustrated almost beyond being able to speak. But Saer pressed a single fingertip against her lips to still her retort.

"Mind ye, I still think we'll end in me bed, because ye have a passionate spirit I have no intention of ignoring."

She shook her head to dislodge his hand.

"Make yer choice, lass, but if ye decide to challenge me with an argument, I do nae promise ye'll have anything to wear by dawn."

He released her skirt and reached down for a dagger resting on the trestle table set for supper. The last of the sunlight glinted off its sharp edge.

"Savage," she muttered, but shook her head, because she knew he enjoyed the label, and she wasn't sure if she intended to admonish him or praise him. "And do nae ye dare grin at me for calling ye that." She moved toward the *terrazzino*.

"I wish to wash me hair. Alone."

She didn't look back to see his response. She was better off not knowing. Of course, that was only because she enjoyed the passion he stirred in her as much as he did—that was what she had to make sure she never let him know. She'd never escape if she did. And she needed to escape; there was no way she would accept his authority.

None.

⁂

"Did nae expect to see ye tonight." Baruch reached up and pulled on the corner of his bonnet when Saer appeared in the Hall.

"I'm trying to be"—he sat down and rolled his eyes—"a suitor."

Baruch choked on his laughter, earning a scathing look from Saer.

"Do nae start on me, man," Saer barked. "That woman is stubborn."

Two women began serving the high table as the MacLeod retainers broke bread at the long tables filling the Great Hall below.

"I believe that's one of the qualities ye enjoy about her."

Saer bit into a piece of meat and chewed thoughtfully. "Aye and nay. I expected her to accept our match by now."

Baruch stroked the side of his beard. "I'm nae sure arriving with the lass tied around ye is quite the way a man brings home a bride."

Saer grunted. "Aye. I won't say I'm sorry. Me actions fit our relationship."

Baruch broke off a piece of bread from the large round placed in front of them. "Ye're no liar, that's for certain. More than one man would have trouble admitting that so easily."

"I take responsibility for me deeds."

Baruch nodded approvingly. "A quality that makes ye a laird worth serving. The lass likes that about ye. Her gaze follows ye."

And keeping his gaze off Nareen was a challenge he'd underestimated. His men were taking good long looks at him while they ate. The women serving the tables were equally curious. Saer found himself watching the doorway at the end of the main aisle.

"Is the lass joining us?" Baruch asked.

Saer shut his eyes, biting back a word of profanity for just how exposed his feelings were. He was laird, a position that wouldn't be his very long if he appeared weak.

"No." He lifted his hand, and his head of house came over. "Send supper up to me chambers for Mistress Grant. She's to be afforded every courtesy."

Gitta lowered herself and made her way toward the kitchens.

"And freedom?" Baruch inquired.

The other captains sitting at the high table all turned to look at Saer. It pleased him, because his place had not been an easy one to assume. There were plenty of men among the MacLeod who didn't care for seeing the lairdship pass to a bastard.

But the alternative was to see the clan splintered. There were three cousins who all had equal claims to the lairdship after Saer. Blood would be split and no mistake. A bastard laird was better than seeing what remained of the MacLeod's torn apart from within.

"I intend to wed Mistress Grant," he told them. "Her brother agrees to the match, but the lass needs time to adjust to the arrangement, and I've no taste for a weeping bride."

Several of his captains nodded in agreement.

Saer wished it were as simple to convince himself that Nareen would adjust. What bothered him most was just how important the matter was becoming to him. It was almost as if he needed her to choose him.

His mother had loved his father, and it had taken her into ruin. He would never make such a mistake with his own life.

It was a weakness he could never afford.

❦

The water was cold but refreshing. Nareen used the soap twice in her hair before deciding she was clean enough. The wind chilled her when it hit her bare skin, raising goose bumps. She'd have to suggest some shutters to block it.

She frowned. She wasn't staying with Saer. That simply couldn't be.

"Mistress?"

Nareen started. She pulled a length of linen off a hook and wrapped herself in it. She heard footsteps approaching from inside the chambers.

"There ye are." An older woman appeared in the arch. She had wrinkles around her eyes and mouth, but her hair was still dark where it peeked out from beneath a cap. "I'll stir up the fire, mistress."

It had been a long time since she had been called mistress. Nareen paused, tempted almost beyond measure just to let Saer have his way. His offer was a good one.

She moved into the chamber. A flash came from the hearth as the woman struck a flint, and brilliant sparks fell into a small pile of tinder she'd placed in the hearth. She bent down and blew on it. Smoke began to rise in thick tendrils until it burst into a bright orange flame.

"I am Gitta," she offered as she added wood to the growing fire. "I served the laird's sister, Daphne, but she's wed and with her husband these days." The fire cracked and popped as it caught. Heat began to fill the chamber.

"I've been acting as head of house," Gitta offered gently as she moved to close the *terrazzino* doors nearest the hearth. She moved on and closed the next set as well. "I'd best find ye a dressing robe before yer supper arrives."

The chamber was magnificent, but Nareen realized it lacked wardrobes. There was only a single one near the bed, and when Gitta fitted one of the large keys hanging from her belt into the lock, she opened the doors to reveal precious little.

"After Sauchieburn, we were raided several times," she said in explanation.

There was only a single dressing robe, and Gitta pulled it out. She brought it to Nareen, holding it wide for her to slip her hand into the sleeve. Nareen hesitated, the time she'd spent serving Abigail making it feel strange to be served.

Someone knocked on the outer door, and she thrust her hand into the sleeve. She turned just as the doors were opened and Gitta finished closing the robe around her bare front.

Two maids and a young boy entered. They all stopped and lowered themselves.

"That is nae necessary," Nareen said.

The maids' eyes narrowed in confusion as they each carried a platter to the table. The boy held a wooden goblet and earthenware pitcher. He set the pitcher down and used a pressed square of linen to wipe the inside surface of the goblet before he set it down. One of the maids had placed a small bowl of salt on the table. The boy took two pinches of it and sprinkled them on the plate the maid had set out for Nareen. He broke off a piece of bread and wiped the salt around the edge of the plate.

He moved behind the large chair and pulled it out for her now that the plate was cleansed of any poison. The ritual made her shiver, because it meant Saer was not completely confident in his place.

Of course he would be concerned.

She sat down, and the maids lifted covers off the dishes they had brought. There was meat, cheese, and fruit. It was nothing compared to the feasts laid out in the Ross castle. But it was more than enough.

The maids lowered themselves, then left. Nareen started eating before she realized Gitta was standing behind her.

"I do nae need service."

The older woman looked skeptical.

"I am very well on me own."

She knew the woman's feet must be aching from the long day. No head of house was idle. It was a coveted position, the ring of keys hanging from Gitta's belt a symbol of her authority. Those keys unlocked the cabinets where costly things, like spices and clothing, were kept. If anything went missing, Gitta would have to answer for it.

Gitta finally nodded. But she went to the large bed and turned down the bedding. When she finished, she stopped in front of the table Nareen was seated at.

"Do ye wish private meals?"

Nareen shook her head before she realized she was agreeing to appear in the Hall. Gitta didn't notice though. She'd lowered herself and started for the door as Nareen battled the idea of sitting next to Saer in front of his clan.

The fact that she hadn't accepted his suit wouldn't matter. Actions spoke louder than words. Of course, Saer preferred action too. But if she didn't appear in the Hall, she'd be saddling the servants with the chore of bringing her meals to her. No one needed to do tasks that were not essential. She'd be selfish to add to the burden of the staff.

She sighed and took a long look around the chamber. It was sparse, but even the lack of carpets impressed her. Saer was earning his way. He was proving himself worthy of the position of laird.

She stood and moved over to the wardrobe Gitta had left unlocked. Inside were only three shirts and a single doublet of thick wool for winter. She lifted one of the sleeves and found the cuff worn. It had been repaired, and the patches were almost worn through.

Saer was wise. He was building up his fortress before spending resources on luxuries like new clothes and carpets. After all, what good were fine things if you could not protect them? He was also building a clan.

She walked out onto the *terrazzino* and looked over the half wall at the courtyard below. Small fires burned to provide light. The workers were enjoying tipping back their mugs as music filled the yard. Some couples danced, and others moved off into the shadows to enjoy each other's company.

She felt herself turning to look at the bed. Just like Saer, it was large and solid.

The night breeze picked up her hair, helping to dry it. She tipped her head back and filled her lungs, but she still saw the bed.

Saer wanted to found a dynasty in it. With her.

Was that so bad?

Maybe he had a point about what sort of life she would have if she returned to Grant land. Yet nothing was without cost. If she stayed, she'd have to promise Saer obedience.

She wasn't sure she could keep such a vow.

Fatigue was pressing her. With her belly full, the comfort of the bed called to her.

She walked back into the chamber. There was no reason to be stubborn. Gitta had left out a wooden comb. Nareen pulled it through her hair before climbing into the bed. The sheeting was smooth and fresh smelling. The scent of heather quickly lulled her to sleep.

She'd decide how to leave in the morning. Or maybe, she'd just decide.

Something.

❧

She was a beauty, Saer thought as he stood beside the bed and contemplated Nareen. It was little wonder her cousin had tried to sell her.

Her hair was as black as a raven's feathers. When she was awake, her emerald eyes made for a startling combination. He moved closer to the bed, reaching out to stroke her cheek. Her skin was creamy and flawless. Her black eyelashes made a perfect half moon against her cheeks.

But that wasn't what drew him to her. It was something else, something deeper. And it pleased him greatly to find her sleeping in his bed. For certain, trust was growing between them.

He set his sword against the wall by the side of the bed where he usually slept, and sat down in one of the chairs to take off his boots. The fire had died down to cinders, leaving the room lit mostly by the moonlight coming through one of the open doors.

He smiled as he felt the breeze blowing in. She hadn't shut the door. They had more in common than she wanted to admit.

He finished and stood up silently, resisting the urge to wake her. His cock was standing firm when he removed his kilt and shirt, but he forced himself to slide into the bed without jostling Nareen.

Desire she'd already admitted to. What he craved was an admission of trust. Entering his bed of her own will was just that. He moved closer and filled his lungs with the scent of her skin. His cock ached, but he smiled. He was more content than he could ever recall being. At least since he was small enough to think the solace of his mother's embrace was all he needed.

He buried his face in her hair, inhaling the scent. It sent a spike of arousal through him and a need to have his skin in contact with her.

Any way possible.

❧

"Look here…"

Nareen kicked at the bedding, but the dream was too strong. It closed its claws around her and dragged her deep into the nightmare where her cousin Ruth's face rose up to torment her.

"So sweet and fresh…" Ruth exclaimed gleefully. "A tight virgin."

Nareen tried to smother her whimpers, detesting her fear. But it was like a demon, overpowering her and taking command of her senses.

"She's full of spirit too…"

Someone reached for her. From out in the darkness, where her cousin laughed merrily at her torment.

"Yer spirit is what I crave…"

Her fear exploded into terror as the groping hands were suddenly attached to Saer. She thrashed, trying to fling him off her, losing the battle to scream as she felt him closing his embrace around her…

❧

"Nareen!"

There was a sting against her cheek, and it broke the hold of the dream. She opened her eyes, screaming when she looked into the dark eyes of the man from her nightmare.

"Come back to me, lass," Saer demanded. He cupped the sides of her face, drawing in a harsh breath when she dug her claws into his bare chest.

"'Twas a dream," he said softly.

"A...dream..." Her tongue felt clumsy in her mouth, and her heart was pounding so hard it was almost impossible to draw in breath. Her lungs hurt, and her body ached like she had been straining.

"Easy, lass..." he cooed softly, stroking her hair back from her face. "It was a dream."

"A nightmare." She managed to swallow and rolled her lips to moisten them. "I'm well." She pushed against him, but he shook his head.

"Ye are nae."

She glared at him, recognizing his tone too well. "I've had a bellyful of demands, Saer MacLeod. Let me be."

His eyes narrowed, but he surprised her by releasing her head and rolling onto his back. "So why don't ye make some of yer own?"

"Ye never listen to me demands."

"I do indeed," he answered softly, enticingly. "When ye wrapped yer thighs around me hips and demanded satisfaction, I met yer demands well and truly."

She growled at him. "And ye believe now is a good time to remind me of that?"

He nodded firmly. "The alternative is to fight off going back to sleep, because ye know that memory will be waiting for ye. Come here and make a new one, one with ye in control."

He was far too perceptive. His proposition had a
tantalizing appeal. But she started to shake her head. "I
told ye, I cannae trust any man. Ye must understand."

He rolled onto his side and stroked the side of
her face. It was a tender touch, but she flinched, still
caught in the hold of her nightmare. She knew he was
watching her, so she swallowed and felt the tension
easing. When he stroked her skin again, it was slower.
A shiver moved through her, but one that pleased her
because it banished the world of her past in favor of
the moment she was in.

"I understand," he whispered. "I understand waking
in the dead of night and wondering if the wolf I hear
growling is going to tear me throat out before I kill
him." He smoothed her hair from her face and softly
kissed her cheek. "I know I hear that wolf from time
to time and feel the sting of regret for having to kill it,
because it was just as hungry as I was."

He rolled back onto his back. "And I know that
the only way I ever found peace was by training
hard enough to ensure that I had the strength to
defend myself."

Confusion held her in its grip until he tossed the
bedding off his body. His cock stood up, swollen
with need.

"Come here, Nareen. Do everything ye feared
having done to ye. Demand what was demanded of
ye, and grow strong enough to nae fear anything that
might have been done to yer body."

It was ludicrous. Sinful to be sure. Wanton. But the
idea felt surprisingly right and pleasing.

Boldness took hold inside her, burning away the

remnants of the nightmare. It was an addictive feeling. It grew so quickly, she was already moving toward him before she decided how she wanted to touch him.

But her memory offered her options. The same words that had been rising up from her nightmare, like suggestions from the devil himself, became ideas capable of reclaiming control over her emotions.

Nareen rolled over and reached for his member. It was smooth and hot and thick. He sucked in his breath, stiffening as she teased it with the tips of her fingers. His skin was so soft, like velvet beneath her fingertips. But it covered a staff that was hard as steel. She grasped him and slid her closed hand down to the base of his cock.

Saer's words rose from her memory, pleasing her immensely. She enjoyed that memory far more and was eager to make new ones to bury the past beneath their weight.

She came up on her knees next to his belly and pumped her hand along his length a few more times. His face was drawn tight, and she felt her lips curl up with delight.

"Ye said 'everything'?" she questioned boldly.

"Aye," he answered roughly.

Anticipation tightened in her belly, sending a twist of need through her passage. Her body was heating up, making it comfortable to leave the bedding behind.

"Even wrap me lips around yer…cock." She forced the word out, refusing to be afraid of it any longer.

His expression tightened, anger glittering in his eyes. He sat up and grasped her shoulder. "Did that bitch make ye perform that service?"

He was furious, the rage hot enough to feel. But she stared at it, fascinated by the protectiveness in him.

"Nareen?" he growled. "Tell me."

She shook her head and stroked his member.

"Then how do ye know about frenching?"

"Me cousin offered to sell it, and I was at court."

"I should have hung her," he snarled.

"Yet ye know what it is…" Nareen stroked his cock again. "And the look in yer eyes tells me ye have experience with it…"

His eyes narrowed. "So I am being overly offended? Is that yer point, lass?"

She drew her hand up to the top of his length and teased the spot beneath the crown with her thumb. When she raised her gaze back to his, his lips were pressed into a hard line as he fought to maintain his composure.

"I believe me question is, do ye want me ignorant? For if ye do, I'll remind ye that I asked to be taken home to me brother, for I will never play act the part of a simpleton."

He grabbed another pillow and put it behind his head, then settled back. The position was less relaxed, less submissive, and she felt a response ripple through her. It was just there, in defiance of everything she had decided she wanted. Without question, she enjoyed his arrogance.

Damn her weak flesh.

But she was going to use her own cravings to serve her needs tonight. She toyed with his length, stroking it with just her fingertips before closing her hand around it again. His expression changed, becoming more rakish, and her breath caught. There was a pleasure to be had in seeing him enjoy her touch, and it filled her with boldness.

She lowered her gaze to his cock. The crown was marked with a ridge of flesh and a slit. She teased it with her fingers before leaning down to lick it.

"Christ," he growled, his breathing labored.

She looked up to find his chest rising and falling quickly. Moonlight spilled in through the open doors, making her smile. This was no pitch-black chamber making her feel like she was locked away.

She leaned down again and licked all the way around the crown. He hardened even more, becoming rigid. Saer gripped the sheet beneath him as she watched him through her eyelashes. She opened her mouth wide enough to take him. His skin smelled clean and was silken smooth against her tongue. She licked the slit and watched him go as tight as a bowstring.

It was arousing in a way she'd never expected— part power and part enjoyment of knowing he liked what she was doing. She leaned farther down, taking more of his length inside her mouth. He jerked, thrusting toward her face as she heard him demand, "Enough, Nareen."

"Nae nearly so," she instructed him softly. With his cock wet, it was easier to work her hands up and down his length. "I think it is far past time for ye to be the one being driven mad."

He curled up and caught her hair. "I have been, lass. Why do ye think I left me land to find ye?"

There was a force in his eyes that sent a shiver through her. She wasn't even sure if it was physical or emotional, only that it was so intense, she nearly moaned.

She tilted her head, and he released her hair. Leaning over, she drew her tongue along the side of his cock, lapping him from root to crest in one long swipe.

"Aye…" he rasped.

It was more of a sound than a word, and it pleased her greatly. She leaned over the other side of his length and licked it too. When she made it to the top, she opened her mouth and sucked him deep inside.

"Aye!"

She tightened her fingers around the portion she couldn't take, pumping her hand up and down as he began to thrust again. The first drop of his seed filled the slit, and she licked it away with a bold lap.

He groaned, his body tightening even more. But she didn't release him. She sucked harder, until her cheeks hollowed against his cock. Her fingers moved up and down on the base several times before he snarled and his seed began to fill her mouth. She swallowed it. Sucking every last drop of it away as he cursed.

He didn't relax onto the bed, but sat up and slid his hand into her hair again. He rose right up onto his knees, taking her with him. Their bodies pressed against each other, sending a jolt of need through her. Her bud was throbbing, while her passage felt empty.

"I do nae care if ye've enchanted me, I only fear ye'll stop."

He kissed her, licking his way across her lower lip before thrusting his tongue into her mouth. He teased her, tormenting her with the motion she craved. His cock was hard again. She played with it, teasing the rod and purring as it remained rigid.

Saer clasped a hand around her waist and rolled her onto her back.

"No," she said, refusing to let him part her thighs.

He lifted his head and glared at her.

"Ye said I might do everything I pleased with ye," she said.

She pushed at him, earning a grunt, but she lifted her chin stubbornly. "On yer back. Ye'll be the one ridden tonight."

His eyes narrowed, but his face softened with understanding. The bed bounced and the ropes creaked as he rolled onto his back. His cock stuck up from his belly, making her ache with the need to feel it inside her.

"Come, lass, if ye think ye can manage a full stallion."

When she rose up, his gaze flashed with excitement. She was trembling with it as well, her motions clumsy as she lifted one knee and swung it over his wide hips.

He cupped her waist, taking some of her weight and easing her into position.

"Gaining the saddle is the hardest part."

"I hope not," she answered as he moved her back and the head of his cock slipped between the wet folds of her slit. Moonlight flashed off his wide grin as she pressed down.

He didn't let her sheath his cock. His grip stayed firm as he thrust up into her with a controlled motion.

"Ye are still tender."

"I am nae," she argued and lifted herself off him. Her clumsiness vanished as she became accustomed to the motion of riding him. This time she pressed farther down and felt her passage stretching to accommodate

him. She gasped, the fullness a sweet balance of pleasure and pain.

"As I said, Nareen," he cautioned her. Saer didn't
wait for her rise, he lifted her off his cock.

But she was impatient for more, fighting against his
grip. "No, I say what will be between us tonight."

He shook his head, an arrogant grunt escaping his
lips. "Ye're mine, lass." He thrust up into her to prove
it, holding her suspended above his hips.

She gasped, wanting to argue with him, but she
was caught in the rush of sensation that being full of
him unleashed. He pushed deep and withdrew before
thrusting again.

"Savage…" she choked out at last.

"Hummm…" he agreed. "Do ye truly crave one of
those weaklings from court?"

"I crave ye," she confessed. It probably wasn't the
wisest thing to say, but it clearly pleased him. She leaned
forward, and his attention switched to her breasts.

"I see merits to letting ye set the pace, lass."

He lowered his hips to the surface of the bed and
let her sheath him until she was sitting on top of him.
Releasing her waist, he reached for her breasts and
cupped them.

"Aye, benefits I will enjoy well."

He massaged the tender globes, making her impatient for friction. She lifted herself up and plunged
back down. The first time was bumpy, but she braced
her hands against his shoulders and tightened her
thighs around his hips.

"Very enjoyable…" He pinched her nipples gently,
grinning when she increased her pace.

"Stop trying to control the pace, Saer."

She rose and fell a few more times, the hard length of his cock sending pleasure rippling through her. Her nipples were contracting, the swirling need inside her belly making her ready to burst.

"That is something I cannae promise, lass." He slid a hand around her torso and sat up. He bound her to him, with his cock driven deep inside her as he turned and pressed her back against the bed. She growled at him, but he pulled free and thrust back into her, sending a shaft of delight through her.

"I dreamed of ye here, when I told the carpenter how I wanted the bed made..." He thrust again and again with more power. Her eyes were trying to slide shut, but she resisted because he was taking control of her.

She needed to refuse.

But she couldn't. Her need was too great, and he knew how to push her over the edge. Pleasure spiked through her, ripping away what she thought she wanted as her body took what it craved. She twisted and cried out before she lifted her eyelids to find Saer watching her.

His face was full of primitive satisfaction.

"I wanted to make ye mine in this bed."

He leaned back and started thrusting again. He hadn't spilled his seed yet, and he eased the contact between his length and her sex.

She gasped when she realized he was driving her back up to another peak.

"Saer..."

He impaled her with a hard thrust that sent the air from her lungs.

"I wanted to hear ye cry out me name in this chamber…"

The bed groaned as he thrust harder and deeper into her spread body.

"Dreamed of ye clinging to me here…"

"Stop…" Her lips were dry, but her body was arching toward his. "I cannae…nae…again…"

"Ye will," he informed her ruthlessly. "I'll drive ye back to ecstasy, Nareen. Again and again."

It was savage—he was savage—but she couldn't seem to resist. He leaned over her, pinning her hands to the surface of the bed as he hammered into her. He surrounded her, held her down, and rode her harder than she thought she might endure.

But her body blossomed beneath the onslaught, pleasure tightening even deeper inside her. She was straining toward him, every fiber of her being part of the effort. Saer let more of his weight settle on her. She whimpered as he pressed harder against her button. Her lungs burned, and her heart felt like it might burst, but she didn't care. It was madness, and it tore her away from everything.

Her cry echoed off the ceiling. Saer snarled against her ear, burying himself deep as his seed began to flow into her. He pumped it inside her, and pleasure wrung her like a wet linen. Her passage contracted, milking him of every last drop.

She didn't have any strength left when the pleasure receded. The bed cradled her body, and she didn't even have the energy to brush the tangled hair from her face. Sweat coated her skin and Saer's. His scent filled her senses, adding to the satisfaction glowing inside her.

He rolled over, landing heavily on the bed beside her. She curled onto her side as her heart began to slow, ready to relax back into sleep, the nightmare that had awakened her completely forgotten.

"Ye did nae answer me, Nareen."

Her body was warm and glowing with satisfaction. The last thing she wanted to do was discuss memories she'd worked so hard to banish.

Saer rose up behind her, pressing her onto her back so he could lock gazes with her. "Did yer cousin force ye to service a man with yer mouth?"

"I did nae obey her when it came to the men she wanted me to entice," she muttered and shut her eyes. "Ye were right. Choosing me own lover is the way to stop being afraid."

"It matters a goddamn lot, because I'm going to choke the life out of that bitch if she had ye suck off one of her clients."

"She didn't get the chance." Nareen opened her eyes and shot him a hard look. "I made sure of that. I was nae going to wait in that locked room for the day when Ruth found a man willing to pay what she wanted for me," she said. "So do nae say again how much ye dislike Abigail, for I used her as much as she did me."

He bit back his next question, fighting for control.

"How did ye get out to meet Abigail?" he asked suspiciously.

"She was one of Ruth's customers," she explained. "Me cousin made me serve the table, so the men might get a good look at me. Abigail was complaining about her maids, so I made sure to serve her and be noticed."

Nareen rolled onto her side, but Saer cupped her shoulder and pulled her to her back.

"What else did she do to force ye to her will?"

"Let it be, Saer."

He slowly shook his head.

"It matters naught now. For I am here, not there any longer."

"It matters a great deal." He planted a hand on the other side of her torso to keep her from rolling away from him. "Ye mean a great deal to me, lass. Do nae begrudge me protecting ye."

His words struck her hard. She hadn't realized how much she needed to hear that he cared about her, until the words were spoken. She reached up and flattened her hand over his heart. "I am here. If I tell ye she threatened to beat the bottoms of me feet with a rod, and even gave me a taste of it—"

"That bitch!" he roared.

Nareen moved her hand to cover his mouth, but her fingers felt small against him. "Did yer sword master never beat ye? Or yer training mates who were born with the blessing of the Church? Did they nae remind ye of yer place with more than words?"

He blew out a long breath but admitted, "Aye."

"Ruth claimed it was how the Moors kept their harem girls obedient without marking them where their masters might see. It matters naught, because I grew stronger with every strike. I never performed for her, but I enjoyed knowing just how to drive ye as insane as ye make me. So I cannae hate completely being there. I would nae be who I am if I had not known that time in me life."

He was still angry, but his lips twitched, and he shook his head. She sat up and pushed him onto his back and rested her head on his shoulder. He held her close, smoothing his hand along her waist and down to cup her hip. She curled onto her side, rubbing his chest before drawing in a slow breath that filled her senses with his scent.

For the moment, she couldn't recall why she was not perfectly content.

Five

THE CHURCH BELLS RANG EARLY ON MACLEOD LAND.

Nareen opened her eyes and blinked. The horizon was just turning yellow. Saer groaned before sitting up and swinging his legs over the side of the bed.

"I begin to see why some of me men argued over the timing of morning Mass." He lifted his arms and stretched. "I find me bed more enticing this morning with ye in it."

Nareen found herself distracted by the prime picture he made. She was often called a beauty, but she found Saer's body majestic. She'd never wanted to stare at a man before, but with him, she seemed to need to fight the urge.

"Stop looking at me like that, woman..." He looked over his shoulder and winked. "Ye'll have me braving the displeasure of the good Father Peter to spend the next hour laying with ye instead of providing a good example to me clan by being at service."

He stood up, and she blushed as his cock stuck out, hard and ready. It wasn't the sight of his member that sent heat to her cheeks; it was the way her sex began to throb with anticipation.

"We need the man to agree to wed us," Saer muttered as he pulled on a shirt.

Nareen had sat up and started to stretch. She froze at the word "wed."

"I cannae wed."

Saer stiffened. He'd leaned over to begin putting his boots on but straightened to glare at her.

"Explain that, Nareen."

She looked for the dressing robe but it was gone, leaving her holding the bedding against her nude body. "I did. I told ye I will nae vow to be obedient."

"In private, I have no quarrel with that."

He leaned over and finished closing his boot. He tugged sharply as he tightened the lace around the antlerhorn buttons, considering the matter settled. Nareen sighed; he was granting her a concession, but it was not enough.

"I told ye, I cannae belong to anyone."

Saer's body went tense. He didn't answer her but tied his second boot before standing up and moving over to the trestle table. The remnants of her dinner were pushed off to the side. His kilt was pleated and waiting for him. He slid a wide leather belt beneath the wool and picked it up. In silence, he buckled the belt in one practiced motion, then made sure the fronts of the wool covered him.

"I mean ye no insult," she offered as she crawled to the edge of the bed in search of the dressing robe.

"No, ye mean to drive me mad with the chase ye are leading me on. I have matters to attend to, and have no time for games."

She found the edge of the dressing robe at last and

tugged it free. Saer picked up his knitted bonnet and tugged it down over his head.

"I explained me feelings to ye," she insisted as she tied the robe closed and faced him. "Very clearly, before ye brought me here."

"Ahhh…" He crossed his arms over his chest and gripped his forearms. His knuckles turned white, proving he was fighting the urge to remain where he was. "Yer feelings. Women change their feelings often."

"I know me will and told ye plainly." And so it began, just as she'd known it must. He thought the matter settled and was beginning to dictate his will to her. "There will be no wedding, and I am nae fickle."

He closed his eyes, looking like he was struggling to maintain control. He drew in a deep breath and let it out before opening them again and locking gazes with her. "I never accused ye of such." He walked toward her, kindness returning to his eyes. "And I have been gentle with ye."

She scoffed. "Ye have also been demanding."

He shrugged, his eyes glittering with hard purpose. "Ye enjoy me nature. I dare ye to deny it."

She opened her mouth, but he raised one hand to silence her. "Shall I go below and find a few witnesses to yer cries last night? Stone walls funnel sound very well, lass."

Her cheeks felt like they'd caught fire. He laughed softly and stroked one hot surface.

"I enjoyed making ye scream, Nareen." She was staring into the savage side of his nature as he impressed his will on her. "Now dress and come with me for the blessing of matrimony. By nightfall, there will nae be a soul wearing me colors who does nae know ye spent the night here. I would nae shame ye."

"Yet that is what ye have done." She scooted back when he tried to slide his hand into her hair.

"Do ye nae think me men did nae know what we were about beneath me kilt, Nareen?" he pressed. "Their duty is to guard me back while I sleep."

She shook her head, her body shuddering with anger. "I told ye, I would nae trust...and I will nae take vows that will make me yer property."

She could not bear it. So she turned away, unable to look at what she was rejecting.

"Ye belong to me..."

She jerked her attention back to him. But he was already closing his hand around the tie of the dressing robe. One hard tug sent her tumbling into his body. She brought her hands up to fend him off, but only ended up with her arms trapped against his chest when he locked his arms around her.

"Ye belong to me because I am the man who moves ye to ecstasy and boldness."

She strained against his hold, and he waited until she realized it was a futile effort.

He leaned down until his breath brushed her lips. "And I shall be happy to prove it to ye as many times as necessary for ye to yield."

He crushed her retort with a searing kiss. It was hungry and demanding and hard. She felt like she was starved for it, which enraged her. She wiggled, trying to escape as he claimed her lips in a kiss that stole her breath. The bells changed tone, signaling the beginning of service.

Saer released her, and she stumbled away from him. It was a retreat. There was no way to hide it.

He nodded with satisfaction. "I enjoy the look of ye breathless from me kiss. It's sure to haunt me throughout the day until I can return to chasing ye."

"What are ye going to do now?" she demanded, hating the way her nipples were stabbing into the soft fabric of the dressing robe. "Set yer men to guarding me? This fine chamber will be naught but a prison if ye do."

He lifted one dark eyebrow. "And that will only help ye hold on to yer ideas of marriage being the same as being owned?"

"It is."

He moved over to the wardrobe that was still open. "No MacLeod retainer has time to stand at doors."

She realized she'd been holding her breath, and let it out in relief.

"This is a private matter between us, one I'll be dealing with. Ye have me word on that."

He reached into the wardrobe and grabbed the pieces of her dress. But he didn't bring them to her. He walked right past her and reached for the door, stopping to scoop up her boots where Gitta had placed them by the hearth.

"Wait! Ye cannae mean to—"

He paused with his hand on the doorknob. "Take yer dress? Aye, lass, I do. There is nae a single unused garment on me land because of the raids we suffered, so if ye sneak out of this chamber, be prepared to be seen in yer chemise."

He opened the door and took her clothing with him.

"Saer!"

He shut the door in answer.

Damn him.

Curse him.

Savage!

༄

Baruch was waiting for him at the bottom of the tower steps. Saer thrust the clothing at his man, ignoring the incredulous look on his face.

"Make sure no one sneaks that back to Nareen."

Baruch looked like he was contemplating dropping it, but settled for bunching it up into a ball and handing it to the younger captain standing beside him.

"Make certain that does nae make its way back to Mistress Grant."

Saer growled, low and ominously. "Ye do it, Baruch. I need to know that woman is here, nae running across Comyn land for that bastard Morrell to get his hands on."

Baruch took the clothing back, but his expression was one of disagreement.

"What is yer argument, man?" Saer demanded loud enough to be heard throughout the inner yard.

"Having an excuse to run Morrell Comyn through would be right welcome."

Saer poked the wadded-up dress with a thick finger. "Nareen belongs to me. Ye'll have to find another reason."

"Aye, aye," Baruch agreed, then smirked. "We heard that plain enough last night. Although I think it was more of a wee-morning-hours sort of thing. I'm guessing she was nae waiting to give ye a warm welcome last evening."

Baruch didn't flinch when Saer sent him a deadly look. He just bundled the clothing tighter against his chest. "I'd best get to service. Father Peter is a strict one. Hands out penance far too easily for a man of poverty."

"I'm going to service," Saer snapped. "Ye deal with that dress before ye show yer face."

"Aye, Laird." Baruch tugged the corner of his bonnet with a twinkle in his eye. The man would never be subservient toward him, but Saer wasn't looking for that in a captain. He needed a man he could always trust, no matter the situation.

Even securing a damned dress. Saer felt his temper straining as he watched Baruch carry the clothing away.

He wanted to go back up to his chamber, but he fought the urge. Winning a fight took more than brute strength; it took strategy. Especially when it came to Nareen.

His pride was stung, and something else, but he ignored it as just more injured pride. He could not allow himself to feel more than that. Love had been his mother's downfall. He could not make such a mistake.

That gave him the discipline to move toward the church and enter it. The service was in progress, but Father Peter still noticed him. Saer pulled on the corner of his bonnet.

Women loved. It was something that allowed them to settle into the changes life demanded of them. But it was still damned frustrating, because he had no idea how to cultivate something he didn't have.

But he'd never backed away from a challenge, and Nareen wouldn't be the one to change him.

She'd settle in.

❧

Nareen screeched at the closed door.

She ran toward it, but the slap of her bare feet made her stop.

The beast had even taken her boots!

The door wasn't locked.

She could still leave. But she didn't move toward the door. Maybe the man didn't have his retainers posted to keep her inside the chamber, but she didn't doubt she'd be returned there the moment someone noticed her. It would hardly be difficult to notice her if she appeared below in a dressing robe.

She snarled and stomped across the room to one of the sets of doors that led out to the *terrazzino*. Sunlight was washing over the inner yard. Everyone was in the church, which was through the old gate and inside what was the outer yard. The masons had worked up until the last of the daylight the night before, their tools lying where they had been working. The huge wooden wheels that worked the cranes stood with loads of cut stone stacked neatly on their load-bearing platforms, waiting to be lifted up to the growing walls.

Only a few retainers were posted on the walls. They moved back and forth as they scanned the cleared area surrounding the castle. None looked in her direction, because the loch was behind her. There had to be a man posted above her to keep watch for water invasion.

All of it was impressive. And she detested it completely!

That was a lie...

And it shamed her.

She couldn't begrudge Saer the respect he'd earned. She'd never heard of such a feat, never thought a clan might find a way to recover so quickly from the loss the MacLeod had suffered. So many of their number had perished at the battle of Sauchieburn that it should have taken a generation to rebuild their ranks. Saer was making it happen within five years.

People began to return from the church. The yard was soon full of conversation and sound as they ate. No one lingered over the meal, though. Soon, the steady clip of the hammer and chisels was heard again. Beyond the inner yard, she heard men calling the young men to training. Some of the youths eating with their families below her hurried to grab their wooden swords and run toward the gate.

Saer offered them a great deal. There were not many places where a mason's son might be trained to be a retainer. A stoneworker simply didn't make enough money to pay for the training or to outfit his son with a sword and mail.

Saer was making sure it happened. It told her more about him and his struggle with life than any conversation might have. He was a survivor and intended to make sure his clan survived too. The masons took to their work with zeal in gratitude for everything being offered to them. Loyalty would never be a problem for Saer.

There was a soft rap on the door. A moment later it opened.

Gitta held it as two maids and the young boy entered again. Nareen tightened the robe's belt and stayed on the *terrazzino* while the boy performed his duties. Gitta was quick to point him toward the door.

"I see why ye were nae at services," the head of house remarked as she oversaw the maids.

They finished setting the table and moved onto the bed.

"I need a dress to wear," Nareen said sweetly.

Gitta offered her a slow shake of her head, proving Saer had already spoken to the woman.

"But I did bring ye something to keep yer hands busy."

Nareen watched as the woman unfolded a bundle. It was soft and creamy linen. Nareen reached out to run a finger across its surface, smiling at the texture.

"Agnes will be up with the sewing tools in a moment. She had to go across the yard to the old tower where the laird's sister kept her solar. There were a few things that did nae get taken, and the laird is in need of shirts."

"I'll nae be sewing the man a shirt," Nareen declared with her hands on her hips. Such was a personal duty a wife or sweetheart did for a man. An intimate chore.

Gitta drew herself up, folding her hands in front of her. Nareen swallowed and made sure her tone was even.

"Perhaps ye might bring me some wool, for a dress?"

Gitta shook her head. "All the fleece was woven into tartan this season for the new retainers."

Of course. Protection of the castle folk came before new dresses.

"I have no authority to tell ye what to do, but it does seem a shame to have ye do naught for the entire day," Gitta exclaimed.

There was another knock on the door before Agnes entered with a small basket. She was a younger girl with freckles sprinkled across her nose and onto her cheeks. She smiled brightly and lowered herself.

"Agnes has asked to serve ye," Gitta explained. "Her mother serves in the kitchens and has taught her daughter well."

Agnes was beaming as she moved to the table set for Nareen's morning meal, and inspected it. She straightened a dish, then moved to look at the bed.

"I do nae need service," Nareen said to Gitta.

The head of house maintained her stern stance.

"But I thank ye for thinking of me," Nareen said at last, relenting.

"It's settled, then," Gitta said firmly. "We'll leave ye to yer morning, mistress. Agnes will bring ye a noon meal. Our laird has strict rules for everyone. We all have duties during the day, for there is much to build."

Agnes was shaking with happiness. The girl moved in front of her and lowered herself before following Gitta's figure toward the door. The head of house was the last one through.

Nareen found herself eating to the sound of the stonemasons working below. The steady pace of their labor frustrated her as she ate. By the time she was finished, she was feeling the lack of activity. It was like an itch that was just out of reach in the middle of her back. She stacked her dishes, wiped the table clean, and found herself pacing.

She used the comb to straighten her hair and braided it, but that took little time also. It was a shame to not earn her bread.

A shame to be a burden on those who were working to make sure everyone had what they needed.

A shame to be idle.

"Oh, fie," she groused and stalked over to the linen. She carried it back to the table and laid it out. She could make something for herself.

But that would be stealing.

No, no it was nae. The man had imprisoned her.

But it would be dishonest to use the linen without permission. At the very least, she'd be taking a gift from him.

She wasn't in the mood to thank him.

But she couldn't do nothing for the entire day. She wasn't doing it for Saer. At least not as a personal service. She was simply earning her meals, like everyone else.

Aye.

That was right.

She went to the wardrobe and pulled out one of the two remaining shirts. One was in tatters. The edges were worn and fraying. Along the sleeves, there were holes from sword training. Many had been darned, but there were new ones. She laid it out and found a measuring stick in the basket. With a piece of charcoal from the hearth, she began to draw cutting lines on the fabric. In the Highlands, fabric was expensive. So she didn't cut into it until she checked her measurements twice.

Inside the basket, she found an iron and poked at the fire to find some coals. She found a log and let it catch so she might heat the iron. Every piece of fabric had to have its edges rolled and pressed and sewn before she might begin to assemble the shirt.

But it was work, and she hummed as she listened to the stoneworkers in the yard.

❧

"Ye've a fine, steady hand, mistress," Agnes said in praise that evening.

Gitta and Agnes were both inspecting the pieces of the shirt she'd made. Her neck ached from leaning over, but two sleeves were finished, with their cuffs neatly attached. The body of the shirt had its neck gores in and was ready for the collar.

"Fine work indeed," Gitta remarked with a tone rich in experience. "Nae a bit wasted, either. That is how to make a shirt properly."

"It hardly seems hard enough work to leave me with such an appetite," Nareen said as she began her supper.

A knock sounded, and Gitta went over to open the door. Maids entered with fresh bedding in their arms. The head of house gestured them toward the bed as Agnes fussed around the table. The meal was simple— a piece of bread, some soft cheese that spread easily over the bread, and some small chunks of meat—so there was little for the girl to do. She finally lowered herself and left.

"Is there any parchment and ink to be had, Gitta?" Nareen asked as the older woman pointed her maids out of the chamber. "I should send me brother word of where I am."

The head of house walked away from the bed and stood in front of the table.

"I'm sure the laird will satisfy whatever needs ye have," Gitta said sweetly.

Nareen blushed as she realized what the woman was implying. There was a sparkle of merriment in her eyes as she lowered herself and made her way toward the doors. Nareen's hand froze on the way to her mouth, because her throat had suddenly swollen shut.

The man had no mercy. But it was her own nature that was turning traitor against her will.

The night air was blowing through the open arches, teasing her with the freedom she was going to be denied now that Saer considered her his.

She glanced back toward the bed, and it made her admit there were parts of the arrangement she did not find terrible. Yet she was torn.

Something caught her eye. She swept the bed twice before she realized the wardrobe had something hanging in it. Gitta had lit a small tin lantern on the far side of the chamber. The little slashes of light from the lantern danced over something hanging inside. Pushing the chair back, she moved toward it and smiled when she realized it was her dress. She reached for it and pulled it out, making a happy little sound when she found her boots as well.

She tied her hip bolster around her waist and pushed it down into position around her hips. Next came her overskirt, which she laced closed with a few quick motions. She took a moment to adjust her chemise before pushing her hand into one sleeve and then the other. When she pulled her bodice into place, she let out a sigh. She'd never spent an entire day unclothed before. But once she began to lace the front of the dress closed, she almost lamented the need to contain her breasts inside the stiffly boned bodice.

Tears began to sting her eyes when she started to lace her boots. It was ridiculous, but she couldn't banish the sudden wave of reluctance moving through her. The dress being returned could mean only one thing.

Saer was granting her her freedom. Shunning his marriage offer had shamed him, no doubt.

It was for the best, and yet, she had trouble braiding her hair as tears escaped her eyes.

The chamber door opened, revealing the man she'd spent so much time contemplating. He was so vital, it struck her like a blow. She drank in the sight of him, trying to memorize the details of his face, because she was sure it was the last time she might see him.

"Come, lass." He offered her his hand. "Let's take a ride."

"A ride?" she questioned.

He nodded. "I know ye enjoy them. So do I."

Confusion held her in a tight grip.

"So, ye did nae return me dress because ye have tired of me resistance?"

"I am tired of it, truly, but ye have always represented a challenge to me, Nareen." He gestured her forward with a crook of his fingers. "We've talked enough and gained naught. Let's try some action."

She was tempted, the invitation of his open hand delighting her and driving the sting of unshed tears from her eyes. In fact, she was suddenly pleased, the hunger growing inside her so quickly it was unnerving.

It also made her wary.

"Ye're training me," she muttered. "Offering me a treat for obedience."

"Is that nae life?" he questioned. "Does nae even holy salvation come only with penitence?"

She wrinkled her brow as she contemplated his argument.

"Why do ye make me a villain?" He opened the chamber door. "I strive to please ye."

"So I will wed ye."

With the door open, it was hard to recall why she'd argued. Now, she was the one keeping herself inside the chamber. It made no sense at all.

"I want ye for me wife, Nareen, but by yer own choice. Is that nae what ye are struggling to maintain? Yer freedom of choice?"

She sucked in her breath, and he chuckled. "Ye see? I do understand ye."

"I wish I understood myself." The words slipped out before she realized what she was admitting.

Saer tipped his head back and roared with amusement.

"Enough," she groused on her way past him. Somehow, it was easier to do when she didn't have to place her hand in his.

She heard the door close as he followed her. Excitement began to pulse inside her as she hurried down the stairs and felt the fresh air hitting her face.

"This way, Nareen…"

Saer took the lead, and she followed him eagerly.

Aye, eagerly.

❧

Her mare was pleased to see her.

The animal lifted her ears the moment Nareen

entered the row of stalls she was in. She tossed her head and pawed at the ground when she recognized Nareen.

"Me men took her out today, but ye would nae know it to see the way she is acting."

"I suppose I am to blame." Nareen stroked the mare's velvet neck. "The night has been our time together for the last year."

"I miss being able to ride as often as I used to," he confessed.

Nareen looked over the neck of her mare at him. "Ye should be proud of what ye are building here. It is a marvel."

He tossed a bridle over to her and grinned. "I am, but maybe nae completely for the right reasons."

Nareen fitted the bridle onto the mare, grateful for the chance to keep her eyes off him. The man had an unfair amount of handsomeness. Unfair because she needed her senses uninhibited by his dark and dangerous looks.

"Why do ye say that?"

He reached over and pulled the mare from the stall. "Because part of me enjoyment of what I'm building is knowing I am the man no one wanted taking the lairdship. Father Peter would likely have something to say about that if I had any inclination to confess it to him."

Saer took the mare into the yard, where his stallion was already waiting. He turned and clasped his hands around Nareen's waist.

"I can mount meself."

His eyes narrowed, his grip tightening and sliding to cup her hips. "Aye, lass, I know that well, but I thought ye wanted to get outside the castle for a bit?"

Heat curled through her, sending her heart accelerating with excitement. "I do."

He pushed his lips into a pout. "Oh, well…" He lifted her up and placed her on the back of the mare. "Ye do have a talent for wounding me."

"Only because ye—"

He held up his hand and shook his head. "Let us ride, lass, or I will take great delight in kissing ye until ye forget what it is we're arguing about."

She settled her skirts and guided her mare away from him. "There…that is exactly why I do nae wish to wed. Ye'll assume whatever I say has no meaning because ye can overwhelm me."

He swung up and onto the back of his stallion. The animal shifted as it took his weight. But he controlled it with the sure and steady command he seemed to have over everything.

Including her.

"Perhaps I think ye are the woman I should honor above all others, because together we drive each other to ecstasy."

"I mean no insult to ye, Saer." Yet she was shamed by her actions, for she *was* insulting him.

His lips curled into a grin. "Ye'll have to work harder to wound me, lass, and as I promised ye this morning, I do nae back down from challenges."

"Oh, I heard ye plain enough," she said. "But taking me clothing was…it was…"

"Savage?" he suggested.

Her eyes narrowed, and she turned her mare

toward the gate. Her blood was heating, her temper flaring up, and there was only one thing that was going to lead to with Saer MacLeod.

Passion.

If she didn't avoid his bed, she'd be wedding him for certain when her belly rounded.

So she leaned over the neck of her mare and let the horse carry her away. Once she was through both gates, she raced across the open ground that served to protect the castle by offering no hiding places for approaching armies. The wind chilled her cheeks, but she didn't lose herself completely to the ride.

The reason was Saer. She felt him watching her. Some might call her a fool for saying she could feel a gaze on her, but she did. There was a connection between them she couldn't seem to ignore.

Beyond the clearing, there was forest. Saer passed her and took the lead as they slowed down to allow their horses to make their way around the trees. There were clouds tonight, blocking out most of the moonlight. Saer looked back at her. She smiled at him and enjoyed the look of approval that spread over his face.

He turned his horse and nudged it closer to hers. Time began to move slower as she became aware of tiny details. The way his hair moved, the motion of his eyes as they narrowed when locking on hers. Her heart accelerated, increasing her respiration and pulling the scent of his skin into her senses. It was intoxicating—her grip on reality loosened until all she cared about was how soon his fingers would brush her skin. He was reaching for her, his leg brushing hers. She lifted her chin, tilting her head slightly so his kiss might fit perfectly.

But something moved behind him. She blinked, almost too far gone to make sense of the warning going off inside her head. But she opened her eyes, trying to focus on the motion.

"Look—"

She didn't get the chance to finish. Saer reacted instantly, turning with a vicious cry. Someone dropped from the tree limbs above, dragging Saer off his stallion. There was a hard sound as they hit the dirt, and then another growl of rage as Saer jumped to his feet and flung the attacker off.

"Ride!" he commanded her and slapped the flank of her mare. It was an icy tone, one that had no room for disobedience.

Except she had not promised him obedience.

He turned and pulled his sword, but there were more shapes in the night. They surrounded him, crouching low.

Nareen pulled the dagger from her belt and slid off the mare. She patted her flank so the animal would move away.

"Are ye mad, woman?" Saer demanded of her.

Someone lunged at him, and he lifted his sword, swinging it in a wide circle above his head before bringing it down in a slicing motion across the body of the man. There was a dull thud, and then another, as he dropped to the ground in two pieces.

The scent of blood filled the air, turning her stomach, but she tightened her grip as one of the remaining attackers turned on her.

"Here, pretty lass... I'll give ye that kiss ye were wanting..."

Saer attacked, raising his sword high, but the man behind him lifted a dagger and made a lunge toward his unprotected back.

Nareen dove under his raised arm, bringing her right arm up to lodge against the attacker's plunging hand as her brother had taught her. She cried out as her forearm took the force of impact, but grabbed the man's bent elbow on the inside and pushed forward with all her might. The dagger was inches from her face as she twisted and dropped him on his arse.

There was a clang as swords met behind her, but she didn't dare risk turning around to look. The man at her feet snarled and struggled to rise.

"I'll give ye a lot more than a kiss when I get ye on yer back, bitch!"

Gaining his feet, he opened his arms, intending to grab her. She stood her ground, letting him get close enough to think victory was his before she sank the dagger into his neck. He gurgled, blood spurting out from the neck wound to coat her hand.

But she held steady, pulling the blade back so the wound was deep and wide. And fatal.

He convulsed before collapsing to the ground. The meager light shone on the four bodies. Nareen looked at them all to make sure none of them moved, before looking over at Saer.

Saer was watching her with a hard expression. It chilled her, but not because she feared he'd report her to the church. No, it was far more personal. He was likely glad she had not agreed to wed that morning.

"Who taught ye how to do that, Nareen?"

There was a body lying behind Saer, but he was focused on the one at her feet.

"I warned ye"—she wiped the blade of her dagger on the dead man—"I was nae the right choice for wife. I knew ye'd disapprove of me nature once ye were tired of the challenge."

"Disapprove?" he questioned. "Is that what ye think?"

"I know ye do." She drew in a deep breath and tried to banish the lament attempting to strangle her. "It's unnatural, but I am nae sorry me brother taught me."

"Yer brother, I should have guessed. Kael is a man who puts sense first, and it makes sense no' to leave ye helpless. The only daughter of a laird can be a coveted thing."

He grunted before kneeling down to inspect the body. When he stood back up, he sent her another hard look. "Did yer father know about those lessons?"

"No. He'd have forbidden them, since I am a woman."

"I begin to see why Kael promised ye free choice in who ye wed. He has never treated ye like a female."

"He sent me to Ruth, because he thought he'd made an error and it was time for me to be mentored by other women."

She thought she had let the betrayal go, but it still burned inside her.

"So that is why ye stayed with that brat, Abigail, so long." He wiped his sword on the fallen man and slid it back into the sheath strapped to his back. "Ye do nae trust yer brother to honor his word."

"He will."

But she was not completely sure. That hard truth

sliced through her feelings, leaving a red-hot trail of disappointment inside her. It felt like the ground was crumbling beneath her feet.

"Ye cannae approve, I understand, but I could nae ride away with ye outnumbered."

Saer reached out and cupped her cheek when she looked away, and brought her attention back to his face. "The only thing I disapprove of is ye spent the day plying a needle when ye could have been training some of the younger lads on how to use a dagger."

"I do nae understand..."

"Ye will," he stated firmly. "On MacLeod land, being productive is more important than anything else. As ye can see, we will either grow strong or die at the hands of our neighbors. Since ye know how to use that dagger, ye can teach the skill. That's more important than making a shirt."

"Even if I'm a woman?" she asked, incredulous. "Won't the Church have something to say about that?"

"Father Peter will keep his peace, or I'll remind him that his church will be ransacked, along with the rest of the castle, when it falls. We need God's grace and strong retainers to hold our land."

He let out a whistle. His stallion answered with a snort. "Forgive me, Nareen, but it seems I cannae indulge either of us in this nighttime ride. It was a foolish risk, for I know well the Comyn think to take me land by slitting me throat. No doubt they have noticed I enjoy nighttime rides."

"Aye," she agreed. "Ye must no' be predictable. Yer enemies will use it against ye."

He stroked the neck of his stallion, looking like he was saying good-bye to the beast. "Aye. 'Tis time I acted more like the laird I am. Baruch has been badgering me for months to stop taking off without an escort. But I do nae care for it any more than ye do."

"And ye came out tonight for me," she said quietly.

Saer shook his head. "And meself, lass. I wanted to please ye, but I should have thought the matter through."

"We both should have. I was raised to know the dangers of leaving the Grant castle alone."

He nodded and mounted. "As I keep telling ye, lass, we have much in common."

"Aye, we're both reckless," she replied and heard him chuckle. "I'm sure Baruch will have something to say about that, which is nae pleasing." She went after her mare and mounted.

"I find ye pleasing, Nareen Grant." His tone was strong and sure. "Every single thing I know about ye. Make no mistake about it."

She locked stares with him and felt her resolve crumbling. For just a moment, they were so alike, it felt as though she might trust in their commonalities.

But she was still so unsure.

On the ride back to the MacLeod castle, a heavy sense of reality was weighing down on her shoulders.

Why was life so often cruel?

There was much to crave in Saer, so was it not the cruelest of things to fear binding herself to him?

⤡

"Ye're bleeding."

Nareen moved closer to Saer. Once they were back

inside his chamber, there was enough light to see what the night had hidden. She reached up and cupped his shoulder to turn him, so she might get a closer look at his back. Along his right shoulder blade, his shirt and jerkin were sliced open several inches, the edges stained dark with blood.

"This needs stitching."

He chuckled at the horror in her voice. "Ye have a fair command of a sewing needle, so Gitta tells me."

Saer walked farther into the chamber and took his sword off. She heard him draw in a stiff breath as he moved his injured shoulder.

"Ye should have told me."

"Why?" he asked as he sat down and unlaced his boots. "Besides, it was me own fault."

"I wanted to go."

"Aye." He stepped out of his boots and began to unbuckle his kilt. He held his tongue while stripping out of his clothing.

She was shamed, doubly so when she looked back at the wound on his shoulder. He went out onto the *terrazzino*, and she heard the water splashing down onto the stone as she found the sewing basket and pulled a needle from it.

But she needed other things too.

She turned and left the chamber, hurrying down the steps on her way to the kitchen. Many of those who worked in the kitchens also slept there. The large hearths still had embers glowing red to help her see as she rummaged around, looking for what she needed.

"Who's there?" a woman asked as she raised her head from her pallet in one of the corners.

"Worry nae. I've found what I need," Nareen assured her.

Nareen gathered up her supplies and hurried back into the keep.

She heard Saer cursing the moment she touched the first step. He snarled viciously in Gaelic before almost running into her on his way down the stairs.

He jerked to a halt and stared at her as though he could not believe his eyes.

"Where the devil did ye go?" he demanded, his tone harsh and full of accusation. He had only his kilt on, the pleats in disorder.

"The kitchen, for whisky and—" She realized why he was cursing. "Ye thought I left?"

"Of course I did, woman!"

There was a pounding of footsteps behind her, and a flood of light as several retainers converged on them with torches.

"What goes on here?" demanded one of them.

"Naught," Saer responded. "Return to yer posts."

The retainers were already responding to his command when one of them stopped and pushed the torch he held closer to Nareen.

"Her hands are covered in blood," he roared.

Swords were pulled as the retainer reached for her, but Saer slid in front of her, blocking the man with his body.

Unfortunately, the retainers behind them clearly saw his shoulder.

"The laird's back is sliced clean open!"

Everything in her hands went flying as the retainers yanked her away from Saer. He growled, but they flooded in front of him, pushing him back with their sheer numbers as more and more people came running to investigate what the disturbance was.

"Christ's cock! She did nae slice me!" Saer roared. His curse drew gasps from the women and silenced the retainers. "Now clear the path and give me back me woman."

The retainers standing in front of her didn't want to obey. They parted reluctantly, allowing Saer to see her.

He drew in a long breath. "We met with some Comyn in the woods. The blood on her hands is theirs."

Doubtful looks were cast her way. Some took to stroking their beards. Saer bent down to retrieve one of the things she'd taken from the kitchen. He looked at the jug for a moment and nodded.

"Scotch. Exactly what I need."

The women began to search the floor and collected the other items Nareen had dropped.

"Good night," Saer said, dismissing them all before standing aside so Nareen might precede him up the stairs.

For Nareen, the first step felt impossible to take. Everyone stood still, watching to see what she would do. Saer made a low sound, and she moved, her first steps jerky.

"She's got a dagger in her belt…"

"Its blade is stained…"

The whispers followed her up the stairs, until Saer shut the chamber door.

She turned on him. "Ye did nae trust me."

He frowned at her. "I suppose…"

"Ye did nae."

"Why are ye so angry, woman? Ye're the one who does nae want to trust me. Why do ye demand what ye will nae give?"

She was shaking. "Me reasons are well founded, thought out, and rational."

"So was me reasoning that ye had taken the opportunity to ride off into the night, because ye've made it plain ye are no' content."

"What do ye expect when ye bring me home tied about ye like a prize?"

He was looming over her, but she wasn't going to back down. She rose up onto her toes to get her face closer to his, but it wasn't enough. She lifted her hand and poked him in the center of his bare chest.

He exploded, roaring before capturing the back of her head and kissing her.

She tried to escape, but he followed her, his mouth hot and demanding against hers. She tried to turn her head, and he gripped her nape. The kiss was punishing and sent a flood of desire through her.

Nareen let out a growl. It was low and more primitive than any sound she could recall willingly making. It came up from inside her, from the center of the swirling vortex of desire he stirred up. She reached for him, grabbing a fistful of his hair and holding him in place as she thrust her tongue up into his mouth.

"Ye're mine…" he insisted against her open mouth.

Her need for him was mad, like someone had spilled oil and touched a flame to it. The heat was searing, and the only relief was to reach for what she craved.

She grabbed his kilt, pulling it up to reveal his cock. The fabric frustrated her, drawing a hiss from her lips before she was able to wrap her fingers around his rigid length and satisfaction filled her.

He grabbed her skirt and yanked it up, letting the night air brush her thighs before he hooked them and lifted her off her feet.

She gasped, losing hold of his length. He drove her back against the wall, pressing her to it with his wide chest.

"Mine…" he repeated as he spread her thighs wide with his hips. "I'm going to make sure everyone knows it again and again, until ye admit it."

She didn't care what he said, only worried he wouldn't satisfy the need tearing her apart. She wrapped her arms around him, straining toward him as she felt his cock nudging the folds of her slit.

It was hard, and she craved more of it. "Yes…"

He bared his teeth at her, and she snapped at him. His chest shook with something that might have been a rumble of amusement, but he thrust into her, stealing away every thought she had. There was only his hard length and the motion of his hips as he drove it in and out of her.

She was ready to climax, but he denied her a quick release. Instead, he held her still, controlling the speed of their coupling. She jerked and strained toward him, but he pinned her to the wall with his chest, making it impossible for her to gain the hard pressure she craved.

"Damn ye…" she cursed as sweat began to coat her skin.

"Tell me what ye want, Nareen…" He held back

the last inch of his length, tormenting her with just enough fullness to keep her passion burning her alive. "Tell me how to please ye…"

"Satisfy me!"

The words were torn from her, but she had no will to deny him. In that moment, she lived only for the pleasure he could grant her.

"Aye," he growled against the top of her head as he impaled her completely and deeply.

She moaned, the hard thrust almost enough to fill her with ecstasy.

"Aye!" he snarled louder and thrust into her body again.

She hooked her hands onto his shoulders as he labored to please her. Every muscle seemed to be working toward that common goal. She arched, her spine feeling like it was on the verge of snapping as she tried to angle her lower body to take even more of him inside her.

"Mine…" He claimed her as he drove her over the edge. She screamed. The sound bounced off the walls, and she didn't care. There was too much sensation ripping through her to contain it. She felt like a log dropping in the hearth; when she hit bottom, a shower of red and orange sparks went flying out. It was that hot, that searing.

"Completely mine…" he continued as he thrust against her, riding her through the storm of ecstasy. Just as it began to ebb, he groaned, the sound deep and male. The first spurt of his seed sent her into another climax. It caught her by surprise, tearing her back into the swirling vortex as Saer filled her full.

This time, her heart was going to burst, but she didn't have any strength to care. In that moment, she accepted anything he chose to do with her, because she was absolutely his.

~~~

He kissed her, slow and sweetly. Nareen opened her eyes, slightly unsure of how much time had passed. Saer kissed her temple and then her forehead, and her heart settled into a steady, slow rhythm.

"Now ye're tender," she accused softly.

He tilted his head and nipped the column of her throat. "Ye did nae want tender, lass, any more than I did. I satisfied ye. A selfish man would only use ye."

"I know." The words were soft, and he nuzzled her ear for a moment before lowering her feet to the floor. Her knees were shaky, but satisfaction was glowing inside her, making it all seem perfect.

"I suppose I should have ye stitch this before I ruin the linens." His shoulder. How could she have forgotten?

"Sit down." She hurried over and grabbed the lantern near the wardrobe. Once she had it near Saer, she opened the latch on the little tin side to let more of the candlelight out.

Blood had seeped down his back. She picked up a wash basin and went out onto the *terrazzino* to fill it. Saer had taken off his boots again by the time she returned. He took a drink of Scotch, and then a second one.

She used a piece of soap to wash her hands before she dunked a linen napkin from her supper into the water. As she began to clean his back, he braced his hands on his knees and leaned forward to give her better access.

She threaded the needle and held it over the flame of the candle for a moment.

"This is going to hurt," she warned him.

"Nae nearly as much as finding ye missing did."

Her hand began to tremble, the admission cutting straight through her well-thought-out reasons for refusing him. But she drew in a deep breath and began to stitch.

"I suppose taking yer dress was nae a way to endear ye to me."

She cut off the thread and doused the closed wound with the whisky. He stiffened and drew in a sharp breath.

"I suppose refusing to wed ye did nae endear me to ye, either," she offered softly as she washed her hands.

He chuckled as she bound the wound with a length of cloth for the night. Once she finished, he pulled her into his lap.

His embrace was perfect. She just couldn't think of anything else while his arms were locked around her.

"It seems we both need to learn to trust," he said at last.

A yawn caught her by surprise, and he grunted before standing her up. But he caught her hand before she moved away.

"Promise me the rest of the harvest season to convince ye, Nareen."

His expression was guarded, his tone too. He wasn't a man accustomed to negotiation, and the effort touched her deeply.

"If ye will nae wed me before the first snow flurries begin to fall, I'll send ye home."

It was a vow, one she had absolute faith in.

"Agreed."

His eyes narrowed, and his grip tightened. "That simply?"

"I've never questioned yer honor, Saer." She leaned down and kissed his hand. "Only me own ability to make peace with placing meself under a man's rule. It has never been yer failing, but mine. I would nae disappoint ye and see ye grow to hate me."

She watched the understanding dawn in his eyes. His lips curled up in a wide grin, and he caught her up in an embrace before twirling around in a circle until she squealed.

When he put her down, she was breathless and teetered off balance.

"I'll win ye, Nareen."

His eyes were glittering with delight, and for a moment, she truly hoped he would.

Six

"THOSE BELLS RING TOO EARLY," SAER GROUSED AT DAWN.

Nareen rubbed her burning eyes and tried to move. Her body complained bitterly.

Saer had no mercy and tugged the bedding off her, exposing her bare skin to the brisk morning air.

She yelped and rolled over and onto her feet. Once she was standing, she glared at him.

"Ye have duties to attend to," he said without a hint of remorse. "I want to see what else ye know before I assign ye a group to instruct."

She found her chemise and pulled it over her head. "Ye cannae be serious?" She struggled with getting her arms into the sleeves and brushing her hair out of her face.

"Why nae?" he questioned as he tossed aside the fabric she'd bound his wound with. He offered her the bottle of Scotch and turned his back so she might disinfect the line of stitches again.

In the light of day, she winced at the sight of the red edges.

"What is yer concern?" He pressed her for an

answer as she poured a small amount of the liquor on the wound.

"That yer Father Peter is going to insist I be locked in the pillory."

Saer grunted and pulled on his shirt. "He'll keep his peace, as he has with the other changes I've made to restore the MacLeods to full strength. Everyone on my land will make adjustments in their thinking. Ye've been trained, and well. That is nae a resource I intend to waste."

He turned and shot her a wicked look. "Even if I prefer the idea of ye sitting here, waiting for me in naught but yer shift."

She threw a pillow at him, but it only made a soft sound when it hit his chest and slid to the floor. "I doubt Father Peter will be the only one who points out I am a woman and nae minding me place."

"The Comyn are bastards, who have raped more than one of me clanswomen," Saer informed her bluntly. "If that is the place of a woman, I say it should be changed, and I am laird of the MacLeods."

He was that. It was in his bearing, and now, as the daylight was brightening the chamber, she could see him focusing completely on his responsibilities. That was the reason she felt like power radiated from him. His thoughts were aimed completely on whatever it was he was doing or seeking.

When it was directed at her, it was overwhelming. When it was his clan, it was awe-inspiring. The combination produced a man who was quickly becoming too great for her dismiss.

❧

They hurried into the church as the opening prayers were being sung. Nareen tried to stand at the back, but the MacLeod women all moved out of her way, leaving her facing the priest.

Father Peter stumbled over his words when he saw her. His cheeks darkened as he looked away from her, and his voice returned to a steady, even tone. There were no benches in the church. Women stood in rows on one side while men stood on the other. The only furniture was the altar with wooden candleholders set atop it. Along the sides of the church, there were alcoves where relics or statues must once have sat. They were empty now.

The service finished, and Father Peter made the sign of the cross over his flock.

The women parted again, none of them willing to step in front of her. Everyone strained to get a look at her, many of the women holding up their daughters so the little ones might get a peek as well.

"Mistress Grant?" Saer offered her his hand.

She took it gratefully, and he escorted her from the church. Whispers rose behind them as he took her into the Hall. The scent of the morning meal was drifting through the air, and women hurrying about as they set out bowls of steaming porridge. Men were crowded onto the benches, laughing and enjoying the moment of rest.

Everyone froze when they saw her. The activity around the hearth came to a halt as everyone tried to get a look at her.

"Sure ye do nae wish to wed now?" Saer asked beneath his breath.

Her cheeks heated as he escorted her up the aisle to the head table. "Do nae enjoy this so much, Laird MacLeod."

His eyes glittered with mayhem. "Now that is simply something I cannae promise to do, for I enjoy ye being here too greatly."

He did. It was there in his eyes and in the way he held her hand so formally in front of his people. A perfectly proper escort position. No one would have reproached him for taking the lead, for he was laird, but he shared the moment with her. Making it clear she was the woman he was setting above all others.

Even a wife could not always expect such. She might demand it, but the power was the laird's.

By the time they reached the head table, a retainer had pulled a heavy chair out for her. Saer needed no assistance. The moment they sat, the staff began to serve the table. It began with a bowl being offered to Saer. Once he put his hand over it, another boy poured water from a pitcher onto his hands. A third servant offered a linen to dry them.

It was a level of service she'd seen and helped perform many times at the Ross castle, but somehow, hadn't pictured Saer demanding. She realized he wasn't demanding anything. She caught him biting his lip with impatience as his plate was salted and cleaned before being placed in front of him.

As the meal progressed, the servants hurried to serve Saer and her. They did it out of respect for the place he offered them and the opportunities promised to their children. On MacLeod land, a son might have a better life than his father. It was a rare thing.

It was something that endeared him to her. He was

far more complex than she'd realized. Far more than just a man who had decided she belonged to him. She might have contemplated it further, but he rose from the table the moment he'd finished and offered her his hand.

"Now, lass, let's see what else Kael taught ye."

There was a challenge in his voice that she warmed to. "I am looking forward to it."

No man should be able to move so freely with a wound on his shoulder.

Nareen bit back a harsh word as she stumbled past him for what must have been the tenth time, because he moved out of her way so easily. But she turned and kept him in her sights.

"Good," he said. "Kael taught ye nae to let yer opponent get at yer open back."

"That can prove deadly."

Saer nodded and came at her again with a wooden training dagger. This time, she cut to the side and swung her closed fist at his temple. Pain snaked up her arm from the connection, but Saer was knocked out of his stride. If only for two paces. He jumped around with a chuckle, his kilt rising up to flash his thighs at her. "Well done."

His captains began muttering behind him. They hung back, but Nareen still felt them judging her.

Well, let them. She knew what she was doing.

Dust rose up as he continued to attack. By the time they finished, her hair was matted with sweat and dirt. But she was satisfied, because Saer looked just as taxed.

He watched her brush at some of the dirty splotches on her dress.

"I'll have Gitta find ye something else to wear. If ye're training, ye'll need a change of clothing."

"Ye'll need new shirts, since it seems ye have no intention of letting that wound heal."

He shrugged. "I've had worse."

He looked past her at Baruch. "Let her work with the tens after dinner. They could use a bit of dagger training."

Nareen was surprised to see it was almost time for the main meal of the day. The sun was directly above them.

"I have to inspect the walls," he told her, pausing for a moment near her. He reached out and smoothed some of her hair back. "Ye astound me, lass."

"Most men would be disgusted." It was the truth, and she wanted to see what he'd say when others were listening.

Amusement danced in his dark eyes. "Many were disgusted by my bastard birth and happy to tell me I did nae belong training next to the righteous. I do nae give a damn for their opinions. Strength interests me. Ye have that in abundance."

It wasn't the sort of compliment she'd ever envisioned enjoying. Nor was it like any of the flattery so many men had lavished on her. But it pleased her more completely than any words ever had.

Saer rubbed her cheek a final time before he left. His captains fell into step with him, attempting to converse with him. His position of laird was more than title; it was there in the way he was taking charge.

And he offered her a place too.

It was more than she'd ever thought to have—certainly more than she would have if she returned to Grant land. There she would care for her father until his death, and then become the unwed sister of the laird. Kael would wed, of course, and his bride would expect to be mistress.

The title didn't really interest her. Knowing she had more purpose than warming a bed did. So what did it mean?

She wished she knew. Her feelings were so complicated, and still, Saer was cutting through them with an ease that relieved her as much as it frustrated her.

The bells began to ring in the tower, announcing dinner. Everyone started to make their way to the Great Hall. Nareen looked back and saw Saer up on one of the new sections of wall. He was listening to a man as they looked at one of the rising towers.

The laird was magnificent.

❧

The youths she was assigned to teach stared at her with suspicion. Nareen walked to the portion of the yard reserved for boys ten to twelve years of age and discovered it packed. But not just with boys.

Every single one of their mothers was there, many of them making the sign of the cross over themselves when they saw her. They frowned, obviously distrustful of a woman being given charge of their sons.

"I heard she tried to kill the laird…"

"I hear he was impressed by the attempt…"

Nareen swallowed the lump in her throat. Several of the boys puffed out their chests to make a good showing.

She just tried to keep her knees from knocking.

With a deep breath, she tried to recall how Kael had begun teaching her. There were a few confused looks before she worked out what needed to be done. Small steps. Break the knowledge down and teach every step until you might put it together. By the time the sun was setting, she had neat rows of boys practicing defense against a downward plunge attack. There were cheeky grins as some of them succeeded, and proud looks from their mothers.

Many of the women left once they were assured she wasn't some demon who would spread evil to their children. Around her, the stonemasons continued their work, and the older boys worked with swords as their training masters called out commands. The scent of sweat was high as dust rose from their activities.

Her sleeve was wet from the number of times she'd wiped her brow on it. She longed for the freedom Saer had to simply roll his sleeves up to the shoulder. But at least she had been able to remove her oversleeves. They'd ended up draped over a barrel before her class was half finished. One of the older women, who had been carding wool while watching the class, brought them to her at the end.

"Rather well done. Of course, ye'll have to stop teaching once ye ripen with child…"

Nareen froze. The thing that had tormented her rose up in response to the woman's comment.

Sons… It was the thing Saer craved from her most of all.

The older woman smiled, then moved off toward the Great Hall for supper.

Doubt needled her as she followed.

There was no place in life that was free of responsibility. If she returned home, she'd owe her brother's wife deference and respect.

But if she stayed, she'd face Saer's expectations of sons.

It was his right, of course. He was not wrong to wish for such, but what weighed on her shoulders was the need to be done with living in uncertain circumstances. If she wed him, she'd have to accept uncertainty.

She honestly didn't know if she could.

But she had given her word, and the time frame eased her worry. She did not have to make any decision right now. That granted her the freedom to enjoy the moment.

If nothing else, she'd have a fine memory to keep her warm once she left Saer for the cold life of a spinster.

◦⟡◦

By the end of the week, Nareen ached in more places than she thought possible. Her forearms were bruised from blocking so many times. Her fingers were raw from pulling back the bowstring. At least her feet proved worthy. All of the hours of standing behind Abigail had strengthened them. As the sun began to set, she made her way up to the tower's top chamber, happily anticipating being able to wash the sweat from her skin.

The chamber was quiet, the doors open to the *terrazzino*. She happily stripped away her filthy clothing, wrinkling her nose at the stench. Perhaps she should have just stood beneath the water in her clothing.

The water in the buckets would warm during the day. She'd learned by the end of the week to use water wisely so her bath was warm. Not that chilly water would have stopped her from using the device every night. It was a godsend to be able to clean herself so easily. What were a few goose bumps?

She pulled the length of linen off the hook and wrapped it around herself. But she froze when she entered the chamber, because something was laid out on the bed. She moved closer and found a new chemise waiting for her.

"Ye can thank some of yer students' mothers for that."

She jumped and turned to find Saer sitting in one of the chairs.

"Ye're here before sunset…"

He nodded. "Old Maud climbed up onto the wall to give that to me. I think she nearly frightened half me captains to death by appearing at the top of the ladder. She's a highly respected elder of the clan, and there would have been hell to pay if she'd fallen."

"Why didn't she give the chore to another?" Nareen wasn't really thinking of Maud. She was busy fingering the new chemise, shivering with delight over the idea of not having to put her filthy one back on.

"She was making a point to me."

Nareen lifted the chemise and put it on. It settled into place, falling to just above her knees. The stitches were even and tiny.

"She was making sure I did nae overlook the fact that I've forgotten to see to yer basic needs." He was gripping the arm of the chair. "Why did nae ye ask for clothing?"

"I… I've nae had much time really to think on it. Besides, ye told me there was none."

He watched her, weighing her response.

"Why are ye looking at me as though ye doubt I am speaking truthfully?" she asked.

The way he remained in the chair set off a warning in her head. The man was rarely still.

"And why are ye sitting still?"

He gave a short bark of laughter and stood up. It felt like the chamber shrank, because he was finished trying to lull her into a sense of calm. "Ye know me too well, Nareen, but I hope ye'll give me credit for attempting to have a gentle conversation with ye."

"From ye, it is an effort I cannae overlook." She pulled the comb through her hair and watched him. "But ye are frustrating me, for I have no idea what is on yer mind."

"Are ye still intent on leaving? Is that why ye did nae ask for another dress?"

The comb fell from her fingers and clattered onto the floor. "The agreement is until the snow flurries appear."

He looked at the comb, judging her by her actions instead of her words.

"Is it so difficult to speak yer fears to me?" he asked. "I see something in yer eyes, lass, that ye continue to leave unspoken."

"Some men would consider it a blessing that their choice of woman did nae badger them with every concern she had."

He reached out and laid his hand against her cheek. "I've told ye I want to wed ye."

She turned away, nodding, but turned back when she heard him following her.

"That will nae happen until ye resolve what troubles ye." Determination edged his tone. "So I will ask and ask again until ye tell me. It frustrates me that ye will nae voice yer concern and give me the chance to answer it."

She drew a deep breath and gathered her courage, for she was acting like a coward by remaining silent.

"Ye've also told me ye wish for sons," Nareen stated clearly.

His eyes narrowed. "And ye said ye like children."

"Some women do nae conceive, Saer, and ye are nae one to be denied what ye set yer mind to getting. Every moment I have known ye, it has been part of yer quest to have sons. What will happen if I give ye a daughter? As yer father's bride did?"

Surprise registered in his eyes, and he reached out to cup her cheeks. But she jumped back, earning a dark frown from him.

"Ye are everything to me, Nareen. If ye present me a daughter, I will welcome her."

He said it easily, so easily that she was tempted to believe.

"And what of no children? Will ye send me back to me brother if fate is truly unkind toward me?"

"Since that is what ye have claimed ye wish to do, why would it matter if I did?"

"It would matter." She clamped a hand over her lips when she realized the words had slipped out.

His expression suddenly softened; the tension in his body eased. "Ye have affection for me at last, Nareen."

She looked away, but he cupped her chin and brought her face back toward him. "Do nae try to stem it. I would have ye happy."

Her lips were dry, so she rolled them in to moisten them. The desire to believe in happiness was stronger than it had ever been since she left Grant land. It almost felt as though it might become bright enough to banish the doubts lurking in the shadows of her mind. "And do ye return me affection?"

He lifted his chin and lowered his hand to hook his fingers around his belt.

His expression became guarded, sending a warning snaking through her. "I will honor yer love, Nareen."

"But ye do nae intend to return it?" He didn't want to answer her. She could see the reluctance in his eyes. "Now who has thoughts unspoken?"

"It's a weakness I cannae afford." He drew in a deep breath. "I'll nae repeat me mother's mistakes."

She stood silent, unable even to think.

"But it pleases me to know ye have softened toward me." He nodded again. "Pleases me very much. I understand women need such tender feeling to be content. I wish ye to be so."

"But nae to experience such things yerself?"

His brow furrowed. "Highlanders do nae follow weak lairds. Now, Gitta is fetching ye a fresh dress to wear to supper. I must make sure she gives Maud cloth in exchange for what was used for that chemise."

He turned and walked toward the chamber doors. His kilt swayed with his powerful strides, but for once, she wasn't distracted by his physical prowess.

All she felt was an overwhelming need to collapse.

Her knees weakened, and tears stung her eyes. The sound of the door closing behind him was like a cannon shot. She felt it vibrating through her, shattering the contentment she'd woken up with.

She sank down, losing the battle to control her tears as well as her legs. Hot little drops of saltwater left tracks down her cheeks as she swept the chamber with her gaze, seeking any shard left of the comfort she'd decided was there.

She found it, lodged deep in her heart. No matter what she wished, there was a feeling burning there that would not heed her demands. It was hot and made her ache as she heard Saer's words again.

He'd meant what he said. He would never love her.

And she knew, without a doubt, that she had fallen in love with him.

❧

The outer gate wall bells began to ring during supper.

Nareen chided herself for how relieved she was.

Hiding her hurt from everyone took effort, and she knew she wasn't fooling Saer completely. He knew her too well already. Before she'd taken more than two bites, he was cutting her a sidelong glance.

By the time her meat grew cold because she was only picking at it, he'd reached under the table to squeeze her thigh.

She forced her smile into place and ignored the questioning looks from him.

What was there to say? I love ye, but like so many men, ye believe love to be a weakness? He defied the teaching of the Church when it came to the role a woman must play, but he still fell prey to the notion that love was soft and a form of madness.

Once more, they had much in common, for neither was willing to change for the other.

Perhaps she should wed him and prove she was willing to trust. The idea needled her for what felt like hours as she remained undecided.

Saer stood up, making his way down the aisle, along with many of his men. The Hall hushed as they waited to see who was at their gates. The Comyn had had time to send a raiding party in retribution for the men she and Saer had killed.

She itched to get up, but if she did, everyone would follow her. The Hall was a sanctuary, and it was her duty to make sure the women of the clan stayed there.

No matter the cost for her.

❦

"Open yer gate, Saer MacLeod!"

Saer arrived and heard his name being shouted by whomever was locked outside.

"Ye've got me sister, and I've come to thrash ye for it!" Kael Grant swore.

"He has a unique way of trying to entice us to lift the gate," Baruch remarked.

"Aye," Saer answered as he waved to the men at the top of the gate towers. They began to turn the huge wheels that wound the chains and lifted the heavy iron gate. It groaned as it rose and revealed Kael Grant and a hundred of his retainers.

Saer frowned. "Did ye come here for a fight?"

Kael rode in and slid off the back of his stallion. His

boots had barely hit the dirt before he sent his fist into Saer's jaw.

Saer stumbled back but righted himself quickly. "Explain yerself, Kael!" he snarled as his men rushed forward and the Grant retainers prepared to fight.

"Ye'll be the one explaining about how I hear ye brought me sister into yer castle tied around ye!"

Saer wiped blood off his chin and held up his hand. His men didn't care for the command to stand their ground, but they backed up, grumbling.

"Nareen is settling in well."

Kael had the same black hair as his sister, but also had black eyes. His chin was covered with several days' growth of beard, proving he'd wasted no time in making his way to MacLeod land.

"Me damned cousin Ruth claimed much the same thing!" Kael roared.

Saer threw a punch at Kael and sent him stumbling back.

"Ye'll nae compare me to that bitch." Saer pulled back, allowing Kael to gain his balance. "I should have choked the life from her when I had the chance. I'm still thinking it's worth the time to ride down to the lowlands to see it done."

Kael growled but held himself back. "Why?" he demanded.

"I'll tell ye, but nae before ye swallow some of yer anger, man," Saer warned. "Ye knew full well I planned to wed yer sister."

Kael shook his head. "I agreed to yer suit. Nae to a claiming." He pointed at Saer. "I'll beat ye senseless if ye have her locked in a chamber somewhere. I swear I will!"

"She's been teaching some of me younger lads how to defend themselves against dagger attacks."

Kael pulled himself up straight, frowning as Saer's words sank in. "She told ye about that?"

"She proved it when some of the bastard Comyn tried to kill me."

Kael's expression tightened again. "What the hell was me sister doing in a precarious position like that?"

Saer drew in a deep breath. "I was nae brought up to be a laird like ye, Kael. I forget that a ride through the woods just might end with me having me throat slit because me neighbor covets me land."

Kael froze while Saer's words sank in. A moment later, he let out a crusty chuckle. "Nae so wonderful a life, is it, lad?" He laughed long and loud. "Bet yer mother did nae tell ye about that part of being a laird's son, now did she?"

"No."

Kael nodded. "Now about this bringing me sister home tied around ye. Tell me it's nae true, and I'll be content."

A few of his captains cleared their throats. Kael's eyes widened. "Saer?"

"Come inside, Kael. If ye do nae care for me reasons, ye can thrash me, but our men do nae need to be involved."

Kael popped his knuckles.

But the crowd around them had begun to return to their supper, allowing him to see Nareen standing in the gate between the inner yard and the outer one.

Two MacLeod retainers stood in front of her, refusing to let her go any farther until Saer made a motion with his hand. They moved back, leaving her facing her brother.

She took a step forward but stopped, her teeth set into her lower lip.

Grant and MacLeod alike waited to see what she'd do, the yard going quiet as all eyes turned to her.

"Remember, yer actions will lead others no matter if ye want them to or no'. That is what being a laird's daughter means. Ye must always think of the example ye set. For everyone shall look to ye for the way they should behave."

She hadn't heard her father's words for a long time. It should have been a welcome relief from Ruth's vicious taunting, but Nareen felt just as controlled.

Her brother was laird in all but name.

Her rage was burning bright at the sight of him, but she could not show it. Saer had made her mistress of the MacLeods, and they would respond to her anger.

Everyone in the yard was waiting for her to greet her brother. To show that Grant and MacLeod might be united through her relationship with Saer.

She'd been raised to expect such an arrangement.

But the last time she'd seen Kael, he'd sent her off to Ruth.

It was done with.

And yet, it wasn't. For she had yet to face her brother.

"Mistress?"

It was old Maud who spoke, age making her tone

crack. The older woman leaned on a cane near the gate, expectation in her eyes. She flicked one time-withered finger toward Kael.

It was a subtle reprimand, but the weight of it was great.

Nareen moved forward, covering the space between Kael and herself. She stopped in front of him and lowered herself.

She could see men nodding with approval, smiles appearing on their faces.

"Welcome, Kael."

❧

Nareen was asleep by the time Saer made it to his chamber. He was no stranger to climbing the stairs halfway through the night. But he'd never felt so relieved when he arrived.

He smelled her delicate scent before he made it past the trestle table. She'd left the doors open again, endearing herself to him because she didn't fear the night the way so many others did.

But the best part was seeing her in his bed, her chest rising and falling slowly. It was the place he'd prepared for her, every detail planned and checked. The bed built large enough for two, and the sheets made of soft fabric so as not to chafe a woman's tender skin.

And she was perfect.

MacLeod and Grant were happily drinking together below because she'd known the part to play. There was a reason noblemen arranged their weddings. They needed a woman who could run an estate and perform under the demands of her position.

Nareen had excelled.

He sat down on the side of the bed and slid in beside her. She shifted, and he pulled her close.

Aye, perfect.

He buried his face in her hair, inhaling the scent. It sent a spike of arousal through him and a need to have his skin in contact with hers.

Any way possible.

He stroked her cheek and along her jawline before smoothing along the column of her throat. She muttered in her sleep but raised her chin so he might reach all of her neck. When he stroked her a second time, she let out a soft sound of enjoyment.

He moved close, allowing his erection to nestle between her thighs. She muttered and shifted from side to side as she searched for him. He cupped her breasts, toying with her nipples and pressing his chest against her back.

"Hummm…so nice…" she muttered.

Her nipples drew tight before he smoothed his hand along her body to the plane of her belly. Her skin was smoother than the finest silk, filling him with a need to possess her.

But not yet.

He stroked her belly more, listening to the sounds she made as she came closer to consciousness. She thrust her hips forward, and he didn't deny her what she craved. He teased the curls crowning her mons before gently stroking the folds of her slit.

She hissed, arching back so he could look down the front of her body. Her breasts tempted him with puckered nipples, making his cock jerk. The need to bury himself inside was strong, but he resisted it, enjoying the bite he gained by fighting off his baser impulses.

Her eyelashes fluttered as he stroked her slit again, this time burrowing between the folds to find the center of her pleasure. She thrust toward his hand, little sounds of delight coming from her lips. She grew warmer, her slit wet.

"What…are ye doing, Saer?"

He rubbed her bud and kissed the side of her neck. "Pleasing ye…"

He watched her tongue appear and move across her lower lip. Her body drew tight, but she never closed her thighs.

"Aye…ye are…" she admitted.

She began to tremble and lifted her bottom. His control crumbed, and he thrust forward. She was so wet, he penetrated deeply on the first thrust. But he pulled back because her sheath was too hot, too tight for him to last within its grip.

"More," she insisted.

He was powerless to deny her, for it was the same desire pulsing through his body. There was only the need and the satisfaction to be gained. He thrust again and again, gritting his teeth against the tight clasp of her passage around his cock. She moved with him, lifting her bottom for every motion. His balls were tightening, the impending explosion beginning to darken his thoughts. He rubbed her harder and felt her sheath tightening with the first hints of ecstasy.

His seed began flowing, burning a path through his cock as he pumped his hips back and forth, burying himself as deep as possible as pleasure tore through

him. It was hard and gripping, dropping him back
into reality with a jolt because it had been so intense.
Nareen's passage had tightened around his length,
pulling the last drops of his essence forth.

He smoothed his hands over her, covering her lips
when she began to speak.

Her spirit was rising again, but the moment was
too intimate to shatter with pride. So he kissed the
side of her neck and smoothed the hair away from her
face before he heard her sigh and surrender back into
sleep's hold.

Tomorrow, Nareen would be finished with arguing
against her place beside him.

❧

There was a crash outside their *terrazzino* at dawn.

Saer jerked and was on his feet as voices began
shouting below. "Stay here." He grabbed his sword
and rushed outside.

Nareen wrinkled her nose at him and followed
once she'd found her chemise.

One of the cranes had lost its load of stone. The
cut blocks were scattered over one of the tables, but
there didn't appear to be anyone hurt. Several of the
stonemasons were yelling up near one of the large
wooden wheels used to operate the machine. Two
younger boys stood with their heads lowered.

"I'd best get over there," Saer groused. He turned
and glared at her. "What are ye doing out here in that
chemise, woman?"

"It's more than ye have on," she pointed out.

He wasn't wearing a stitch.

"Maybe ye shouldn't look like ye're enjoying it so much," he teased. "At least nae unless ye're going to make an honest man of me at the church door."

Women's voices joined the tirade.

Saer went inside and began to dress. He finished quickly, leaving her looking for her dress while he ran out the door. It was missing. She even searched the *terrazzino*. The church bells began to toll as she wrestled with her temper.

Had Saer decided that leaving with her brother presented too much of a temptation? Perhaps he had more feelings for her than he'd admitted.

Someone knocked on the door.

"Come in, Agnes."

But it was Kael who pushed open the door.

"I am in a foul temper, Kael."

Her brother didn't even blink. He strode into the bedchamber and planted himself in front of her.

"And I am nae dressed," she warned.

"So, put something on, Sister. For I am no' leaving."

Nareen ground her teeth together. "I cannae," she was forced to admit.

"I thought ye were serving the Earl of Ross's daughter. Did ye wear out yer fingers in a year's time?"

"Nae," she snapped. "Me dress is gone; that is why I cannae put it on, and the other one I had was taken by Bastian MacKay when his men abducted me and Abigail."

Her brother chuckled mercilessly.

"It is nae funny," she scolded. "Saer took it away before too, because he did nae trust me to remain and would nae waste the men to guard me the day through."

Her brother was turning purple in his attempt to keep from roaring with laughter. "I suppose… that's an effective method of making sure ye'll be noticed leaving."

"But I gave him me word," she finished, so disappointed that it made her ache.

Kael sobered. "And it bothers ye that he does nae trust ye to keep it?"

"Aye," she admitted.

"It bothers him that ye do nae trust him enough to wed him."

Nareen stiffened. "Ye may leave if all ye are going to do is lecture me. Ye promised me choice when it came to whom I wed, and I'll be having that."

Her brother looked at the bed behind her.

"Ye are no virgin, Kael, so do nae try to shame me."

"I'm trying to point out that ye took yerself off to his bed while he was sitting with me last night."

"So what if I did?" she argued. "The pair of ye did nae need me there."

"Ye were avoiding me," Kael said.

Nareen lifted her chin. "Maybe I was. Ye should really thank me for that, for it gave me temper time to cool."

"Ye went to his bed to find sanctuary."

"Do nae place too much importance upon it. Everything is in short supply on MacLeod land. There was no other bed to go to."

Kael tilted his head to one side, as he often did when he was about to question her logic. "Ye found yerself a position as a servant in order to escape a situation that most would have found impossible, only to tell me now ye could nae find another place to lay yer head?"

"I do nae care what ye think of it."

Kael nodded. "That's the truth at least."

"I'm nae a little girl any longer," she informed him.

"But ye're furious with me."

She closed her mouth and bit her lower lip.

"Say what is on yer mind, Nareen, I've come a long way to hear it."

He stood ready. She recognized the look in his eyes from years of standing together while their father handed out punishment. Kael was his only son, and imperfections were not tolerated. Many of hers had been forgiven, but never Kael's. It had formed him into a man who expected nothing less than perfection from himself.

She shook her head and felt her anger bleed away. "Truly, I am at peace with it. Ye did nae know, and in truth, it was ye who helped me escape."

"I do nae see how," he said with confusion.

"Ye taught me to fight." She grinned at the memory of more than one bloody nose. "It made me strong and even saved me life."

Her brother was silent for a long moment She stared straight at him, letting him see what was in her eyes. He nodded at last.

"I'm going to be paying Morrell Comyn a little visit today," Kael informed her. "Because I do nae care to hear that his men tried to kill me sister."

"Do nae be overprotective," she said. "It's Saer's duty now."

"He's nae yer husband, Nareen."

She cut her brother a hard look. "Because I refused to wed him."

The words were out of her mouth before she realized she was playing into his plans.

"Why did ye refuse to wed, Nareen?"

It was a hard question.

"I had good reason, doubts about what might happen."

"Be plain, Sister," Kael demanded.

She lifted her hands and gestured around her. "Look about, Kael. Saer is nae a man to be disappointed when it comes to what he plans. Do ye know what he told me? That he desired me because I had spirit, and he knew I would give him sons because of it."

"What is wrong with that reasoning?" Kael asked.

She sighed. "I simply could nae find meself willing to trust in the future."

"Because I failed ye."

"Do nae," she said.

Kael crossed his arms over his chest.

"I'm changing me mind on the matter, it just took time."

"Like forgiving me?" He let out a long breath. "I suppose that makes sense."

"So, ye see, everything is well enough." Except Saer had left her without clothing again.

"I will take ye home, Nareen, if ye wish."

She shook her head. "I gave Saer me word, and he gave me his. I'm here until the snow flurries fly to see if we can come to an agreement."

"I do nae care. Ye're me sister. If ye want to leave, I'll take ye."

Kael hadn't forgiven himself completely. She could

see the guilt burning in his eyes. He meant what he said, even knowing the cost would be the end of his friendship with another laird.

"I love ye for that, Kael."

&

Saer rubbed his temple.

His head was aching as the tenth witness stepped up to have his say. He was grinding his teeth but had to sit through the man's story or risk offending him. The boys who had been playing in the crane wheel were feeling the wrath of the entire community. He didn't think he could come up with a punishment worse than making them stand through the retelling of their transgressions. Both looked ready to vomit.

"Thank ye," Saer muttered as the man finished. "I believe I understand the facts of the matter."

Two more hands went up, but Saer stood. "Father Peter will have the instruction of these boys for the next month, since it's a blessing no one was hurt. They will serve in the church to show how grateful they are."

The priest was standing in the corner with his hands clasped and hidden in the sleeves of his sackcloth robe. The boys looked up, their eyes widening as the priest gestured them toward him. They dragged their feet as they followed him out of the kitchen.

Saer wasn't far behind.

"I thought that was going to last all day." Baruch voiced what Saer had been thinking.

But they stopped when columns of Grant retainers passed them by.

"What in the name of Christ?" Baruch asked.

A huge cloud of dust was kicked up because of the number of retainers Kael had riding with him. Saer climbed up the steps of the new tower and looked through the open inner gate to see how far the line stretched.

"He's taken all his men."

"Aye, it looks that way, Laird."

Saer turned and looked into the Great Hall. The head table was empty, sending a shaft of dread through him. He turned and took the steps three at a time.

❧

The door to the chamber exploded inward.

Nareen jumped and screeched as Saer made it halfway into the chamber before he spotted her.

"What the hell are ye doing eating up here, woman?"

"Why did ye take me dress away again?" she demanded.

She had to work to shove the heavy chair back from the table. By the time she made it to her feet and around to face Saer, he had returned and shut the door.

Nareen met him in the middle of the room with her hands on her hips. "I do nae like having me word questioned, Saer MacLeod."

"I do nae like thinking ye took off with yer brother," he answered back.

"What are ye talking about?" she asked.

"Kael just rode out with all his men, and ye were nae in the Hall."

"Because ye"—she stabbed him in the middle of his chest—"had me dress taken away again."

"I did nae." He swept her hand aside.

"Well, it is gone," she said, "leaving me here in naught but a shift."

"I like ye in naught, woman!" he growled. "But more importantly, I like ye in naught…in me bed."

He scooped her up and carried her the few paces to the bed. She bounced in a tangle of limbs as the church bells began to toll in the distance.

"Saer—"

"I'm going to appreciate God's creative work right here this morning."

"Saer MacLeod!" She admonished him.

He wasn't repentant in the least. With a snarl, he pressed her back and cupped her knees. He pressed them wide, kneeling between them as her chemise rose up.

"I believe it's time to repay the favor of frenching."

Shock held her dumb, and he took advantage of her paralysis. He flipped the edge of her chemise up, baring her mons.

"Can men do…such a thing?" she gasped at last.

He looked up her body, his expression full of determination. "Indeed they can, lass."

Excitement nearly tore her in two. It shredded every argument she had before any of them fully formed. She made a half sound of protest that transformed into a moan as he brushed his fingers over her cleft and along her slit. She gasped and recoiled because the sensation was too intense, but Saer held her still.

He leaned closer and licked her. She cried out as his velvet tongue swept along the seam of her sex before he used his fingers to part the folds and expose her. The little nub was throbbing insistently, and he didn't ignore it.

The first lap sent the breath rushing out of her lungs.

She was sucking it back in when he drew the little bud into his mouth and sucked on it. Pleasure knotted in her belly as her passage felt like it was contracting, seeking any sort of penetration. The motion of his tongue against her was driving her mad. Her heart hammered away as she lifted her hips off the bed in a desperate attempt to find satisfaction.

Saer wasn't willing to grant it to her. Just as she felt it beginning to crest, he left off sucking and licked his way to the opening of her passage.

She cried out in frustration.

He chuckled wickedly.

"No' yet, lass. I want to make sure ye know why ye need to stay with me." He thrust one finger into her body, sending a jolt of need through her. "I am the man who will always satisfy ye, Nareen. Always."

His tone grew rough with determination.

"Then do so," she demanded. "I want more than yer finger."

"Is that so?" He stood up and lifted his kilt. His cock was rigid and ready. "Is this more to yer liking?"

"Aye!" she answered, unashamed.

He unleashed something inside her that had no limits and no regrets. She opened her arms in invitation, and he came to her.

He cupped her bottom as he sank into her spread body. She closed her eyes, no longer having time to process the sense of sight. She was too absorbed with the hard thrusts of his body into hers. The filling and stretching of her passage and the way it sent delight through her.

She strained toward him, bucking with every thrust and moaning with satisfaction as she felt him slide completely into her. In that moment, they were part of the same soul, each one connected by the need burning inside them. He snarled, and she opened her eyes to see his teeth bared at her. The muscles along his neck were corded as he strained to hold back his seed.

He thrust harder and deeper into her. He touched some spot deep inside her passage that was so sensitive, she burst into a shower of delight. The moment she cried out, his seed began to fill her, hot and searing. She gasped, struggling to fill her lungs as she was tumbled and twisted by rapture.

They ended up sitting on the floor and against the edge of the bed. Saer cradled her against his chest and tucked her head beneath his chin.

"Ye are the only woman I have ever enjoyed fighting with."

"Ye should nae have doubted me word."

He smoothed a hand along her shoulder. "When I saw yer brother riding out like the devil was on his heels, all I could think was that ye'd left me."

Her thoughts cleared suddenly, and she lifted her head so she might look at him. "I was talking about the dress, but that is even worse. I gave ye me word."

He frowned at her. "For the last time, I did nae take yer dress."

But he'd still thought she'd left.

"Kael did offer to take me," she admitted.

Saer cussed and stood up. "He would."

"He is me brother, Saer. Ye would do the same for Daphne."

Saer reached over and helped her up. He held on to her biceps, massaging them softly as he contemplated her.

"I am glad ye stayed, Nareen."

His voice was thick with emotion. The wound he'd opened on her heart the day before soaked it up, giving her hope that he might have affection for her after all. "Why? Could ye nae replace a woman who does nae keep her word? Even one with spirit?"

"I could never replace ye," he declared softly.

She opened her mouth to try and make him say the words she needed, but he touched his forehead to hers and closed his eyes.

"I do nae know what…this…is between us, Nareen." He opened his eyes and locked gazes with her. "Only that I need ye to be here, with me. I need ye to trust me… I…need…ye."

"I love ye."

Her words were soft, but she watched them hit him. He stiffened, his grip on her biceps tightening as he drew in a breath. A moment later, he bent his knee and lowered himself in front of her. He hugged her to him, placing his head against her belly. She pushed her hands into his hair and held him tight.

"I do nae know if I can love, Nareen."

She heard the doubt in his voice and recognized it well. "I still do nae know if I can trust completely, but I am here," she offered in return.

He stood up and wiped the two tears that had fallen from her eyes off her cheeks.

"We are well matched."

She offered him a smile. "Aye, we are."

There was a knock on the chamber door. Agnes opened it before waiting for someone to invite her in.

"I've found ye a dress, mistress. It took me longer than I thought it would, but yer other one smelled something terrible."

The girl had her arms piled high with clothing and didn't see Saer until she was already inside the chamber.

"That solves the mystery of the dress," he muttered.

There was another rap on the chamber door. It wasn't really closed, and Baruch peeked in.

"Laird, the stone has arrived from the Earl of Ross. They are bringing it across the green now. It's a heavy load. Kael Grant stopped to give a hand with the wagons. One of them has broken a wheel."

"It seems the day demands yer attention," Nareen said.

Before moving toward Baruch, Saer gave her hand a squeeze. "I'll see ye tonight."

"Indeed ye shall, Saer MacLeod."

⤞⤝

Outside the main gate, Saer could see the line of wagons. But they weren't moving toward the castle. One of them had broken a wheel, and the Ross men were trying to mend it. Kael suddenly sent the bulk of his men back to the castle as Saer mounted his horse to go out to greet them.

The Grant retainers happily made their way to the

tables in the inner courtyard to enjoy the meal their laird had made them leave without.

Saer rode out, eager to inspect the stone. It took a lot of time to shape rock. The amount of finished blocks the earl had promised him gave Saer the chance to see the new section of wall finished before the snow started falling. The towers wouldn't be finished, but the yard would be secure.

Only Baruch rode with him, but Kael was standing next to the broken wheel. He looked up as Saer arrived.

"Ye should have brought a carpenter. These Ross seem to have no method of repairing this. What sort of man ventures out without mending tools?" he finished with an expression of disgust.

The Ross had freed all the horses from the carts and held them off to one side, which did not make sense either. But they were also the men who had allowed Abigail and Nareen to leave without a proper escort. The Earl of Ross's son had best get home before his inheritance was eroded away by his father's inattention to details. The Ross retainers needed to be taken in hand.

Saer slid off his stallion and crouched down to look at the wheel. Cut stones had spilled out of the two-wheeled cart, and he couldn't resist running a hand over one. The work was perfect.

"Laird MacLeod?"

Saer turned his head and found the Ross captain behind him. "Aye." He began to rise, but the man struck as he was moving.

He saw the flash of morning sun on the blade of

a short sword the man was gripping behind his leg. Saer threw himself away from it, but there wasn't time to escape completely. The sharp metal slid into his side, leaving a red-hot trail as it sank into his flesh.

"A token of gratitude from the earl for leaving his daughter in the hands of Bastian MacKay!"

Saer let out a roar that had Kael jumping into action. Every Ross was ready to fight, their ambush well planned. Baruch snarled and pulled his sword free, jumping forward to place himself in front of Saer and drive the Ross captain back. Saer heard the sound of swords locking before Baruch buried his blade deep in the Ross captain's chest.

"That's what we do with men who attack without warning!" Baruch yelled.

The Ross weren't ready to give up, but the Grant retainers fought them back fiercely. Saer whistled for his stallion, the animal responding quickly in spite of the fray going on.

He could feel the blood spilling down his side, feel his strength pouring out of him along with it. Men screamed as he hooked his hand into the saddle and swung his leg over the back of the animal.

He barely made it into the saddle and slumped forward, unable to straighten his body. Kael's men surrounded him, but they were outnumbered. Behind him, he could hear someone ringing the bells on the outer wall frantically, but they'd all be dead by the time men arrived from the castle.

The Ross had planned their attack well.

But they also had no wish to die. The Ross suddenly

bolted, fleeing back to their horses and into the woods. Kael gave a cry and sent his men after them.

It was the last thing he saw clearly before his vision began to fade and he turned his horse toward the castle.

❧

Nareen had just sat down at the high table when she heard the bells. Their frantic tempo chilled her blood. She ran back down the aisle and through the large arched doorway that led to the open yard.

The masons were pushed off to the side of the inner yard as men and horses tried to form into lines. Everywhere there were boys struggling with saddles and bridles. Too many of those preparing to mount were only youths.

A commotion started at the gate between the two yards. She saw her brother and his men pushing their way through. They carried someone. Horror filled her as she realized it was Saer.

His shirt was soaked with blood, the creamy linen a terrifying crimson. Even his kilt was stained dark and glistened in the morning sun. Kael and his men hurried to bring him up the stairs and into the tower. She swallowed her horror.

"Make way!" she yelled at the women behind her. They scurried to clear a path as Saer was carried through the doorway.

"Nareen."

His voice was edged with pain and his eyes framed with creases. His was reaching for her, his fingers seeking hers.

She put her hand into his and gasped at the strength of his grip.

"A priest," he gasped as the motion of being moved sent more pain through his ravaged body.

She mustn't cry.

"Yes. I will get Father Peter."

But Saer didn't release her. He pulled her closer. "Wed me."

"What?" She was struggling to keep up and stay in place beside him while his men carried him. "Now is nae the time…"

"Now is the only time!" he exclaimed. "Stop!"

His men didn't listen to him. They bore him up the stairs and into his chamber, and he dragged her along by his grip on her hand.

"Do nae…let our child be…bastard-born…"

"I'm nae with child," she said numbly.

"Ye could be." His voice was failing, his pallor turning gray. "Wed me."

"Ye need last rites," she argued.

There was a flutter of sackcloth in the doorway, relieving her. Father Peter was making his way through the crowd, trying to organize help for their laird.

"Father Peter is here, ye must take yer last rites, Saer."

"Wed us," he growled, but his voice was weakening. "Ye could be…with child… I cannae face God knowing I left it…bastard-born."

The look in his eyes was determined. Tears escaped her eyes as she saw his strength fading while she watched.

"As ye wish," she relented, horrified by the fact that she was granting his last request.

But it filled his eyes with satisfaction. She stared into

them as Father Peter married them. Trying to absorb the last moments of the man she loved.

"Ye are now married," the priest informed them.

Saer looked at the priest, and Father Peter nodded to confirm the deed was done. He looked over to where Kael stood, and received another nod. By the time he looked back at her, his fingers were going slack, his body relaxing until he was limp.

She let her tears fall, and someone moved her back. The solemn tones of the priest intoning last rites mixed with the sharp commands of those trying to tend to his wounds.

But it was likely a useless fight.

Seven

"I DOUBT HE'LL LIVE TO SEE DAWN." THE BARBER surgeon was an old man. He looked at Saer, seeking something else to do, but there was nothing. He gathered up his tools and laid a heavy hand on her shoulder before leaving the chamber.

"Perhaps…ye are with child?" he asked her hopefully before making his way toward the door on shuffled steps that echoed because of how silent everyone was.

Saer's captains were clustered near the door, and he gestured them out with his old hands. Once their footsteps faded, the chamber was left in silence. Even the yard was free of noise as everyone waited on word of their laird.

Nareen moved slowly toward the bed. The wound was stitched and bound, but she could still smell the scent of fresh blood. Saer was a ghastly shade of gray, his lips bloodless. Someone had covered his lower body with a length of MacLeod plaid and laid his sword by his right side.

As a Highlander should be when he met his end.

No. She wouldn't let him die.

She pulled one of the heavy chairs over to the bed and sat beside him. She lifted the bedding off the floor and covered him. Rubbing warmth back into his hands as the day crept by so slowly. There wasn't a single chisel strike to be heard, only silence and the shallow breaths Saer seemed to struggle to take.

Kael came at last. He stood behind her, but she refused to turn to him. She lifted her head from where she'd rested it on the bed.

"I do nae need comfort; he is nae going to die. Ye do nae know how strong he is."

"It was an ambush," he told her at last. "Those bloody Ross wanted blood for Abigail's plight."

"At least...I did nae...pay...for the...stone."

Nareen gasped and turned to find Saer's eyes half-open. He reached for her hand, but his motions were slow and clumsy. She clasped his hand, smiling though her eyes were glassy.

"I'm happy to say we hauled every last stone into the outer yard and even kept the carts," Kael informed Saer.

"Good." His voice slurred. "Water..."

She hurried to fill a cup from the pitcher on the trestle table. Kael helped lift Saer so he might drink from the goblet. He swallowed only a few mouthfuls before going limp again.

"Ye see, Kael? I told ye."

Her brother only laid a hand on her shoulder. She fought back tears and tried not to think about how much experience Kael had with battle wounds.

She'd not lose hope.

It was a wife's duty to keep hope alive.

❧

Fate decided to be kind to her. Saer lived through the day and into the night. Nareen slept sitting in the chair with her head beside him. In the darkest hours of the night, she felt his hands in her hair. She opened her eyes to see him watching her.

"The silver is beneath the corner stone…" He gestured across the chamber behind her.

"What silver?"

He managed a weak grin. "It's there. The Sutherlands returned part of me sister's dowry, since it was so great and we had nothing."

"That's how ye were going to pay for the stone."

He nodded. She reached for the goblet and helped him drink from it.

"There is enough…for ye…if ye are wise…"

"I won't need to be," Nareen insisted gently. "Ye will be here to help guide me."

He tried to reach for her cheek, but lacked the strength to lift his hand from the bed. His eyes slid shut, and she stifled a sob.

෴

The church bells woke her.

Dawn was brightening the horizon and warming the air.

She frowned, realizing the heat wasn't coming from the sun. It came from Saer. She reached for his brow and sucked in her breath.

His body was flushed with fever.

She hurried out to the *terrazzino* and pulled up cool water from the loch to bathe him with. When Agnes arrived with food, Nareen left it untouched.

But some time later, there was a scratching at the door, and then a scuffed step on the floor. Agnes held the door open for Maud, as two other women followed the old woman. One held a steaming kettle, and another had a basket over her arm and a large wooden bowl in her hands.

"Agnes says there's fever."

Nareen nodded.

The old woman pointed at the trestle table. The basket and bowl were set before her.

"Ye were nae taught healing arts," the old woman muttered as she rummaged through the basket, pulling several things out and putting them in the bowl.

"Me mother died when I was three," Nareen answered. "I was taught to stitch and bind wounds, and some medicine. Little really."

Maud nodded. "Me mother was a healer, even if the Church liked to tell her only God had such power. She used to say God had given her wits to know how to use what he'd created. She knew every plant in the forest."

She directed Agnes to crush what she'd put in the bowl. "Time has stolen the strength from me fingers, but not the knowledge from me head."

There was a crunching sound. Maud nodded approvingly and pointed at the kettle. "Just a bit, to form a paste."

Agnes used a wooden paddle to mix it.

"Unbind that wound," Maud directed.

Nareen used the pair of sewing scissors and sliced the fabric away.

"I can smell it festering," Maud informed them.

She moved over to look at the wound. "But it is nae too bad."

She spread the paste over the line of stitches. "Bind it again. Tonight, we'll wash it off and apply more."

She shuffled back over to her basket and took out a small bundle of cloth. It was only as big as her thumb and tied with a cord.

"Steep this until the water is dark. It will ease the pain if ye can get him to drink it."

Nareen took it and placed it in the goblet. Agnes added hot water.

"I'll come again tonight."

It was such a simple statement, but it offered her a morsel of hope. That slender hope became almost too hard to hold on to as the day progressed and Saer didn't open his eyes again. But she couldn't give up.

To do so would to be to give up on her very life.

She suddenly stood, unable to bear the silence. The first few steps were the hardest, but she went through the door and down the steps until she stood in the double arch opening at the base of the keep.

People looked up, standing out of respect, for they thought she was there to tell them their laird was dead. Women covered their mouths with their hands, steeling themselves for bad news. She drew in a deep breath to steady her voice.

"Build," she commanded them.

Frowns marred the faces of those watching as many of the masons looked to one another to decipher her reasoning.

"Build," she repeated louder. "Yer laird has a vision

for the MacLeod, one he offers ye all a place in. Lay
stone and let him hear that ye have no' abandoned his
dream. Let him hear that the Ross have no' stopped us
from doing what we will."

There were nods and then more nods before men
started to walk toward the half-finished walls. The first
sounds of chiseling filled her with relief. It grew louder
when she reentered the chamber, because the doors
were open to the *terrazzino*.

She nodded with satisfaction and returned to the chair.

"We're…well matched."

Saer's voice was thin and his eyes only open a slit.
She lifted the cup to his lips, supporting his neck as he
took some of the brew Maud had left.

"Aye, we are," she confirmed when he'd settled
back down. "So do nae plan on leaving me."

The crane began to groan outside in the yard. A
dull sound of wood and rope. Saer turned toward it,
his lips lifting into a half smile before he drifted off into
unconsciousness again.

❧

The bells on the wall began ringing in the middle of
the next day.

There was a rushed, hurried step on the stone
outside the chamber. Someone pushed in the doors.
Nareen looked up as Baruch made it three full
strides into the bedchamber before he remembered
to tug on the corner of his cap. His attention was
on Saer. He stared at his laird's chest, making the
sign of the cross over himself when he realized Saer
still drew breath.

He turned as soon as the information finished moving through his brain, leaving her alone.

The bells stopped, but Nareen went to the archways and out onto the *terrazzino* to look into the yard. She hadn't thought she could feel any worse, but below her, were two neat columns of Grant riders arriving.

There could be only one reason they were there. Her father had not been well for many years.

Kael met them. The captain dismounted and ran up to her brother, tugged on his cap, and leaned in close to speak.

What terrified her was the way the man reached out and clasped Kael on the shoulder.

Her belly knotted, and she turned to walk toward the door. She stepped into the hallway as she heard her brother's boots making firm sounds on the stone. His head came into view, and he paused when he found her waiting for him.

His expression tightened, and he bore down on her. He hesitated again before speaking.

"Say what must be said," she instructed him.

He nodded. "Father has suffered a brain seizure. He is nae expected to survive much longer."

She stiffened, longing for Saer's embrace, for it was the only safe place she could think of.

But there would be no comfort from her husband.

"Ye must go, Kael."

Her brother shook his head. "I'll nae abandon ye again, Nareen."

"Go home, Kael. Ye must be a son now. Nae a brother."

Her brother frowned at her. Nareen drew in a breath. "I mean it, go home."

"Ye should be at father's side as well," he answered.

"Saer has no one else to be at his side." She nodded. "Me place is here."

Something flickered in her brother's eyes, and she realized it was doubt. Nareen lifted her chin.

"I am a woman, Kael. Me place is here by me husband's side, and yers is by our father's. We were both taught our duty, and the time has come to see it done."

Her brother's complexion darkened. "Aye." But he reached out and captured her hand, gripping it with his larger one. "Ye have a place on Grant land, and I swear I will nae make any match for ye."

It was his solemn vow. She heard it in his tone and witnessed it in his dark eyes.

"Thank ye."

Kael shook his head. "Never thank me for doing what I should have. Ye cannae absolve me of failing to protect ye, Nareen. No one can."

There was a finality in his tone that tore at her heart. She understood his rage, shared a deep understanding of the pain that ate at him. Feeling one's own confidence shred was worse than any pain inflicted by another.

"I hope ye forgive yerself someday, Kael, for I have. Know I am happy here."

He jerked, making a hiss as he pulled his breath through gritted teeth. He wanted to argue; she saw it flicker in his eyes. But he offered her only a nod before turning and striding down the passageway.

She felt him leaving as much as she saw it happening. But there was something else, something stronger pulling her back into the chamber where Saer fought against fate's desire to tug him away from life.

It was a battle, too.

His body was bathed in perspiration, and he jerked as he struggled to wake. She moved closer, picking up a cloth and pushing it into a bowl of water.

"Shh…" she cooed softly and stroked his forehead with the cool cloth. "There are times ye must be at peace, my love."

Her voice was choked with tears, but it didn't matter, for there was no one there for her to worry about seeing her weakness. She let the tears slide down her cheeks as she rinsed the cloth.

"Do nae weep…"

She jumped, afraid Saer had lost his battle in those moments she'd looked away. But his eyes were open, glittering with all the raw determination he always seemed to have.

"Say…say it…again…"

He was struggling to keep his eyes open, the muscle along his jaw twitching.

"I love ye." She shuddered, and her eyes closed, but she forced them open, not wanting to miss her last moments with him. She caught his hand and pressed it against her breast. "I love ye."

His lips twitched. But he lacked the strength to actually grin at her. For a moment, his fingers moved against the swells of her breasts, but it was a fleeting thing. His eyes closed, and his arm went limp.

A sob escaped her, and then another, as tears flowed down her cheeks freely. Peace settled over him as the sun set. She felt his strength diminishing, along with the light, and she began to feel the coldness of separation biting into her.

Why was fate so unkind?

～

"So I lived to see another day…"

Nareen turned to find Saer watching her the next day. She blinked, unable to understand that he was still alive.

"Ye're keeping me here," he teased her.

"Nay," she argued gently as she offered him more of the remedy Maud had left. She lifted it to his lips and watched some of it disappear. "Ye are too stubborn to die."

"Ye are too stubborn to let me."

"Thank Maud." Nareen offered him more of the remedy. "She knows things I do nae. Things I should know."

"I want to thank ye…for wedding me."

He reached for her hand, and she clasped his.

"Ye told them to work," he muttered as his eyes began to droop.

"It's the sound of the future," she confirmed.

"Go…see what progress has been made… I want to know…"

～

The stonemasons didn't hesitate to show her what they had accomplished. But the stone from the Rosses was stacked outside the new curtain wall, abandoned. She stared at it as two of the senior masons watched her.

"Bad luck stone." One muttered.

His comrade nodded.

"It was paid for in blood," she informed them. "Lay it on the outer wall, so everyone knows their laird will bleed for them if necessary."

They tugged on their caps before she returned to the tower room. She paced back and forth, unable to sit in the chair for another day.

She sensed the battle Saer was waging, would have sworn she felt the struggle he was engaged in. Sweat glistened on his forehead as his fever rose even higher.

Maud pressed her lips together in a frown as she tended to him.

Nareen took his hand and pulled it close.

"Ye cannae leave me," she muttered. "Nae when I have finally found someone to trust again."

He jerked, but his eyes did not open.

"I trust ye, Saer MacLeod, do ye hear?"

She convinced herself he did, speaking to him of all the things they had left to do in life.

She just wished she wasn't running out of hope.

An owl screeched and woke her.

Nareen lifted her head and stared out the open doors of the *terrazzino*.

The bird was perched on the half wall, watching her with eyes that reflected the yellow light of the moon.

"Ye cannae have him," she informed the bird. "Do ye hear? Saer MacLeod is nae going to die."

But his hand was cold.

She gasped and reached out to lay her hand on his chest. The heat was gone, and for a moment, she feared the life had left him while she slept.

But his chest filled, rising up and delighting her. She slid her hands over him, inspecting every inch of him to make sure the fever was truly gone.

"I do...enjoy yer touch..."

His voice was raspy, but more dear to her than any sound on earth.

"Maud did it...ye did it..."

He tried to sit up but managed only to lift his head. "I cannae seem to do anything."

She lifted the goblet to his lips. "Ye survived. For now, that is enough."

⁂

Kael Grant held his father's hand. The old man fought to draw breath and could no longer close his grip.

But he opened his eyes, and there was a clarity in them Kael hadn't seen in years.

"Yer sister?" he asked. "Is she content?"

"I believe she is."

His father clicked his tongue, as though he was having trouble controlling it. "Ye'll make...certain?"

"I will never leave it to chance again," Kael promised.

"Good."

His father was straining, his breath becoming more labored. "I am proud of ye...both."

He succeeded in closing his hand around Kael's. The pressure registered just a moment before his father shuddered and went still. Kael sat still for a long time before easing the signet ring off his father's hand. His laird was dead. He stared at the ring, unable to put it on for a long time.

But he heard the retainers in the yard coming in after training, and the bells striking the changing of the guard along the walls.

He pushed the ring onto his hand. The way to honor his father was to become the man his father had wished him to be.

Laird of the Grants.

∽

The Earl of Ross looked up as his men came into the Great Hall. It was only noon, and he'd just finished his first goblet of wine.

The men stopped and pulled on the corners of their bonnets, but there was something wrong with them. There were only three, and they were tattered and dirty, one wearing a bandage around his leg. One of them walked up the steps to the high table and laid his short sword on the table in front of him.

"What is this?" the earl questioned. He peered closer at the blade. "Is that dried blood?"

"Aye, as ye instructed. It is the blood of Saer MacLeod. The captain was slain after carrying out yer order to ambush Laird MacLeod. The wound looked mortal, but I did nae see him die."

The earl's face transformed into one of horrified remorse. "What are ye saying? That I ordered such a thing?"

"Ye did." The other two men nodded.

The earl sank back into his chair, his wine goblet

forgotten on the table. He looked like he was withering before them, and he died with his eyes open.

There was no weeping on Ross land, only a deep sense of relief.

◈

Saer MacLeod didn't care for resting.

Two weeks later, Nareen was ready to scream at the surly nature of her husband.

Three weeks later, she woke to him trying to dress.

"Are ye mad?" she asked as she kicked the bedding aside.

He glared at her. "I will go mad if I stay in this chamber another day. There is work to do, woman."

"I knew ye were too stubborn to die."

She helped him with his shirt and kilt. He sat down for her to lace his boots, because he still could not bend over without pain.

His people greeted him with a cheer that filled the Great Hall. But her husband was eager to get into the yard. Once there, the sunlight seemed to restore him. His captains clustered around him as the master masons waited their turn to confer with him. Nareen drank in the sight before turning to begin what she'd promised she do if he survived.

◈

"The tens need archery lessons today," he called after her.

Nareen turned and offered her husband a slow shake of her head. His brow furrowed in confusion. She moved back toward him as the group waiting for him backed away.

"I'm off to the stillroom for lessons with Maud."

"Why?"

She pressed a hand against his chest. "Because ye know the art of being a husband, and I need to learn the art of being a wife. That is the way to make a better future for the MacLeod. I'll be making sure the women of this clan are skilled and knowledgeable."

Saer covered her hand with his. "I would nae see ye feeling forced into a place, Nareen."

"I love ye for that." She lowered her voice so her words stayed between them. "And I am happy to be yer wife. So I am off to become a better one."

"No regrets for taking a woman's place?"

"I plan to stand beside ye, Husband, and I like that place very much."

He nodded approvingly. "So do I."

His eyes glittered, looking for a moment like they were flooded with unshed tears. He pressed her hand to his chest with more force, the level of emotion going through him too intense not to feel.

"I love ye, Nareen."

She stiffened. "Ye do nae have to say that."

He slid an arm around her and pulled her close. She froze, worried that she might cause him pain. But he chuckled wickedly.

"I see uses for this wound at last. Never did I think there was a force strong enough in the Highlands to bring ye to heel," he whispered.

"Ye'd be bored to tears within a month if I remained docile."

"True." He placed a kiss against her lips. "Ye kept me alive with yer love, lass. I understand me mother now and pity me father for nae being able to hold on to the woman he loved. I will nae make the same mistakes he did."

They were surrounded by the morning activity, the steady chipping of stone and the grinding of the cranes. His voice was low and soft, for her ears alone.

"Ye won't?" she asked.

He shook his head, and she slid her hands along his jaw. "I won't be making the mistake of thinking me past must control me future. I trust ye, Saer MacLeod."

His eyes brightened, and his embrace tightened. For a moment, she was sure there was nothing in the world except for the two of them.

And their love.

✎

She refused to scream.

Nareen drew in a deep breath and blew it out in a long stream. She opened her eyes and looked at the stars above her, smiling as she felt her baby squirming inside her.

Two maids came onto the *terrazzino*, their eyes wide as they took in the fact that Nareen had ordered the birthing chair to be set up outside. It was summer, and the weather warm.

Her belly began to tighten again. She felt it moving across from her hips to her mons as her labor increased.

She still refused to scream. Only a grunt escaped her lips.

"Bear down…" Maud instructed. The older woman stood near while two other, younger midwives stood by to help catch the babe.

"I see its head, mistress…this next pain should see it done…"

Nareen felt it coming and gulped a breath before pushing. She felt the baby moving, dropping into the world as one of the midwives squealed with delight.

"'Tis a boy! A fine lad."

The baby let out a wail as he took his first lungful of air.

Nareen gripped the armrests of the birthing chair and leaned back as the midwives tended to her. Sweat was beaded all over her body. Her chemise stuck to her. She eyed the bathing shower with longing.

But first she'd greet her son. The trestle table was outside too, and draped with cloth. The midwives had laid the baby on it to clean him.

"Oh sweet mother of Christ…"

Nareen opened her eyes and sat up. One of the midwives was staring down at the new baby with wide eyes. Maud frowned and leaned closer to get a good look at the infant.

"More light," the elder commanded.

"What is it?" Nareen demanded. "Let me see him."

Her voice rose as Maud took a candle and lowered it so she might see something on the baby clearer. No one answered Nareen, sending alarm through her.

It was more than that. It was true fear. She already loved her child, couldn't bear the idea that something might be wrong with him.

"Maud…tell me what is amiss."

Her voice rose, and there was a crash as the door of the inner chamber was shoved in. Saer charged into the chamber in defiance of the tradition that women attend to birthing.

"What is wrong?" he demanded.

"Naught," Maud proclaimed.

She turned, leaning on her cane, and displayed a crooked smile. "I believe everything is now perfect."

She waved one of the other midwives forward. The woman carefully scooped up the newborn babe and brought him toward his parents. Nareen held out her arms, but Saer had to help her hold the baby because she was shaking from the effort of the birth. They cuddled him close as they inspected him, counting his fingers and toes twice.

Maud made her way closer. "Look at his right temple, mistress."

Someone held up a candle, so its yellow light illuminated the new child.

There on his temple was a red mark. It was red and slightly raised, and in the form of a cross.

"It's a sign that the MacLeod made the right choice for laird," Maud proclaimed. "God has put his mark upon yer son to prove he has divine favor."

The women all made the sign of the cross over themselves. One ran to the half wall of the *terrazzino* and leaned out. "A son!" she yelled to those waiting in the courtyard below. A cheer rose up, but Nareen was too busy looking at her child.

Saer kissed her temple. "Ye astound me, lass."

"I'll be having a daughter too," she informed him softly.

He smoothed the hair off her forehead. "Of course ye will."

Music started up below in the courtyard, in spite of the lateness of the hour. The wail of bagpipes lifted into the air, and her son opened his eyes wide and stopped fussing.

Saer stroked his cheek with one fingertip. "That's a fine Highlander lad. Welcome to the MacLeods."

Read on for an excerpt from

The Trouble with Highlanders

MacLeod land, late summer 1488

"YE ARE NAE ME HUSBAND..."

"Maybe I want it just that way, marriage is boring..."

Daphne MacLeod kicked at her bedding, but the
dream held her tight. Part of her was content, maybe
even eager to sink down into the memory of being in
Norris Sutherland's arms.

*"I want ye demanding and passionate, nae filled with
duty, lass..."*

She twisted again, feeling his arms around her. His
strength had been impressive and arousing. Never had
she imagined how much she'd enjoy being pressed
against a man, beneath him or when she decided to
straddle his hips and take charge of their pace. Just as
long as she felt his hands holding her as though letting
her go might devastate him

"And I want ye to stop telling me what to do..."

Need and yearning filled her. It traveled along her
body, teasing parts of her she hadn't known could feel
so good. The sensation was building, twisting tighter

as her body neared the point where it would burst into a shower of pleasure.

Instead, she jerked out of her sleep, escaping the hold of the dream only to discover that her freedom was cold and dark. She pressed her fist against her mouth to silence her cry. The chamber was silent, and yet it felt as though Norris was in it. She could sense him, would swear she felt him close enough to reach out and touch.

But there was no need to light a candle. The wind rattled the window shutters, blowing inside through the broken glass to chill her arms. She lay back down and pulled the bedding up. Her thick comforter was a luxury, and she snuggled beneath it gratefully. But her belly growled, reminding her there had been little comfort set out at supper. The stew the cook produced had been more water than anything else, but it had needed to fill many bowls.

It was a sure bet Norris Sutherland, heir to the Earldom of Sutherland, wasn't awake in the dark hours of the morning with an empty belly. Even his accommodations in a military camp had been grand, the bed on which he'd taken her maidenhead a comfortable one.

Ye mean the one ye joined him on as his lover…

She closed her eyes and ordered herself to sleep while she might. The summer days were long, and there was much to do. Once winter closed its icy fist around the Highlands, there would be naught to do but seek out her bed for warmth.

She certainly wouldn't be seeking out Norris Sutherland. No. She might have enjoyed the time she spent in his bed, but she could not ever forget that she had gone there to avoid wedding a man who loved another. She must not forget, because a man such as Norris certainly did not lack for willing bed partners. She would not join the ranks of his mistresses.

Even if she did dream of the man.

❦

Dunrobin Castle, Sutherland

"Is there anything else ye desire, me laird?"

The serving girl was pretty, and she had curves in all the places Norris liked women to have them. Her dress was open enough to allow him a generous view of her breasts.

"Nae."

Disappointment flashed across her face, her gaze sweeping his chest before she picked up his empty mug and placed it on her serving tray. When she turned around, he was treated to a view of her backside as she descended the four steps leading down from the high-table landing to the floor of the great hall.

Yes, definitely curves in all the right places, and she moved with a sultry motion that should have sent heat through his veins. But his cock lay slack and uninterested beneath his kilt. He reached for the fresh mug of ale the serving lass had delivered but didn't lift it to his lips. This was becoming tiresome—exceedingly so.

He scanned the hall, catching the smiles of other lasses all watching him to see if he would summon them forward. There were dark-haired ones and blondes, even a redhead, but none of them sparked even a twitch from his cock. The thing had been use-less for nearly three months.

"I'm growing worried about ye, me boy."

There was only one man who would call him boy and not get smashed in the face for it. Norris stood as his father appeared from the archway that led to his private study that was hidden behind the raised floor at the end of the great hall. Norris had helped outfit the room to give his father a sanctuary when he needed a few moments of rest. It would never do for the Highland earl to appear fatigued in front of his clan. The chamber had become the earl's favorite for business, but Norris did wonder if part of the appeal was being able to sneak up on his son.

Lytge Sutherland walked straight to his chair, even if he did it slowly. Norris didn't sit until his father was settled in the huge, ornately carved chair set at the center of the high table. Even so late at night, they showed respect to each other, for there were many watching.

"Ye have naught to worry about, Father."

Lytge reached for the mug of ale Norris had left untasted and drew off a long draught. He nodded then set it down. "Nonsense. Ye have nae been the same since returning from Sauchieburn." His father settled against the high back of the chair. "I went to so much trouble to secure ye that royal-blooded bride. Ye allowed her to ride out of here wearing the colors of the MacNicols."

"She was in love with Broen MacNicols…"

Lytge stroked his beard. "Ah yes. The same reason young Daphne MacLeod used to explain why she did nae wed Broen MacNicols as her father arranged. Ye seem to have helped Broen twice in the matter: once by taking Daphne to yer bed so she could be disgraced, and again when ye allowed yer own bride to escape the consummation of yer union."

Norris reached for the mug and took a swig. "I wondered how long it would take ye to hear of the part I played in helping Broen out of his betrothal with Daphne."

His father grinned, as arrogant as any man half his age, but his hair was completely gray now. "I've known, boy. Everything ye do is important to me."

There were men who would have bristled, but Norris returned his father's grin. "Sometimes helping out a friend is a pleasant duty."

His sire's eyebrows rose. "I imagine it was a fine bit of fun to help Daphne MacLeod lose her virtue so her betrothal might be broken, but what did ye gain from it? What did ye bring home to yer clan, me boy?"

Norris felt the bite of his father's displeasure. It was there, glittering in the older man's eyes. What made it sting was that his father wasn't railing at him. The subtle stab was more wounding than a raised voice rich with insults, because his father was speaking to him like the future leader of the clan. A laird never forgot to weigh the benefits of any situation.

"Securing the loyalty of Laird MacNicols is worthy of note," Norris offered.

His father nodded. "Aye, it is."

"And Clarrisa may have been royal-blooded, but she did nae come with a dowry," Norris finished.

"True enough. But blood has its worth. Why do

ye think I keep Gahan near? He's me bastard, and Sutherland blood is valuable. Yer bride may have cost me, but she was a York bastard, and yer offspring would have been kin to the King of England." His father tilted his head to one side and returned to stroking his beard. "The MacLeod lass, according to Gahan, she's a fair sight to behold."

"A fact she despises."

His father chuckled. "That's her youth blinding her. Time will steal her beauty soon enough. Ye learn that by my age. Best to enjoy what ye have when ye have it. I hear ye did that well enough when the lass was in yer keeping."

She'd been passionate too. Norris looked toward the hearth and signaled one of the serving girls forward to avoid having his father witness the flare of excitement that went through him. Daphne had blonde hair but dark eyes, which fascinated him. When he locked gazes with her, he had the sudden feeling he might lose himself in those dark orbs and be shielded from all life's travails. He'd never been one to shirk his duty, but he would not deny how tempting it was to seek her out again and lose himself in her enchanting embrace until dawn broke the spell.

"Gahan seems to have had a great deal to tell ye," Norris groused.

"As I said, he has his uses, and being the head of yer retainers is one of them," Lytge stated. "But he is nae the only source of information I have. In fact, Daphne MacLeod is the subject of interest at many a table in the Highlands. The rumor is that the lass has a fortune for a dowry, one nae discovered when the MacLeod land was raided by those clans who claimed victory at Sauchieburn."

"Who raided her lands?" Norris demanded.

"Comyn, Campbell, Lindsey. Does it matter? Her father fought on the losing side, and those who backed the young king took their pay out of the lands of those clans who did nae make so wise a choice."

Rage heated up inside Norris. It turned white-hot before becoming a rapid boil.

"Why do ye care, Son?"

His father was astute and too keen for Norris's mood. The serving girl delivered another mug of ale, and he lifted it to his lips. "It does nae matter."

"A fortune for a dowry matters. I hear her father had a bastard, and the man is set to inherit the MacLeod lairdship. Being wed to his only sister would be a good alliance." Lytge leaned forward and lowered his voice. "If there is a fortune involved, that is."

Norris sat up, the idea immediately taking root in his head. He realized he shouldn't, but still he couldn't seem to squash the urge to see Daphne again. No, he wanted to let that urge loose and follow it.

"Perhaps I'll ride out and see if it's true."

His father grinned. "And ye think she'll tell ye? Do nae be thinking one night between her thighs will endear her to ye."

His cock was hardening. His temper rose along with the organ. Still, he stood. Becoming a slave to his impulses was dangerous, but the opportunity was simply too tempting to ignore. He winked at his father. "Then maybe I'll have to charm me way into her bed again."

❧

"I do nae take orders from ye."

Daphne MacLeod had heard the same from more than one of her father's retainers. She sweetened her expression, fighting back the urge to call the man a fool.

"I am suggesting ye recognize the logic in helping me round up the sheep before they stray too close to Comyn land. Their wool will be one of the few things we can harvest this season."

Keith MacLeod frowned. "Better that ye should have used those honey-coated looks on Broen MacNicols. If ye had wed him, we'd nae have suffered being raided after the battle of Sauchieburn. If ye were the wife of another Highland laird, no one would have dared even to think about taking what was ours."

"My father stood on the defeated side," Daphne argued, dropping all hints of sweetness. "We'd have been raided, have no doubt. My actions had naught to do with that."

"But we'd have a strong ally to protect us. One that might have made some of the smaller clans think twice before trifling with us. The MacNicols are vassals of Sutherland."

"So are we." Daphne lifted her head, drawing her back straight and glaring at the men standing before her. "I believe we are strong, and I will go after the sheep myself. I am not afraid, nor am I content to sit here and pity me plight. We were raided and have lost much—all the more reason to make sure we lose no more."

She turned her back on Keith. She could feel him

and his men staring at her, but she never falter
Her cousins were still seated at the tables that fill
the great hall. All three of them claimed they wer
the rightful heir to the MacLeod lairdship, and they
were using their blood ties to her father to spend the
day doing nothing of value. She passed them, but not
without shooting them a hard look. They might label
her many things, but they would not call her a coward.

Gitta waited where the great hall ended and the
hallway began.

"Ye are nae endearing yerself to the men."

Daphne didn't slow her pace. "If they cannae see
the need for us to work together to pull in enough of
a harvest to survive the coming winter, I have no time
for them. Arrogance and pride will nae fill bellies. Me
brother is nae here. I am."

Winter would close in on them too soon. Most of
the seed grain had been stolen, and what fields were
planted had been trampled. Some of the young plants
were recovering, but time had been lost, and the yield
would not be great.

"Ye should nae go riding. What if ye're carrying?"
Gitta whispered, panting from the exertion of keeping
up with her.

"I am nae with child." However, Daphne did
slow her pace, and her cheeks heated with shame for
making the older woman rush.

"Ye've nae bled," Gitta insisted. "A Sutherland bastard would give us an alliance—a great one, if it were
a son. The Sutherlands keep their blood close." Gitta
looked at Daphne's belly, reaching out to smooth the
fabric of her skirt flat.

Daphne flinched, jumping back a step. "Enough. If am with child, it will nae be a matter to worry about or many months. Today our sheep are happily on their way off our land with their winter coats still on their backs. We need that wool to buy seed for next year. I will return soon." She left Gitta at the tower steps and stalked toward the stable.

She couldn't think about a possible child. Norris Sutherland was wed. The news had traveled quickly. What bothered her most was how upset she was to know he was bound to another woman. Hadn't she suffered enough at the expense of fate? Everything she'd done had been for the right reasons. If she were shallow or greedy she'd happily have wed Broen MacNicols without a care for the fact that he was fighting with his best friend over her, or that when he discovered her still alive, the man was in love with another woman. Oh no, she would not have cared one bit how unhappy he was in their marriage. Legally, the man had been bound to wed her.

Yet she did not lament her actions to set him free of the contract her father had made with him.

Ye enjoyed the duty sure enough...

Her cheeks heated, and her pace quickened. She'd let Norris Sutherland seduce her so Broen MacNicols might renounce her and wed the woman he loved. Their night of passion had served a purpose. She had no reason to be upset over Norris Sutherland's taking a bride. The man owed her no affection.

Keith wasn't the only man wearing her father's colors who resented her choices. But a child? She didn't need the guilt of knowing she'd forced an innocent to wear

the label of bastard. Even being the child of No[...]
Sutherland, heir to the earldom, wouldn't save it fr[...]
scorn. She smoothed her hand over her belly, searchin[...]
for proof that it wasn't rounding.

What she needed was for her courses to arrive and
silence the rumors, but they had never been predictable,
so there was no way of knowing if she were late or not.
If she bled, it would make her happy, but she feared it
would be yet another reason for her people to resent her.

At least the horses greeted her kindly. She rubbed
the velvet muzzle of one and muttered softly to it.

"Shall we go and sample some of the fine summer
weather?"

As if understanding, the horse tossed its head, sending its mane flouncing. No one would help her saddle
the animal, but she knew the way of it. The stable
master was a good friend of Keith's and always sent his
workers in the opposite direction when she appeared.

They thought she should be ashamed.

"Ye've a solid point about the sheep."

Keith startled her. She jumped and muffled a curse
when the horse sidestepped nervously. Keith frowned,
but she reached up and took the bit, controlling the
animal with a steady hand.

His disapproval softened. "Even if I think ye should
have been thinking of yer clan when ye broke yer
betrothal with Laird MacNicols."

More retainers walked down the rows of stalls.
Horses tossed their heads and snorted as the men
began to saddle them. The stable was full of the scent
of straw and leather.

"The first time I refused to wed him, I did it to

ent him fighting with Laird Chisholms. There
uld have been a feud."

Keith pulled a leather strap tight before granting
ier a grudging nod. "I agree ye did a good thing
there, even if they be the ones who should be
ashamed for acting like lads no higher than me waist.
We do nae need a feud, especially one started over a
woman, even a laird's daughter. I find meself liking
that bit of action on yer part."

She used the stall rail to help her mount and suffered
the harsh looks of some of the men. She bit back the
tart response she would have liked to make. Pointing
out that she was a foot shorter than any of them would
serve only to remind them she was a female trying to
take on the duties of a man.

"But the way I heard it..." Keith continued as he
led his stallion out of the stable, "the second time, ye
defied even the young king by refusing to take yer
place as Laird MacNicols's bride."

Daphne flattened her body across the horse's neck
to make it through the doorway of the stable and into
the yard. "Which gained us Laird MacNicols's good
will. The man is in love with another woman. He'd
have wed me sure enough and resented me."

Keith mounted and reached up to adjust his knitted
bonnet. He'd been her father's head of retainers and
still wore one of his three feathers upward. By tradition, he should have lowered the feather, since the
new laird would be the one deciding who claimed the
privilege of serving in such a high position. It was just
one more detail that screamed out the lack of respect
her father's men had for her.

"The marriage contracts were agreed upon by yer father and Laird MacNicols. The man should have kept his word or at least made recompense to us, nae left it to ye to disgrace yerself so he might be happy."

"He didn't. I made the choice." And she refused to regret it. "Enough. I know yer position on the matter. Ye've told me plainly enough. Let's get the sheep."

Keith surprised her by grinning. He was a fair-enough-looking man when he wasn't scowling at her. His hair was a dark sable, and his eyes a warm brown. There was a thin scar running along the right side of his cheek, but it served only to make him look capable.

"I do respect yer ability to recognize what we need to survive."

She turned her horse toward the gate and rode through it. A smile graced her lips even as she leaned low to flow more fluidly with the motions of the animal. She rode a mare, but a young one with plenty of spirit. The animal took to the uneven ground easily as Daphne guided her toward the border of her father's land. The wind was warm, and it tore at her blonde hair. She'd cut it off a year ago, and the strands were only a foot long now. They didn't want to stay in the braid Gitta had woven at sunrise, but slowly worked free.

Well, it suited her, for her hair wasn't the only part of her that didn't want to be contained. She'd grown up with Broen MacNicols and hadn't wanted to be his wife. The single kiss he'd pressed against her lips had left her cold.

Norris's kiss had sent her heart racing…

She might never have known the difference—or worse, learned of it after she was wed. Maybe the Church was wrong about infidelity. Maybe those who strayed from their wedded partners were to be pitied because they'd been locked into unions with the wrong person.

Ye're going to get locked in the stocks for thinking like that...

Well, only if she was foolish enough to voice such ideas. She raised her head and felt confidence rising inside her. Over the last year, she'd learned a thing or two about keeping her thoughts to herself.

Ye've also learned how to take a hand in yer own destiny...

Maybe she was meant to be alone in life. The Church also preached that women should remain humble and yield to a man's authority. Well, she was far past yielding. She wrapped the reins around her fists and urged the horse faster. Maybe she wasn't humble, but her father's people needed someone to take action now.

Maybe she was exactly what she needed to be.

About the Author

Mary Wine is a multi-published author in romantic suspense, fantasy, and Western romance. Her interest in historical reenactment and costuming also inspired her to turn her pen to historical romance with her popular Highlander series. She lives with her husband and sons in Southern California, where the whole family enjoys participating in historical reenactment.

Temptation in a Kilt
by Victoria Roberts

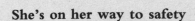

She's on her way to safety

It's a sign of Lady Rosalia Armstrong's desperation that she's seeking refuge in a place as rugged and challenging as the Scottish Highlands. She doesn't care about hardship and discomfort, if only she can become master of her own life. Laird Ciaran MacGregor, however, is completely beyond her control...

He redefines dangerous...

Ciaran MacGregor knows it's perilous to get embroiled with a fiery Lowland lass, especially one as headstrong as Rosalia. Having made a rash promise to escort her all the way to Glengarry, now he's stuck with her, even though she challenges his legendary prowess at every opportunity. When temptation reaches its peak, he'll be ready to show her who he really is... on and off the battlefield.

"Wonderful adventure with sensual and compelling romance." —Amanda Forester, acclaimed author of *True Highland Spirit*

For more Victoria Roberts, visit:

www.sourcebooks.com

X Marks the Scot
by Victoria Roberts

He's fierce, he's proud, he's everything she was warned against.

Declan MacGregor hadn't a care in the world beyond finding a soft bed and willing woman... until he had to escort Lady Liadain Campbell to the English court. The woman needles him at every turn, but he can't just abandon her to that vipers' nest without protection.

Liadain wasn't thrilled to be left in the care of her clan's archrival. It was as if the man never had a lady tell him no before! And yet as whispers of treason swirl through the court and the threat of danger grows ever sharper, her bitter enemy soon becomes the only one she can trust...

Praise for *Temptation in a Kilt*:

"Well written, full of intrigue, and a sensual, believable romance, this book captivates the reader immediately." —*RT Book Reviews*

"Filled with everything I love most about Highland romance..." —Melissa Mayhue, award-winning author of *Warrior's Redemption*

For more Victoria Roberts, visit:

www.sourcebooks.com

To Wed a Wicked Highlander
by Victoria Roberts

∾

Torn between his duty and his soul mate, what will this Highland bad boy choose?

When a beautiful traitor is discovered under his own roof, Laird Alexander MacDonnell is faced with a decision he never thought possible. He's sworn to protect his clan, but following his duty will mean losing his heart forever to the woman who betrayed him—his wife.

Lady Sybella MacKenzie is forced to search for her clan's ancient seeing stone under the roof of her father's enemy. But when she finally finds the precious artifact, ensuring her family's survival will mean turning her back on the man who has captured her soul.

∾

Praise for *Temptation in a Kilt*:

"An exciting Highland adventure with sensual and compelling romance." —Amanda Forester, acclaimed author of *True Highland Spirit*

"Filled with everything I love most about Highland romance…" —Melissa Mayhue, award-winning author of *Warrior's Redemption*

For more Victoria Roberts, visit:

www.sourcebooks.com

The Highlander's Sw

by Amanda Forester

———— ❧ ————

A quiet, flame-haired beauty
with secrets of her own...

Lady Aila Graham is destined for the convent, until her brother's death leaves her an heiress. Soon she is caught between a hastily arranged marriage with a Highland warrior, the Abbot's insistence that she take her vows, the Scottish Laird who kidnaps her, and the traitor from within who betrays them all.

She's nothing he expected and
everything he really needs...

Padyn MacLaren, a battled-hardened knight, returns home to the Highlands after years of fighting the English in France. MacLaren bears the physical scars of battle, but it is the deeper wounds of betrayal that have rocked his faith. Arriving with only a band of war-weary knights, MacLaren finds his land pillaged and his clan scattered. Determined to restore his clan, he sees Aila's fortune as the answer to his problems...but maybe it's the woman herself.

———— ❧ ————

"Plenty of intrigue keeps the reader cheering all the way." —*Publishers Weekly*

For more Amanda Forester books, visit:

www.sourcebooks.com

The Highlander's Heart
by Amanda Forester

❧

She's nobody's prisoner

Lady Isabelle Tynsdale's flight over the Scottish border would have been the perfect escape, if only she hadn't run straight into the arms of a gorgeous Highland laird. Whether his plan is ransom or seduction, her only hope is to outwit him, or she'll lose herself entirely...

And he's nobody's fool

Laird David Campbell thought Lady Isabelle was going to be easy to handle and profitable too. He never imagined he'd have such a hard time keeping one enticing English countess out of trouble. And out of his heart...

❧

"An engrossing, enthralling, and totally riveting read. Outstanding!" —Jackie Ivie, national bestselling author of *A Knight and White Satin*

For more Amanda Forester books, visit:

www.sourcebooks.com

True Highland Spirit
by Amanda Forester

Seduction is a powerful weapon...

Morrigan McNab is a Highland lady, robbed of her birthright and with no choice but to fight alongside her brothers to protect their impoverished clan. When she encounters Sir Jacques Dragonet, she discovers her fiercest opponent...

Sir Jacques Dragonet is a Noble Knight of the Hospitaller Order, willing to give his life to defend Scotland from the English. He can't stop himself from admiring the beautiful Highland lass who wields her weapons as well as he can and endangers his heart even more than his life...

Now they're racing each other to find a priceless relic. No matter who wins this heated rivalry, both will lose unless they can find a way to share the spoils.

For more Amanda Forester books, visit:

www.sourcebooks.com

Sins of the Highlander

by Connie Mason with Mia Marlowe

❦

ABDUCTION

Never had Elspeth Stewart imagined her wedding would be interrupted by a dark-haired stranger charging in on a black stallion, scooping her into his arms, and carrying her off across the wild Scottish Highlands. Pressed against his hard chest and nestled between his strong thighs, she ought to have feared for her life. But her captor silenced all protests with a soul-searing kiss, giving Elspeth a glimpse of the pain behind his passion—a pain only she could ease.

OBSESSION

"Mad Rob" MacLaren thought stealing his rival's bride-to-be was the perfect revenge. But Rob never reckoned that this beautiful, innocent lass would awaken the part of him he thought dead and buried with his wife. Against all reason, he longed to introduce the luscious Elspeth to the pleasures of the flesh, to make her his, and only his, forever.

❦

"Ms. Mason always provides a hot romance." —*RT Book Reviews*

For more Connie Mason and Mia Marlowe, visit:

www.sourcebooks.com